Make Me An Offer

Make Me
An Offer

Caroline King

First published in 1998
by HEADLINE BOOK PUBLISHING

A HEADLINE LIAISON paperback

1 0 9 8 7 6 5 4 3 2 1

ISBN 0 7472 5866 X

Typeset by Palimpsest Book Production Limited
Polmont, Stirlingshire
Printed and bound in Great Britain by
Mackays of Chatham PLC, Chatham, Kent

HEADLINE BOOK PUBLISHING
A division of Hodder Headline PLC
338 Euston Road
London NW1 3BH

Make Me
An Offer

Prologue

Louisa Dane turned over in bed, stretching out her limbs as far as they would go. Mixed feelings of excitement and trepidation washed over her as she savoured her first waking moments and listened to Andrew splashing about in the bathroom. Slowly she pulled the sheet back from her face and examined the daylight filtering in through wide windows on the opposite side of the room.

Andrew's voice broke through her thoughts. 'It's a murky sort of day,' he commented, as he leant over her, shaking his head and showering her naked flesh with water. Louisa squealed with surprise and grinned up at him.

'No,' she replied, 'it's a lovely day. In fact it's an excellent day, a most resplendent, exciting, satisfying, fulfilling . . .' The words tailed away as Andrew fixed his lips across hers and in an eager response she pulled him down and onto her, the remaining droplets of water transferring themselves from one body onto the other as they rolled across the bed. Louisa shivered, suddenly wanting him inside her, her kisses deepening in intensity until, through the mass of flailing limbs, she realised that Andrew's intentions were not necessarily the same as hers. Reluctantly, she released her arms from around his neck and he immediately reached out to stop the buzzing alarm clock which, in her sudden passion, she had wilfully failed to hear.

'Damn,' he said, lifting the clock into the light. 'Sorry, Louisa, I've got to get a move on.'

'Andrew, no.' She pouted persuasively, running her hands down the sliver of damp hair on his chest and towards his groin. 'Surely we can have just a few more minutes.'

1

'No, honestly. Woah,' he gasped involuntarily as she reached downwards to grasp his clearly excited member, and draw him back towards her sex. 'I have to go.'

Louisa sighed and gave up, releasing her hold on him. There was no arguing with Andrew once he had made up his mind. And he was always quite specific. If he said he had to go now, then he really had to go. Spontaneity, she thought, was never the word she would use when describing his character.

'I'm sorry, darling,' he apologised, sprinting away from the bed and towards the wardrobe, a bit too eagerly, she thought. 'But I've got an early meeting with the partners, and anyway,' he continued with a glance back at her, 'you've got to get to the office and start creating an empire.'

Louisa lay back on the bed once more as her hands, hidden beneath the sheet began to drift downwards. The urge to touch herself was almost irresistible now that Andrew had deserted her, and with delicate surreptitious strokes she began to release the tension within her.

'Well,' she said, 'I don't think anyone's going to mind if the boss is just a few minutes late. Anyway, after today I shouldn't think I'll ever leave the office again.'

Andrew cast her a sideways look as he pulled on his jacket. 'Hypocrite,' he announced. 'Stop trying to sound bothered about being chained to the desk. You know you love it. That's why you took on the capital partners.' He reached over her to give her a final goodbye kiss. 'You wanted to be in charge of a much bigger show. And now you are.' He smiled. 'I know you, you want it all. And I'm sure you'll have it.'

He let himself out of the apartment and Louisa lay back against the chocolate-coloured sheets, her blonde hair spreading out in a halo around her shoulders. The need for sex, raw and hot, flared up inside her groin once again and she groaned with frustration, wishing Andrew could have spared just five more minutes. 'God,' she thought, 'two minutes would have done the job.' Sometimes she didn't want finesse, she just wanted to feel fucked.

The thought of sex was now utterly irresistible. Louisa's

fingers ceased curling her pubic hair and moved to the warmth between her legs, gently stroking the eager swelling bud of her clitoris. Moaning softly to herself as lustful sensations and images intensified, she ran the fingers of her other hand around her nipples, pulling and mistreating them. Gingerly, Louisa let the strokes against her clit lengthen and deepen and felt her way inside her sex. Splitting her thighs apart she slid her cool fingers into the hot, sticky moistness of her hole and then, with a practised ease she increased the pace and violence of her actions, driving herself towards a sharp gasping climax.

She lay on the bed, feeling her senses strung out on the moments of ecstasy that too soon became an ebbing throb and then slowly washed away. She was left somewhat satisfied, but still wishing she had a man there to attend to her sexual needs and also with the lingering wish that Andrew didn't find it quite so easy to drag himself away from her.

Finally Louisa rose from her bed. Pulling a creamy silk kimono around her shoulders she walked through the kitchen, poured herself coffee and strolled out onto the balcony that ran along the side of the building. She looked out over New York which, despite its reputation, still seemed pretty sleepy this morning. It was, after all, only just coming up to six o'clock, and she had plenty of time to get ready for work.

'This is it,' she thought. 'My chance. My time. The moment I've been waiting and working for.' She allowed herself a moment of self-satisfaction and drank down the hot, strong Colombian coffee, before turning indoors to prepare herself for the day ahead.

The Dane Model Agency had been in existence for almost six years. Louisa had devoted that time to building up the business; finding new models, fighting for commissions from magazines, developing the business's name and seeing the whole supermodel arena ebb and flow around her, but always as a fairly small time player in the industry. However, it was her baby and she loved it.

3

Louisa had never been a model herself but she had always loved the glamour and high profile of the fashion business. She was also fortunate in that a reasonably substantial family trust meant she could choose her own destiny, although she still had to make a go of things. Her financial independence did not extend to allowing her to become a dilettante, moving from one project to another. She served her apprenticeship in a series of well known agencies, learning about the business and the industry as a whole and then, when the time seemed right, she committed herself and her funds to creating the business.

Her wealthy East Coast family background, her New York business contacts, a European education, and her Wasp looks – blonde hair, green eyes and a classic bone structure – gave her a head start over much of the competition. But, for all that, she still needed luck. For a long time she was in the position where many of the girls on her books were in the profitable but less glamorous niche lines, showing their nails, hands, hair and faces rather than taking to the catwalk. But now some of the newer models she had brought into the business were finding fame on the catwalks and as cover models, with burgeoning supermodel celebrity status. This had swung the pendulum of success further in her favour and when she had looked for investors there had been a lot of interest. In a way the change in the business had all happened quite suddenly: an overnight success that only took six years to develop.

'Six years,' she thought as the shower pummelled her back, and she moved from there to the dressing room to dry her hair and apply her usual daytime make-up. It was a long time to operate alone and unchecked, and now at last she had chosen to have a partner. She laughed at her ingenuous reflection. 'You liar,' she told herself. 'You would have begged for a partner to bring in this sort of cash.'

It was Andrew who had come up with the goods and had found a suitable venture capital firm, willing to take the risk and put up the money to expand the agency. Her new partners were eminently respectable, and they obviously thought she was going to do well, she told herself with delight. Of course, it was inevitable that they would now own most of the company, seventy-one per cent to be exact, but that was the price for a cash injection of several millions, and she was lucky to retain so much control. The deal was such that, although the third party investors nominally controlled the business, she was in charge unless the business was unable to meet pre-set targets. Or in other words, if she failed. 'No chance of that,' Louisa said to herself. 'I know what I'm doing.'

The investors' primary input at this stage would be to install someone on the board to work with her, plus ex-officio and non-voting directors to assist the two of them in decision-making. Today was the first formal introduction session; she would be meeting her new executive director, a former member of the fashion council in New York and a long-time magazine editor, although now retired, Alex Prince. He would be great to work with, she thought as she buttoned up her blouse and pulled on her stockings, then finished her hair and make-up. He was extremely well-known, his reputation was good, he had terrific contacts in all aspects of the fashion world and he was looking for a business to be involved with in his retirement. So in many ways, the Dane Agency was ideal for him; no personal financial risk, as much involvement as he wanted, and a means of keeping his name on people's lips and in the fashion papers.

Louisa turned away from the wardrobe to examine her reflection in the mirror. She had chosen a creamy silk Armani skirt and blouse and set them against a contrasting olive jacket and she stepped back to admire the overall effect in the long mirror on the far side of the bedroom wall. She looked wealthy, smart and sophisticated: her blonde hair was deeply golden against the olive green of the jacket and beneath the cream silk skirt her long slim legs stretched down to where her feet were stylishly encased in high-heeled Bruno Magli shoes. She nodded with approval. 'Right,' she said. 'Here we go.'

Chapter 1

Louisa's office was based in a smart, well-maintained brownstone on the Upper East Side, where it now comprised two floors of interlocking open-plan rooms and offices. Even though much of the work was done on the client's chosen site, on location or in a meeting at a restaurant, it was always important to have sufficient space for the bookers. These were her most essential group of employees who were responsible for placing models in magazines, fashion shows and advertising campaigns, and who could succeed in promoting the use of a Dane Agency model rather than anybody else's. However it was also necessary to have somewhere for the models to feel at home, particularly the new girls who often had to wait whilst the bookers arranged for them to go on 'go-sees', the trial by audition that most new models have to suffer. Finally, it was highly important to put on a good show whenever potential clients and magazine editors paid a call to the offices, hence her choice of an exclusive address.

When she started the agency the number of employees was so small that there had been no need for much space and initially Louisa had rented just a portion of one floor. However, as the business had grown and the number of permanent staff had expanded, the lack of available space had become an ever-stressful problem, even though they had grown into the offices over the whole of the first floor. At the beginning of the year the opportunity to expand within the building and take over a second floor had arisen and as soon as the venture capitalists' money had come through she had taken over the lease and started building work. However, as everyone apart from the building contractors had predicted, the work was far more intrusive and slower than she had ever expected.

Her other plans on the path to developing the Dane Model Agency into a major-league business meant that she would need more offices in other locations. Louisa was particularly interested in setting up a base in Europe, in London or Paris, but she also wanted to retain the option to open up new offices in Washington, San Francisco and possibly Miami over the next few years. Then, she thought, the business would really have arrived.

She looked up at the tarpaulin on the outside of the building. It was a pain that the builders were still there, but it would soon be completed and perhaps then she should arrange a PR event; a gala opening to show off the offices and raise their profile, with lots of flowers, champagne and beautiful people.

'Yes,' she thought, as she made her way indoors, that was a good idea. As long as the builders stuck to their newly revised version of the already much revised plan. Anyway, even allowing for a delay she should probably get someone to start thinking about such an event and creating a guest list as soon as possible. And getting the right person to do that job was another big issue, she thought, as she settled into her office, examining the papers and files that were piled on and around her desk. Her PA had recently left and there was a yawning gap in the system which was only just barely covered by the agency temps she had been sent. None of these had proved sufficiently effective to warrant being offered a permanent job, and things were starting to get desperate.

Louisa sighed and put the topic out of her mind. There were more important things to do today, she could sort the temp problem out tomorrow. She checked her watch and started to plan out her day's calendar. She had a working lunch with the bookers and administrators to review the month's business and to decide which models should move from being a 'new face' to an 'established name', who should focus on specific magazines and how any 'new business developments', or commercial contacts, were proceeding. Before lunch she had these piles

8

of papers to review, and a conference call with a group of magazine editors, then after the lunchtime meeting she had the introduction session with the venture capitalists, Blake Harrison Development Funds. They were coming to the office in order to formally introduce Alex Prince onto the Board of Directors, and then use the opportunity to settle down to some solid financial discussions and a strategy planning meeting. She had no idea how long the meeting would be going on, but at least the late afternoon timing meant that she could devote most of the day to getting some real work done and finish her preparation for the strategy document with its long range plans to take the business successfully into the next century.

She firmly turned her mind to the immediate business at hand, reviewing papers, magazine credits and profiles; studying the terms of contracts that clients were proposing in order to use specific models to represent them exclusively; examining portfolios and making suggestions about presentation and development. Then there were photo shoots to approve, new models to sign on or send for hair and make-up changes, and their resulting portfolios to review. Although she had been somewhat removed from this part of the business while the funding and venture capital influx had been going through, she was the boss and the owner and as such she needed to keep her finger on the pulse of the business at all times. She also missed working more closely with the models and stylists, and often she would gladly have given up a high-profile power lunch with difficult magazine editors worrying about circulation, advertisements and product placement decisions for a few frantic hours of working with tantrums, dramas and an overexcited photographer on a difficult photo shoot, stuck out in the rain or snow.

At around eleven o'clock Andrew called. 'How are things going?'

'Oh, the usual. Some problems, some good things, but it's OK. I still haven't found a suitable PA though. Did you call for a reason?'

He paused. 'I'm sorry I ran out on you this morning.'

'That's OK,' she said. 'I know you're busy and I know you had an early meeting. It's just—'

'I know,' he said from the other end of the phone. 'You just wish sometimes I'd lose control and do it right there and then.'

Louisa chuckled. 'See, you do know what I want.' There was a pause and Andrew's mobile phone crackled. 'Are you going somewhere?' she asked. 'I thought you were in the office all day.'

'I had a cancellation,' he said. 'And I wanted to congratulate you on the first real day of the new business.' There was a noticeable click as the phone switched off and the door to her office opened to reveal Andrew in the doorway in front of her, mobile phone in one hand, a large bouquet, a bottle of champagne and a shallow box cradled precariously in the other.

'Andrew, darling,' she cried out in delight. 'What a wonderful surprise.'

He smiled at her pleasure and entered the room, depositing his parcels on the desk in front of her as he leaned over to kiss her. 'Hi,' he murmured, then gesturing at the flowers and the box. 'Presents.'

'Yummy. Can I open them now?'

'Let's cancel all calls and visits first.'

Louisa raised her eyebrows. 'And why would I want to do that?' she asked coyly.

'Just do it,' he told her, and turned his attention to the champagne, opening the bottle and removing glasses from the drinks cabinet in the corner of her office.

'OK,' said Louisa, coming out from behind her desk. 'All calls are going to voice-mail, and all visitors are forbidden. I hope you have a good reason.'

She undid the ribbons and opened the large box, wading through layers of crisp tissue paper until she came to a mass of frothy white silk and lace, a strapless basque and stockings in virginal white. She picked them up and raised her eyebrows once again, holding the basque up against her as she turned to face him.

10

'Hold on,' he replied with a smile. 'Keep going.' Louisa gave him a quizzical look and laying the basque to one side she rummaged into the mass of tissue once again. She soon found a second package and withdrew another set of underwear, this time a half-basque of black leather, cut so that it would fasten behind her neck into a studded collar and leave her breasts exposed and supported by a rim of leather.

Louisa ran her finger around the leather edge of the basque. 'Andrew, I'm amazed,' she said. 'I don't want to be offensive, but,' she paused, 'well to be honest I didn't know you had it in you. I mean, you've never wanted to use anything like this before.'

'I was thinking about this morning and leaving you in the lurch,' he replied, walking up to her. 'I want you so much, Loulou, you know that. I don't want to let you down.' His fingers ran along the cream silk of her shirt, and down to the exposed patch of skin at her throat. With deft fingers he began to undo the silk-covered buttons of her shirt, pausing as he reached the base of her breasts to run his hands inside her shirt and around the soft tanned skin of her shoulders.

'So,' she murmured. 'Well you're going to have to do a lot of work to make up for this morning.'

He breathed heavily into her ear as his hands finished undoing the buttons on her blouse, and the skirt below it. 'Whatever you want. Whatever way you want it.'

She drew back from him. 'Let me put this on,' she said holding up the leather basque. 'Then we'll see what you're made of.'

Without another word she drew herself away from him and letting her skirt slip down, stepped out of it and walked over to the door that led to her small private bathroom. Once inside she slipped her lingerie off and replaced the delicate pieces of silk with the aggressively sexual basque. Looking at herself in the mirror she couldn't resist running her hands across and around her breasts; they were full and heavy

11

with soft pink areolae, and the supporting leather circles that surrounded them now lifted them to jut away from her torso. Above her breasts a bronze-studded leather collar was now wrapped around her throat, highlighting the contrast between her femininity, as defined by her make-up and the soft gentle styling of her golden hair, and the overt sexuality of the basque. Beneath her breasts the leather was tightly laced-up as far as her crotch, where a tiny Greco-Roman kilt was made up of short leather strips that just covered her genitals.

Louisa returned to the office, throwing open the door and posing for a moment with her arms outstretched above her, the length of her slim legs exaggerated both by the briefness of her skirt and the high-heeled shoes she still wore. Andrew stared at her from the edge of the sofa.

'My God, Louisa,' he stuttered, rising to his feet. 'You look incredible.'

She stalked across the room to the wide window ledge at the corner of the office, picking up her champagne as she walked and swinging her hips provocatively as she moved past him. Leaning against the ledge the light shone in from behind her, turning her blonde hair into a halo around her face, an image of purity that contrasted wildly with her swollen breasts and prominently erect nipples held above the basque, and the hint of pubic hair and flesh glimpsed beneath the swinging folds of the leather skirt. She tilted her head back to drink her champagne as Andrew followed her across the room.

'Come back here,' he murmured, attempting to lead her back to the sofa, his swollen groin evidence of his excitement and the effect of her outfit.

'I don't think so,' she said, tilting her head and pushing him away. 'This is what you wanted. Well, I want it here. Right now.'

'Against the window?' he said aghast, backing away. 'Louisa, someone might see.'

She tossed her head dismissively. 'Only if they've got a

12

telephoto lens aimed just at this spot. Still,' she added slipping from the seat, 'if you're not up to the job—'

'Oh no,' said Andrew, 'you don't get away with it that easily.'

'So,' she asked, smiling. 'What are you going to do?'

Andrew slipped off his jacket and strode back towards her to place his hands directly over her breasts, kneading them aggressively as he began to kiss her neck, running his tongue along the hard edge of leather that encircled her throat and down to her breasts. She moaned with pleasure as her hands found his buttocks and drew him forwards to grind her pelvis into his groin, finding a solid erection held within his trousers, whilst his hands ran down to find the dampness of her sex. As their lips met again, his tongue moved inside her, enhancing the need she felt for him, a desire for him to fill her up and make her feel whole.

'I want you naked,' Louisa gasped as she grappled with his cuffs and shirt buttons. 'Help me.' Without a word Andrew drew back slightly and deftly pulled off his shirt and kicked off his shoes and socks. Before he could remove his trousers Louisa had dragged him back towards her, reaching for his nipples as he had reached for hers, sucking on them hungrily whilst her hands started to pull at his belt and remove his trousers. As they fell, he dropped to his knees and eased the strips of leather that obscured her sex to one side, spreading her thighs gently apart as he buried his head in her mound of golden blonde pubic hair.

Louisa leaned back against the windows that looked out across the road and onto the street below. Sunlight continued to stream in and she could see the people below, blissfully unaware of the actions going on above them. In the meantime, Andrew's tongue was easing its way into the cracks and crevices of her sex, each movement sending shivers of pleasure deeper inside her body, making her cry out as he explored further inside her sex.

'Touch yourself,' he groaned, standing once again. 'I want to see you touch your breasts. Louisa ran one finger across her mouth, moistening it gently, then ran it around her nipples, now hardened to tiny points in the centre of her breasts. Then she leaned back against the window and slid her fingers between the folds of her skirt, half hiding her actions from Andrew's gaze as she ran her fingers into her cunt. Andrew groaned and tore her hands away from her sex to replace them with his own, roughly rubbing the flat of his hand against her wetness, whilst sucking and biting at her nipples, and bringing her pleasure to a crescendo.

'Andrew,' she begged, breathless with lust. 'Please, I want you to fuck me.' With one last kiss at her nipples Andrew raised his head as Louisa tilted hers back, waiting for him to enter her. 'Please,' she murmured again.

'Not just yet,' murmured Andrew, to her surprise and shock. 'The public are still a little too close for my liking. If anyone's got that camera, it's not going to be my face they photograph.' He reached down for her waist and swivelled her round to face the window, spreading her thighs apart as he ran an exploratory finger into her crack.

'You bastard,' she groaned, shuddering with pleasurable sensations, as he felt inside her methodically, then replaced his finger with his cock, pushing it in between her thighs to penetrate her sex. Andrew groaned as he split her lips apart and she felt the full length of him slide slowly in and then out of her, before he re-entered her with enough force to push her firmly against the window, and started to pump at her with a recognisable rhythm. Held in place between Andrew's body and the window, his encircling arms propped on the window ledge beside her, she was left with nothing to hold onto but the flat window pane. With each thrust from behind her Louisa experienced the power and full force of his body beating against her and both felt and heard the slap of his testicles against the edge of her pussy as he continued to pound his way into her.

'OK, you little exhibitionist,' he murmured into her ear, pumping his cock deep inside her. 'How about this? Does this turn you on?'

She looked down and out of the window and suddenly the passers-by seemed incredibly close. Her imagination saw them stare and point upwards at her and it combined with the sensations that were coursing through her sex, exciting and stimulating her, until they tipped her over the edge of restraint. In moments her orgasm was exploding inside her, absorbing all her senses, so that she hardly heard Andrew's angry cry of satisfaction, coming as it did shortly behind her own whimpers and groans.

At four-thirty she was still hard at work, but beginning to feel more than a little irritated at the late arrival of her new partners. She sighed, examining her watch one more time. Perhaps the traffic had held them up, but this was really rather unimpressive. Finally she heard voices and some laughter from the outer office and her new temp popped her head around the door looking a little flustered.

'Ms Dane, your guests are here,' she began.

'Fine,' said Louisa, 'show them into the boardroom and I'll be right there.'

The temp turned her head to deliver the message and Laura rose to collect some relevant papers, then made her way down the corridor to the boardroom and let herself in. Alex Prince was nowhere to be seen; instead a complete stranger sat at the head of the table, dominating the room with his presence.

She stared at him in confusion. He was young, no more than thirty-five, with dark hair and features, and a Mediterranean complexion. At first glance that was all she noticed, although she did register that his fashion sense left something to be desired. She looked around the table at the members of the Blake Harrison team who were huddled, as though for protection, at the end of the board table nearest to the door, leaving a wide gap between themselves and the unknown stranger. Immediately, all of Louisa's senses warned her of trouble ahead. There were too many people there that she hardly knew; the room was full of tension, and stress was drawn across the face of every person, with the sole exception of the young man at the far end of the table. In contrast he was relaxed and seemed mildly amused by the effect he appeared to be generating.

'What's going on?' demanded Louisa baldly, directing her question at Henry D. Harrison, chief partner of the venture capitalist firm.

'Ah, Ms Dane,' he replied, avoiding her gaze. 'How are you today?' She fixed him with a steely look.

'Will you please tell me what's going on here?'

'Right,' he replied. 'Well, Mr Tessario here is your new associate director, and we felt you two should meet as soon as possible.' He paused and Louisa cut in.

'What's happened to Alex Prince? Where is he?'

'He had another engagement.'

'Really?' she asked. 'What does that mean?'

'I'm afraid there's been a last-minute change to our plans.'

'What sort of change?' she demanded more irritably.

'Alex Prince has declined to join us.'

Louisa stared. 'Why?'

Harrison and the others shifted in their seats, clearly trying to phrase a suitable answer. 'He decided that this wasn't the business opportunity he was looking for.'

Louisa pursed her lips and looked down the table at the stranger. 'So?'

'We, ah, well, we still have a new director to introduce to you.' There was a long and uncomfortable pause.

'Well then,' she said stiffly, 'will you please introduce me to my new director?'

'Certainly,' blustered Harrison. 'Louisa Dane, Paul Tessario.'

The stranger spoke for the first time. 'Paolo,' he corrected, lifting his eyes lazily, and ignoring Harrison to focus solely on Louisa.

'Ah, right,' squirmed Harrison, visibly discomforted. 'Yes, sorry. Well, Paolo Tessario, Louisa Dane.' Louisa sat down at the end of the table directly opposite Tessario and looked expectantly at the stranger's face.

'Perhaps you could fill me in on your qualifications for this

16

role,' she said stiffly. There was another difficult pause and then Harrison rushed to answer for his associate.

'Well,' he began, speaking very rapidly, 'Mr Tessario has a range of experience in business and legal affairs.'

'Specifically?' said Louisa.

'Specifically, how?' asked Tessario.

'Well, have you done anything in fashion, publishing or the modelling industry?' asked Louisa. 'Or some related industry perhaps?' she added.

He smiled thinly. 'Some related industry,' he agreed without any further explanation.

The room went very silent as Louisa and Tessario continued to examine each other from their opposite ends of the table. Louisa's mind was in a whirl. This was her worst nightmare come true, someone completely inappropriate getting their hands on a controlling share in her business. She took a grip of the panic that was rising within her and looked at Harrison sternly.

'Frankly, Henry, this isn't what I was expecting and, no offence intended, Mr Tessario . . .'

'None taken,' he murmured.

'. . . but this seems utterly inappropriate for the Dane Agency.'

Harrison shifted uneasily in his seat once again. 'I, ah I'm not sure I'd agree with you about that, Louisa,' he began. 'Frankly, Mr Tessario has excellent qualifications for this position, and as you will be aware,' he continued, dropping his gaze to stare at the polished wood table top, 'ultimately, this decision is ours.'

'In conjunction with me,' snapped Louisa. 'Or had you forgotten that?'

She looked closely at Harrison and the other members of the team and suddenly realised with clarity that it wasn't her reaction that was making them nervous. It was Tessario. He sat there at the end of the table, apparently impassive and with what appeared to be a complete lack of interest in the conversation. Making a sudden decision Louisa spoke again.

17

'Will you excuse me, gentlemen? As this is clearly going to take some time to resolve I must cancel another appointment. I won't be long.' She stood, and all of the venture capitalists rose to their feet. Tessario however, remained sitting resolutely in his chair. She looked him over once again and left the room.

She went straight to her office and dialled Andrew's office. 'Hi, this is Louisa Dane. Is Andrew there please?'

'I'm sorry Ms Dane, he's in a meeting,' replied his secretary.

'Sarah, this is important,' she answered. 'Very important. Can you please get him out of there now. I need to speak to him immediately.' There was a pause, then the secretary returned to the phone.

'Ms Dane? Hold on.'

Andrew came to the phone.

'Louisa, what's the problem? I'm in a meeting.'

'Thank God,' she said in a rush. 'Andrew, I am in such trouble. Blake Harrison is here – all of them as far as I can tell – and they've brought this guy I've never heard of, to be my partner. But he knows nothing about the business. They're dying to dump me in it and run away, I can tell. Andrew I don't know what to do—'

'Louisa,' he stopped her. 'Take a deep breath and tell me the problem. To start with who is this "guy"?' More calmly she repeated her tale.

'I don't know who he is, but honestly, Andrew, he gives me the creeps, and he's scaring the hell out of Harrison.'

'How do you mean?' he asked.

'I'm not sure,' she replied. 'It's as though they're scared of upsetting him. Harrison got his name wrong at first, he called him Paul, and when he was corrected, well, quite frankly he almost wet his pants.'

There was a pause. 'What did you say his name was?'

'Paul, well Paolo. Tessalli or Tessari I think.'

'Tessari?'

'No,' Louisa replied, 'Sorry, it's Tessario. Paolo Tessario.'

'What does he look like?'

18

Louisa sighed in exasperation. 'He's in his mid-thirties, he's got dark hair and a tan. He looks Spanish or Italian, something Mediterranean. Oh and he's got gold chains hanging around his neck and his wrist and he's got rings. Everything's just too loud and ghastly. And they're saying I have no choice about it. He's in.' There was another long pause from Andrew's end of the phone. 'Andrew,' she said desperately, 'you know these people. What should I do?'

He sighed deeply. 'Listen, Louisa, I can't be sure but I think that they're right. If they absolutely insist on putting this chap on the board then you will have a lot of problems keeping him off. Now don't say anything,' he continued as she began to argue furiously. 'This shouldn't have happened, that's why we went with Blake Harrison, because of their name and their reputation for integrity.'

'Integrity?' she shrieked. 'Look where their integrity has got me.'

'Please, Louisa, listen to me,' continued Andrew insistently. 'For the time being you may have to put up with him, and I only say may,' he continued forcefully as another cry of dismay came over the airwaves. 'But if he really doesn't know anything about the business then the best thing to get rid of him may be to take things easy for now. Perhaps you could sideline him in the business and get him out of there by his own choice.'

'You're joking,' Louisa exclaimed. 'Have you gone completely mad?'

'No, I'm giving you some advice. Just leave it be for now. You've made the deal. It may be best to accept this and work on it from the inside.'

'But—'

'Listen to me, Louisa,' he continued, 'I want you to stay calm, and be very polite to him, to all of them. I need to check this guy out and until I have I want you to stay on good terms with him.'

'Why?' she demanded.

'Can we discuss that later?' he answered evasively. 'I need to speak to some people first.'

'What people?'

'Just trust me, darling. Remember, I'm speaking as your lawyer and your lover.'

There was a silence. 'There's something wrong isn't there,' she said. 'Something's going on and you know what it is.'

'There's a possibility,' he admitted.

'Tell me what it is.'

'No,' Andrew replied. 'Not over the phone and not now. Just please wait. Stay calm and leave things with me.'

'OK,' she agreed. 'I'll stay cool, calm and collected, and I won't argue with them.'

'Good,' Andrew approved.

'But I will tell them I'm not happy and I want to see how this Tessario gets on before there are any final decisions about his place in the business.'

'OK,' he agreed, 'but remember, just be nice to them, at least for the time being. I'll see you at my place later tonight and we can talk more then.'

'Alright,' she said reluctantly, and put down the receiver.

Returning to the boardroom, it was clear that nothing had changed. In fact as far as she could tell no-one had moved from their seats in the intervening period. She took her place without a word, acutely aware of Tessario's eyes upon her.

'Well, gentlemen,' she began in a calm tone, 'to continue our discussion . . .' Her voice tailed off as she realised belatedly that the papers she had originally brought with her into the room had disappeared. She looked up and saw that Tessario had spread them out in front of him and was even now shuffling through them. Louisa bit her lip to prevent the rage welling up inside her from erupting out, but it was a vain gesture. 'What the hell do you think you're doing?' she demanded. 'Those are my notes and papers. Hand them back now.'

Tessario looked up at her with a mildly amused expression at her rage and shrugged. 'Hey,' he said, 'we're partners now. Perhaps you should loosen up a bit and give us all bit of leeway.'

'Us?' Louisa hissed. 'I don't see any "us" around this table, and the only person reading my confidential papers is you. So kindly hand them back. Now!'

Ignoring her outburst, Tessario pulled her strategy plan out from the pile. 'This for example,' he said. 'Lady, this is as unrealistic as hell. You will never make this much business in this space of time.'

'And what would you know about it?' asked Louisa, apoplectic with rage.

'Because I've got a brain in my head and I'm not a space-case bimbo,' he threw back, to a rustle of embarrassment from the other members of the group around the table.

'Excuse me,' Louisa spat out, all thoughts of being polite gone for good. 'I'm the one who's built up a thriving business here.'

Tessario smiled winningly, transforming his darkly aggressive, brooding features with a flash of white teeth. 'Yeah,' he said. 'Using your daddy's money. Not exactly a risk, was it?'

Louisa stood up once again. 'That's enough,' she said stiffly. 'Henry, I'm sorry but I have to insist that this person does not join the board of directors of the Dane Agency. I cannot accept him in any capacity.'

Henry Harrison shifted in his seat, clearly unwilling to answer. Instead it was Tessario who spoke, looking up at her from beneath dark, heavily lidded eyes. 'Here's the deal, Louisa. You can sit down and stop shouting because you don't actually have an option here. I am, and will remain, your fellow director and if I were you I'd get used to the idea.' He leant back in his seat. 'I don't want to upset you, but that's the way it is. Now, let's get on with the meeting, shall we?'

She stared, speechless, as Harrison turned towards her. 'Louisa,' he began, 'you know we value you and your business but Mr Tessario is quite right.' He flashed a look of concern at Tessario, who appeared to be reading a note from the papers. 'We think this is the best way forward for the agency, Louisa,' he concluded unconvincingly.

'Perhaps we could discuss this in private,' said Louisa, now utterly deflated.

'Fine, let's go into your office,' Harrison agreed, but not before Louisa had noticed him getting approval from Tessario with a fractional movement of his head. They left and walked down the corridor in silence. Louisa showed Harrison into her office and shut the door firmly behind them.

'I would like an explanation.'

Harrison shrugged. 'I can't give you one,' he said. 'This decision comes from a very high level, from very persuasive people.'

'What does that mean?'

'Louisa, he is taking that job. Please, I beg of you, let it go. Stop making a fuss and deal with it. At least for now.'

'But you're the venture capitalists. That's your business,' she said helplessly. 'You put the money into my business. You don't think he's right, so why are you foisting him on me?'

'I don't have any choice,' Harrison admitted. Louisa stared at him, shaking her head.

'So you and your band of gutless wonders out there will just sit back and let him muscle in on my agency in any way he wants?'

Harrison drew himself up. 'I am not going to discuss this any more. You have your director, Louisa, and I hope you two can work together. It would be a shame for the Dane Agency to lose someone who has made it such a success simply because they couldn't handle the inevitable changes that came with investment and expansion.'

Louisa stared. 'You're threatening to push me out of my own business?'

Harrison walked to the door. 'Our business,' he said turning shamefacedly back towards her. 'I'm sorry, Louisa,' and with that he walked out and back down the corridor.

Louisa stared at the door, hearing his footsteps departing down the corridor and feeling the world collapse beneath her feet. 'Keep breathing,' she thought. 'Just keep breathing and it will be alright.' But somehow she knew it wouldn't.

At last she felt she could move again, and she slowly made her own way back to the boardroom to collect her papers. To her surprise Tessario was there alone, the rest of the group having long since departed. He looked up as she walked in and raised one eyebrow.

'Everything OK?' he asked, as though their previous conversation had never taken place.

'Not exactly,' she replied stiffly.

'Look, Louisa,' he went on. 'Why don't we go out, have a drink, and try to work this through. I'm going to be hanging around this place a lot from now on, so we could set some ground rules; get to know each other a bit better and talk about the agency.' She stared at him, feeling beaten, and finally she shrugged.

'Fine. Whatever. I'll get my coat and some things from my office.'

'Great,' he said springing to his feet and pulling the papers together. 'I'll bring these with me and we can talk about your future plans as well.' She swallowed.

'Perhaps we could do that another day,' she said through gritted teeth.

Tessario looked at her closely for a moment. 'OK,' he agreed.

From the moment they went to the bar Tessario had chosen in the mid-town area Louisa knew the evening was destined to be a failure. He had a limousine waiting outside the office and confidently directed it to 'ZanZi' on East 54th and 22nd Street. Louisa had heard of ZanZi although she had never been there before. It was new and happening and full of young actors, models, and financiers looking out for the beautiful people. It was also loud, brash, trendy and youthful – not her sort of place at all. They walked past the crowd at the door who were vying for attention, and amazingly the doormen lifted the rope and waved them in without a second thought. They entered to a loud burst of music and her heart sank, but Tessario appeared not to notice her flinching against the noise, and led her confidently through the crowded room to the bar. Then somehow, despite the crush, they were shown to a large velvet-covered couch and a waitress appeared at their table.

'We'll have champagne,' said Tessario. 'To celebrate our new relationship.' Louisa glared at him. 'Will you lighten up?' he asked tetchily. 'How long can you keep this going?' It was on the tip of her tongue to tell him that the sooner he got out of her business the sooner she would be able to drop the unpleasantness, but Andrew's concern finally filtered through to her and she held her tongue.

'OK,' she replied, finally attempting to ease the atmosphere between them. 'I can't say I like it but I am prepared to make the best of the situation as it stands.' Tessario leaned back in his seat, apparently satisfied. 'For the time being,' she added firmly.

He nodded. 'Fair enough,' he said as the waitress returned. 'Here, have some champagne.'

She sipped at the spicy, bubbling liquid and a silence fell. As it grew more intense Louisa groped in her mind for a non-controversial topic of conversation.

'How did you do that?' she asked. 'Get us in I mean. You didn't even have to bribe the doorman.'

He shrugged. 'I have pull here.'

'How?'

'My family.'

'Oh,' she said.

Tessario glanced about him. 'Do you like it?' he asked. Louisa shrugged in response.

'It's not really my sort of place,' she admitted.

'So what is your sort of place?' he asked conversationally.

'Somewhere quieter, more relaxing.'

'Maybe you could decide where we go for dinner.'

'Um, I'm sorry,' said Louisa, 'but no. We agreed this was just for a drink.'

'If you don't like it here and it's too noisy to talk about work,' he said patiently, as though talking to a child, 'then perhaps we should go somewhere else for dinner and talk about the business there. So that we can get to know one another better,' he added with a somewhat lascivious grin that Louisa chose to tactically ignore. 'I'm not that bad really. Not when you get to know me.'

Louisa looked across the room. At length she turned back to face Tessario. 'Right now,' she said, 'I don't know anything about you, or why you're here, and I'd like some explanations. So, I guess dinner it is.'

'Good,' he said. 'Where do you fancy going?'

Louisa shrugged. 'Let's try to get a table at La Risselle. It's an Italian restaurant on 74th and Madison, not that far from the office.'

Tessario shifted and looked uncomfortable for the first time since she had met him. 'I know it,' he said. 'But are you sure you want to go there?' he asked. 'I hear that place can give you food poisoning.'

'Don't be ridiculous,' said Louisa. 'Its got an excellent reputation and I've eaten there several times. Now, will you phone or shall I?'

'No problem,' Tessario reassured her, reaching for his mobile phone. 'I'm sure they'll fit us in.' Miraculously there was a spare table and the two were soon back in the limousine and on their way.

'More family connections?' quizzed Louisa as they arrived at the small, but inviting restaurant entrance, its low-key, slightly shabby frontage disguising the fact that it was both highly successful and that it was much larger than it looked from the street, extending a long way back into the building.

'Sort of,' he admitted, and then went quiet.

La Risselle was, like ZanZi, relatively new in town, but a very different sort of place. Its ambience, menu and prices attracted a great deal of expense-account diners, plus a number of older men with much younger female dining companions. In fact, by Louisa's estimate they were some of the youngest people there, once the ad agency crowd had been discounted. It was only as they walked in that she realised her mistake in choosing this particular restaurant: she saw at least half a dozen faces that she knew reasonably well, and she knew instantly that Tessario's presence would be reported on and investigated first thing the next morning in model agencies and magazine offices about town. As they walked through the tables she had no alternative but to smile and wave at the people she knew while keeping her head up and her eyes on the middle distance, hoping no-one would try to speak to her. Meanwhile she was painfully aware of Tessario's strutting walk, which seemed to be getting worse by the moment, plus his profusion of jewellery, his gold bracelet, his rings and the necklace that had managed to work its way out from beneath his shirt.

She sat at their table and kept her eyes downwards, uncertain whether to hope that the people she knew would think this was a new boyfriend or a potential client with bad dress sense, and decide that in either case they should be left alone together. Fortunately, although a number of people had given them a close stare, no-one had come over to speak to them as yet. Tessario sat down opposite her, apparently equally unenthusiastic about talking to anyone, and a pair of waiters immediately appeared at his side. He looked up at Louisa.

'You're the classy one,' he said with a challenge in his voice. 'You order for both of us.'

Louisa gave him a sharp stare but he seemed genuine enough. 'We'll have the goat's cheese salad, followed by the San Pietro fish and a bottle of the Pouilly Fumé.' The waiters nodded in unison and one glided away to fetch the wine. 'This way, if the food's off we'll both get it,' she said sweetly to Tessario, who nodded back vaguely, letting his eyes glance around the room. The waiter returned with the crisp, fresh wine and they sat in silence for a few moments. It was Louisa once again who broke the silence. 'So, perhaps you should tell me about the work you've done in the past,' she said. 'I would like to know what areas you have particular experience in, so that I don't bore you with something you know particularly well,' she added cuttingly.

'Like I told you,' he replied. 'Its all been in related businesses.'

'Such as?'

'Magazines mostly, distribution, looking after people and guiding careers—' He paused meaningfully, but the meaning was lost on Louisa.

'Anything I'd know of?' she persisted, and was rewarded with a short, sarcastic laugh.

'No,' he said, finishing his wine, and immediately pouring another glass. 'I don't think so.'

'So, basically, you have no experience in this area,' she said, all of his responses confirming her initial suspicions.

'Plenty of experience, just not in "this area",' he agreed, mimicking her tones. 'Jeez, that's some fancy accent you've got,' he said, effectively changing the subject. 'Where'd you get it?' Louisa pursed her lips before replying and for some reason this seemed to provoke him into an immediate reaction. 'Cut that out, will you?' he said harshly. 'God, every time I open my mouth you get that smug little look all over your face. Like you're thinking about just how much to talk down to me.' He paused, glowering at her. 'You know, for someone whose job is on the line you're real sure of yourself.'

There was an uncomfortable silence as the waiter arrived with the hors-d'oeuvres, then with a mercurial switch in temper Tessario clearly controlled himself and continued. 'So, did you get that accent at school?' Louisa nodded. 'Where was that?'

'A private school in Manhattan,' she replied faintly, 'and a year in Europe. Then college at Brown's.'

He nodded. 'Very fancy. Very Ivy League,' he said, continuing to eat. After a few minutes he looked up at her and smiled. 'Excellent choice.'

'Good,' replied Louisa, and they continued eating in silence.

There was a small dance floor in the corner of the restaurant, and a band was playing tunes from the forties. When they had finished eating Tessario looked over his coffee at Louisa. 'Would you like to dance?'

'This isn't a date, you know,' she said stiffly. He smiled in return and stood, holding his hand out for hers. Louisa sighed slightly and joined him. He drew her onto the dance floor, and into his arms. Contrary to her expectations he was an excellent dancer, holding her close but not too tightly, and leading with an innate grace and experience. Her mind wandered

27

as she realised how close she was to his body, to the solid muscles beneath the fabric of his suit and shirt. Tessario was unsophisticated and uncouth, and God only knew what he was doing in her business, but at the same time she couldn't deny that physically he was very sexy. At least he would be if only he'd keep his mouth shut and drop the jewellery, she thought. His smell was masculine, with a slight aroma of expensive cologne, his body moulded easily against hers, and she became uncomfortably aware of his physique, his size and his masculinity. With a shock Louisa realised he was definitely aroused and she looked up to see him studying her closely. She blushed involuntarily and drew away from him.

'I think we should go now,' she said.

The limousine was waiting for them outside, and in the chilly night air Tessario acted out his part as a perfect gentleman, insisting on putting his coat around her shoulders while they got to the car and then holding the door open for her. As they drove towards her apartment block in Tribeca, Louisa realised that she was exhausted from the emotional rollercoaster of the day. She leaned back against the seat and let her head rest and her eyes close, aware that Tessario was very close by, but relieved that for the time being at least, he seemed more preoccupied with his own thoughts and the flow of traffic around them. At least he couldn't read her mind, she thought. A hand touched her knee and she jumped in surprise.

'Hey, come back to earth,' Tessario said.

'I was just thinking about work tomorrow,' Louisa lied, crossing her legs and shaking his hand off her in the process.

'Great, well you can count me in on that.'

'You'll be there tomorrow?' she asked. In reply Tessario shook his head in mock despair.

'Louisa, haven't you paid attention to anything that happened today? I am here for the duration.' He paused and his eyes narrowed as he looked closely at her, then continued in a softer tone. 'You know, I'm sure we could get along. And of course, it would be to your advantage if we did.'

'I beg your pardon?'

'You heard me. How many times are we going to have to go over this. We're stuck together. Hey, I may not have wanted this job any more than you wanted me in it, but I can roll with the punches. That's what you've got to learn to do as well.' As he finished he slid his hand back onto her knee. 'You know,' he continued, 'this could be a lot more pleasant for both of us, if you wanted it to be.'

'I beg your pardon?' she said again.

Tessario laughed. 'Louisa, come on. You know what I mean.' He raised one eyebrow and his gaze ran over her body as he spoke. 'I know your type. You're all ice on the surface and fire underneath.' He raised one finger to run it down the front of her jacket, gently outlining the curve of her breasts as she sat rigidly, pressed into the corner of the seat. 'I could give you what you want,' he went on. 'I know what you want.' As he spoke his voice dropped to barely a whisper. 'You want to be treated nasty, like a bad girl deserves to be treated.' He drew back slightly to observe her face. 'I saw your playthings. I know what you want.'

Louisa stared at him, her face flushed with horror. 'What are you talking about?' she demanded hoarsely.

'The parcel at your feet,' he replied, a grin spreading slowly across his face as he watched her give a furtive glance at the package containing the lingerie Andrew had given her that morning. It looked as though no-one had touched it.

'I don't know what you're talking about,' she stated.

'Sure you do,' he continued, still smiling. 'You just don't want to admit it. That's OK, but you'd better know something, leather really turns me on.' As he spoke he ran his hand further down, onto Louisa's leg and down her thigh. Moving suddenly very fast he reached under her skirt and towards her crotch with one hand, cupping a breast with his free hand as he leaned forward to kiss her lips at the same time. The onslaught caught her by surprise for a moment, and his tongue slipped between her lips, warm and tantalisingly sexual. Then she recovered herself and slapped his face – hard.

'Take your hands off me,' she stormed.

'Woah, calm down,' he replied, recoiling back, apparently mystified by her reaction. 'What's the problem? We were getting on great.'

'We were not getting on great,' Louisa spat back. 'We were not getting on at all. We were simply having a business dinner that you insisted upon. Then you started mauling me.'

'Oh yeah,' he sneered. 'So what was all that coming on to me on the dance floor and just now in the car.'

'I was not coming on to you,' she screamed.

'Oh yeah,' he taunted her, 'all that snuggling up to me, making sure your tits brushed against my arm. Leaning back and crossing your legs so I could get a really good look up your thighs. You're dying for it.'

'Stop the car,' said Louisa. 'I'm not putting up with any more of this.'

'Don't be ridiculous,' Tessario snarled back. 'You wouldn't last five minutes out there.'

'Longer than being in here with you. Anyway, who says I'm the one who's getting out? Now stop the car.'

They glared at each other, then Tessario leaned forward and barked at the driver to stop. 'Thank you,' said Louisa in a frosty voice, collecting her things together.

'What do you think you're doing?' Tessario asked wearily.

'Making myself scarce.'

'Shut up and sit back,' he replied. 'If it's so offensive to spend another moment with me then I'll get out and the car can come back for me.'

'That's quite alright, I will be fine,' replied Louisa stiffly.

'No you won't,' said Tessario dismissively, getting out of the car. 'But I will be.' He leaned into the driver's window. 'Get her to her place, and send someone out to collect me. I'll be in the bar over there.' He ducked his head back out of the car and straightened up. 'Enjoy your ride home, princess,' he said through the open window with exaggerated politeness, then waved the limousine on its way. As the car drew away Louisa swivelled in her seat and stared at his receding figure until finally he turned and walked into the bar.

30

Chapter 2

Louisa gathered her belongings together, slammed the door of the limo shut behind her and stepped through the threshold of her apartment block breathing a sigh of relief that the day was finally over. Nodding a cursory goodnight to the doorman she took the elevator to her apartment and, letting herself inside, she breathed a sigh of thanks that she was finally alone. She walked through the open plan apartment, heading for the bedroom where she was relieved to strip off her suit and replace it with casual and comfortable leggings and a voluminous white cotton shirt. Then she went into the kitchen and poured herself a glass of white wine, turning to the phone as she drank, to call Andrew. Thankfully, he was at home and picked up the phone after only a couple of rings.

'Louisa?'

'Yes.'

'Thank God, I was getting worried. Where have you been?'

She sighed. 'Out for drinks, then dinner. And it was just lovely,' she added in a voice heavily laced with sarcasm.

'Listen, Louisa,' Andrew continued, barely listening to her reply. 'Stay where you are. There are some people coming over to see you. They want to talk about Tessario.'

'Why?' she asked. 'And how do you know?'

'Well,' he went on, clearly somewhat uneasy, 'they have some concerns about Tessario's role in the business.'

'They're not the only ones,' Louisa replied wearily, going back into the lounge, sitting down and swinging her feet up onto the sofa. 'We have got to work something out as quickly as possible. Do you have any idea what sort of afternoon I've had with him? Anyway, who are these mysterious "people"?'

'The FBI.'

Louisa's stomach froze and then flipped. 'The FBI? Why do they want to see me?'

'Look,' said Andrew. 'Now isn't the right time, but they'll explain everything. Louisa,' he added, sounding worried, 'this is moving fast. Just listen to them and do what they tell you to. OK?'

'I'll listen,' she replied, guardedly. 'How soon can you get here?'

'I've got some things I've got to finish off at this end and then I'll be right over. I shouldn't be too long.'

'Thank God,' she replied as the doorbell rang. 'I need you for support. You have no idea how awful this is. And goodness knows what these FBI types want, but whatever it is it won't be good—' There was silence from the other end of the phone and she stopped in mid-step, headed towards the door. 'You know something else don't you,' she stated. There was a pause then Andrew reluctantly replied.

'Not much,' he admitted. 'But enough to be worried.'

'Andrew, you're scaring me,' Louisa whispered. 'What's going on?' The doorbell rang again and she peered at the wall-mounted video screen showing a group of four men, none of whom she recognised. 'Hold on,' she said to Andrew, then she turned to address the men on the screen. 'Yes?'

'Ms Dane?' the foremost, oldest man enquired, flashing a badge at the camera. 'I believe you're expecting us.'

Louisa paused, then slowly pressed the buzzer. 'You'd better come up,' she said. Speaking into the phone she continued, 'Andrew, they're here.'

OK,' he agreed. 'Just remember, listen to them, pay attention to what they say, and call me when they're gone. I'll be with you as soon as I can.'

Louisa put down the phone, and finally responded to the insistent buzzing at the main door. The group of four came in led by the oldest, and clearly the most senior, who introduced himself as 'Agent Krysakow'. He was aged about forty-five, with the calm, relaxed manner of a friendly bank manager, which sat in complete contrast to the edgy unease of the remaining three younger men, Agents Davies, Kelly and Scott, who sat themselves in a row on the far end of the sofa she had previously occupied.

'Andrew tells me he contacted you,' she filled in, hating the silence between them. Krysakow nodded gravely, wandering about the room, apparently absorbed in the decor. 'How did he know how to do that?'

Krysakow turned to face her. 'We approached him a week or so ago.' At Louisa's mystified expression he continued. 'We didn't want to elaborate at that time, but we did ask him to contact us if certain situations developed within your business.'

'My business?' she repeated stupidly. 'That's what I don't understand. Why didn't you just ask me instead?'

'We didn't want to put you into a difficult position too early,' he explained, looking sympathetically at her. 'Unfortunately, the situation has developed much as we suspected it might, and we need to take you into our confidence. For your own protection if nothing else.'

'And what do you mean by that?' Louisa demanded.

Agent Krysakow sighed. 'Ms Dane, you seem to be wilfully refusing to accept the evidence in front of your eyes. You have been sold out by those very nice people at Blake Harrison, and now instead you are involved with some very nasty people.'

'Explain,' said Louisa. 'For God's sake stop messing about and just explain what you mean.'

'Ms Dane,' he continued, 'your new partners are the Mafia.'

For long moments Laura stared at him with her mouth wide open. Then she shook her head, as if to wake herself up from a nightmare. 'What do you mean "Mafia"?' she demanded. Krysakow rose and walked over to her.

'I realise that this will be something of a shock to you—'

'A shock?' she spluttered.

'—But if you stay calm we can help you.'

Louisa sat down on the nearest chair with a thump. 'How exactly? And why should I listen to you?'

Krysakow sat down beside her. 'Because, Ms Dane, we offer you the best, if not the only, chance of staying alive.' Louisa stared at him as long seconds ticked by, then quite suddenly she laughed out loud.

'This is ridiculous. How or why would the Mafia be involved in my little company?'

Krysakow gave a worldweary sigh and sat down bedside her. 'This particular family needs a legitimate business through which to launder money from other more nefarious activities.'

'I don't understand.'

'They bring money into the business, a lot of it. In your case,' Louisa flinched, 'in your case,' he explained, 'it's investment money that they'll probably bring in. Although they might also get your business to use their own suppliers, and in that way they launder dirty money by passing it through a series of businesses until it can't be traced any more. In fact it only needs to pass through three or four businesses before the money is completely untraceable. Then it's clean and legal and can go back to the Family. Very simple.'

'But how do you know about it?' she whispered.

'We have informers.' He shrugged. 'It doesn't really matter. But believe me, Ms Dane, this information is good. The firm of Blake Harrison sold you out to the Mafia to get them off their backs, and now they plan to launder funds through your business. Whether the Dane Agency grows or folds in the long term will be irrelevant to them. If they can make it work, so much the better.'

'And me?'

'You are essential to keep the business going, for the moment. But sooner or later they will make a decision on what to do with the business in the future, and you won't have a say. At that point you'll either be in with them, or out.' He paused meaningfully. 'And if you're out then you could be anywhere.'

Louisa swallowed. 'What does that mean?'

'These are dangerous people, Ms Dane.'

'Who are "they" exactly?' she asked. He stared at her.

'Paolo Tessario for one.'

'Oh come on,' she scoffed. 'He's an Italian-American but that's all. He wears too much jewellery and he's an oversexed fool, but surely he's not really . . .' Her voice tailed away at the expression on Krysakow's face. 'Surely you must be wrong.'

'No, Ms Dane,' he insisted mildly. 'We're not wrong about this at all and you know it already, you just haven't admitted it to yourself yet. Tessario's uncle is Georgio Mazzucello; he's the head of this particular Family. Tessario is clean so far, but that's only because we haven't caught him at anything.

'We know Tessario's mother looks out for him and tries to keep him out of the business, the traditional family business. So far he's been on the legit side of the mob,' Louisa shuddered, 'but now it looks like he's coming out of the woodwork and showing us the real thug inside.' He grasped Louisa's shoulders. 'These are bad people, Ms Dane. You must understand that.'

She pulled away. 'So why are you here? What am I supposed to do?'

'We want you to help us trap them.'

Louisa stared. 'Are you insane? You've spent all this time telling me my new partners are the mob and now you calmly suggest that I should go up against them? You must be mad.'

The ring of the outer doorbell was an abrupt shock to the group, and at the same moment an agent's radio buzzed. He muttered into it for a moment and looked up as Louisa, held back from answering the door by Krysakow, opened her mouth to complain. 'It's Tessario.'

'What do I do?' she whispered, suddenly scared.

'Act normally,' Krysakow replied. 'Don't worry about what to say or do. Just be yourself.'

'I could tell him I know about him,' she whispered desperately.

'I beg you, Ms Dane,' he replied, 'don't do that. It would not be a good idea. Whilst this Tessario is an unknown quantity, the chances are that he's just like the rest of them and that could mean you'd be in great danger.'

She swallowed, and nodded. 'Alright,' she whispered. 'I'll do my best.'

Krysakow smiled down at her reassuringly. 'You'll be fine.' He motioned to the rest of the group who got up and trooped into her bedroom at the far side of the apartment. Turning back to Louisa he continued, 'Just remember, keep him talking, be nice to him, and try to relax. You should probably try to keep him at the door, but whatever you do, try to forget that we're in the next room.' He turned to leave and join his men. 'Remember, you won't come to any harm if you just be yourself, and nothing can happen to you – we'll be here the whole time.'

The buzzer sounded again, and he disappeared from her view. 'Some comfort,' muttered Louisa as she went to the intercom. On the video she could see Tessario looking up at the screen, clearly exasperated. She pressed the button and spoke.

'Hello.'

'Louisa? Hey, I thought you weren't going to answer me for a moment.'

'What can I do for you?' she asked and in response he put on a pitiful expression and gazed into the camera.

'Can I come up? I'd like to talk to you.'

'It's late,' she replied. 'Can't this wait until tomorrow?'

'It's personal,' he replied. 'I'd like to explain. About tonight.' He shifted from side to side and for a moment he almost looked young and vulnerable as he continued to stare contritely upwards into her eyes.

Louisa sighed. 'Alright,' she replied, and pressed the buzzer, looking over her shoulder to where Krysakow was observing her from the 'safety' of the bedroom doorway. 'OK?' she asked.

'Fine. Just keep him talking and we'll see where he wants to go with this "explanation".'

She turned back towards the door as the internal buzzer

sounded and when she cast a final look towards the bedroom Krysakow had hidden away again. 'Great,' Louisa muttered to herself. 'My heroes.' Opening the door she found Tessario casually leaning against the doorpost.

'Hey,' he said, smiling at her as if they had never screamed insults at each other and as if he were here for a cosy chat.

'Hey yourself,' Louisa replied, her nervousness adding to the tones of overwhelming sarcasm.

Tessario looked over her shoulder and into the apartment. 'Can I come in for a moment? I'd rather not do this on the doorstep.' Without a word, Louisa stood aside to let him in. He sauntered across the threshold and looked about him with interest. 'Nice place,' he said approvingly, strolling around the room.

'I'm glad you like it,' said Louisa, once again letting sarcasm drip from her words, 'but I'm sure you didn't come here to admire my taste in wallpaper.' There was a pause as Tessario continued to walk around the room, watching her out of the corner of his eye.

'Yeah,' he said casually, continuing his perambulation around the room and towards her bedroom. 'You're right.'

'You wanted to explain,' Louisa interjected nervously, however this time he made no sign of having heard her. 'Hey,' she said sharply and a second later an even louder 'Hey,' finally brought him to a standstill as his hand was stretching out to open the connecting door to her bedroom. His eyebrows lifted in a query, his hand hovering near the handle as she gestured vaguely at the sofa.

'Look,' said Louisa, 'you wanted to talk, so why don't you sit down and start talking?'

'What's the matter, Louisa?' Tessario asked. 'Got something to hide in there? Or someone maybe?' He gestured at the bedroom door with his thumb, but when she only glared at him without answering he raised his hands in surrender. 'OK. I'll sit. Jeez, get a sense of humour.' He retraced his steps to the other side of the room and sat down on the sofa, looking across to Louisa, who was still standing nervously near the front door. 'You can relax, you know,' he said with a smile. 'I'm not going to jump on you.' She raised her eyebrows disbelievingly. 'OK,' he went on, 'I just wanted to say I'm sorry if I came on a bit strong earlier tonight. You were giving out some mixed signals you know,' he continued defensively. 'It wasn't all my fault.'

'Bullshit,' she hissed, forgetting her earlier nervousness in a wave of irritation at his arrogance. 'There was nothing mixed about my signals and you knew exactly what you were doing.'

He shrugged. 'Anyway, I guess it put you on edge. But you know,' he continued, looking up at her from beneath long dark lashes with a smooth, practised smile. 'You're pretty gorgeous, and I just couldn't help myself.'

'Fine,' replied Louisa. 'You couldn't help yourself. Thanks. I'll remember that the next time you ask me to get into a car with you. Just don't be surprised if I can't help myself when I kick you in the balls. Now,' she continued, 'if you don't mind I'd like to have some quality time to myself, so this is where you leave and don't come back. Anything else you want to say can be said at the office.'

She opened the front door and held it ajar as Paolo rose slowly from his seat. At the threshold of the apartment he paused. 'You seem pretty on edge, Lou,' he commented. 'Is anything bothering you? Something at work perhaps?' He smiled knowingly but Louisa gritted her teeth and refused to let herself be drawn into the conversation. Unperturbed he came closer, so that their bodies were occupying almost the same space. 'You know, I don't want to worry you, but I can give a really relaxing massage . . .' His hands glided upwards to hover at her neck, before he apparently caught himself. 'Whoops,' he said, sighing melodramatically. 'Looks like I've done it again, and I only came to offer the olive branch and say "let's try again".'

'Fine,' said Louisa, staring straight ahead and refusing to meet his eyes. 'Now you've said that, we can say goodnight and I can sleep easier in my bed. I've already told you, anything else you have to say can be said in the office – in the morning.' She finally turned her head to meet his gaze, and was stunned by the depth of his limpid brown eyes and the extraordinarily long lashes that surrounded them.

Tessario smiled lazily, as if in that instant she had exposed her innermost thoughts to him. 'I just wanted to make things right between us,' he said breezily. 'So now we can start the new day on a proper footing. Partners together, at least between the hours of nine and five.'

'Fine,' she replied, petulantly looking away once again. 'That's great. Goodnight.'

'After all,' he continued, ignoring her interruptions, 'we're in this together. For richer or poorer.' He paused. 'And I will give it my best shot at being good. I promise. However distracting it might be to work so closely with you . . .' He let the last sentence hang in the air, then he gave another infuriatingly knowing smile and strolled past her, so close that she could feel the heat from his body, and her shirt fluttered as he went by. 'Goodnight, Louisa,' he called. 'It's been a pleasure, as always.' Finally he left, strutted down the hall and walked into the elevator, giving her a casual wave without looking backwards, obviously confident that she would be there to see him gone.

Louisa felt her rigid muscles sag with relief, and giving a huge sigh of exhaustion she turned back into the living room. Krysakow and the other agents had already emerged from the bedroom and were having a conference in the corner of the room. 'Great,' she said crossly. 'What if he'd decided to come back in for a goodnight kiss?'

'Why? Was that on the cards?' asked Agent Scott with a smile.

'He seemed to think it was,' Louisa retorted. 'And what would you have done? Told him you were my brothers?' She stomped into the kitchen and pulled out a half-empty bottle of Chardonnay, pouring herself a glass and pointedly ignoring the sounds of someone following her. Finally she turned around to face Krysakow, waiting patiently at

39

the doorway. 'Well?' she asked. 'So what's the master plan now?'

He observed her patiently for a moment, ignoring the drink in her hand. 'He's clearly very attracted to you,' he commented.

Louisa snorted in disbelief. 'That man would get his pants off for anyone,' she retorted, sipping at her wine. 'Sorry, but I've just spent the evening with him and I'm telling you, he'll do anything and anyone, any time.'

'And I'm telling you, Louisa,' Krysakow continued. 'Right now any idiot could see that you'd be at the top of his list.'

'So?'

'So this changes everything.' He leaned against the wall of the kitchen and in the ensuing silence Louisa could hear the sound of police cars screaming in the distance, the radios crackling from the next room, and the agents replying in their officious manner. Finally she gave in.

'OK. You clearly want me to ask, so I'm asking. How?'

Krysakow didn't answer immediately. Instead he stared into the distance for a moment, formulating his reply. 'We hadn't appreciated that this attraction would occur. It offers us and you a completely new opportunity.'

'I haven't got a clue what you're going on about,' Louisa said, sipping at her wine.

'Look,' said Krysakow, 'if we can get closer to Tessario we can learn a great deal more about the business he and his family are in.'

'Excuse me,' replied Louisa. 'If "we" can get closer? I think what you really mean is "If Louisa can get closer".'

'Well, yes,' he agreed. 'But we can offer you all the support you might need. We would keep a very close eye on you. All we would need you to do would be to get close enough to Tessario to find out where the important information is.'

Louisa stared at him. 'No way,' she said finally.

'Louisa,' he began, opening his arms wide as if to embrace her into his idea.

'Ms Dane to you,' she snapped. 'No way. That's final. Do

you think I'm mad?' she continued, striding past Krysakow and into the lounge where the other three agents were waiting. 'You waltz in here, tell me I have a mobster for a business partner and suddenly it's, "Hey Louisa, why don't you just cosy up to the bastard?" Thank you but no. I'd like to keep my kneecaps intact and you lot can do your own dirty work. That's what I pay my taxes for.' She opened the door to the corridor and stood, waiting for them to leave. For a moment there was silence, then Krysakow walked over to the door and stood in front of her, looked sad and world weary.

'Of course,' he said, 'you have to make your own decision, but if you are actively working against the state we may find it unavoidable to keep you out of any future prosecutions. After all, you would be working for organised crime.'

Louisa's eyes widened. 'You bastard. You'd never be able to pull a fast one like that.'

'Ms Dane,' he replied, 'we will do whatever we have to in order to prevent the activities of the crime Families. If you choose to actively work with them, then as far as we are concerned you are working against us, and we can only react to that situation.'

'What the hell does that mean?' she stormed.

'It means that you should seriously consider what you are going to do about Tessario,' Krysakow advised her.

'I've told you,' she snapped. 'Nothing.' He shrugged.

'I wish I could say it has been an unmitigated pleasure,' he told her, 'but unfortunately . . .' He spread his hands expressively and smiled sympathetically. 'I'm sure we'll speak again,' he concluded and left the room. Steaming with rage and fury, Louisa held the door as the remaining agents trooped out of her apartment, following their leader. The last to leave was Scott, who passed her saying, 'I've left a contact number on your mantelpiece, just in case you should reconsider your position.' Then he too was gone.

She slammed the door in their wake and, turning back to the sofa, threw herself down on it, staring at the ceiling of the apartment, too exhausted even to cry. When the doorbell rang once again she finally managed to rouse herself out of her stupor. It was Andrew. He came into the lounge and wrapped his arms around her carefully and gently, completely demolishing her veneer of calm.

'What am I going to do?' she sobbed, leaning her head against his chest. Then she grabbed at his lapels. 'And you, you bastard. You knew this was going on and you didn't tell me,' her voice soared to a crescendo, and ended in a strangled cry.

'Oh baby,' he murmured, stroking her hair. 'By the time I knew anything it was a done deal, and to be honest I just didn't believe it. The FBI didn't tell me anything of substance, they just talked about the possibility of "business activities" and made vague comments about your new partners.'

'You're not stupid, you're a lawyer,' she spat at him. 'You must have known something was up.'

'Louisa, I didn't,' he said stroking her hair. 'I'm sorry. As soon as the FBI left my office I ran another check on Blake Harrison and I truly thought they'd got it all wrong. It was only after you phoned me from the office that I began to think something was up.' He held her by the elbows and looked down into her eyes. 'Did you really think I would have kept something this important from you? If I'd had any idea . . .'

She nodded, still sobbing bitterly. 'They said you didn't believe them.'

'What else did they tell you?' he asked, leading her over to the sofa and depositing her there.

Louisa sighed. 'Just that they've never managed to pin anything on him, that he's a thug and, God help me, they think his uncle is the Godfather.'

He sighed. 'Anything else?'

'Oh yes,' she said bitterly. 'Not so veiled threats about how if I don't play their game and spy on Tessario, they'll treat me as a co-conspirator and get me sent down.'

Andrew's lips twitched. 'A "co-conspirator"?' he asked disbelievingly, as he unfolded a handkerchief and passed it to Louisa.

She nodded. 'If I'm not with them I'm against them.'

He laughed. 'That's ridiculous. As of right now, no-one has done anything illegal in the business. They're just trying to intimidate you.'

Louisa glared at him. 'Thank you, Einstein, I had managed to work that out for myself,' she said. 'And guess what? They're really good at it!' Andrew's lips eased into the shape of a smile once again and despite herself Louisa found herself joining in the laughter whilst wiping away the tears from her cheeks. 'Oh God,' she said. 'What the hell am I going to do?'

Andrew wrapped his arms around her and walked her through the lounge to the bedroom. 'You're going to relax, and then go to bed and take time to think things over. Nothing will happen instantly, and it may be that you do decide to talk to the FBI again. Right now they're just trying to pull your chain and we're not going to let them.' He led her to the bed and helped her remove her leggings before laying her down on the cover. Then he curled up beside her, caressing her and stroking her hair; soothing her with his movements. She felt the tension within her start to ebb away as she accepted the sense of his suggestion and as she relaxed in his arms he kissed her gently. She tilted her head to meet his lips for the second kiss, a slow, warming meeting of their lips, then slowly she moved her arms around his head and shifted her body to wrap herself around him. In silence they held each other, both enjoying the warmth and pleasurable understanding between them.

As she lay there Louisa's mind kept going over and over the events of the evening. Without actively wanting to, she found herself constantly focusing on Tessario's clumsy attempt at seduction in the car and the impression of suppressed power and maleness that emanated from his body whenever he was near her, whether it was dancing, standing or pressed up close to her.

Quite abruptly the gentle soothing she was receiving wasn't enough to eliminate the memory and Louisa's sexual appetite

43

overtook her attempt at relaxation and complacency. Without warning she was filled with a sense of passion that had her brain spinning out of control and her body arching upwards for her lover's embrace. She reached out and grasped Andrew's head in both hands, drawing him down towards her mouth, seeking his lips as an intense hunger coursed through her veins.

The unexpected change clearly surprised Andrew but this reaction drew an even stronger response from Louisa. Her hormones and senses went into overdrive as she pushed him back onto the bed and ripped at his shirt, the buttons spinning off into the distant recesses of the room.

'Louisa . . .' Andrew began.

'Shut up. I want to forget today ever happened, so just shut up and fuck me,' Louisa whispered back, dragging the shirt from his shoulders and down his back, fighting with the bedsheets as she tried to roll a still-stunned Andrew forward and backwards to remove his clothes.

'Louisa—'

She finally pulled the last of his shirt from out of the waistband of his jeans and, dragging it from his shoulders, threw it across the room and returned to concentrate on unbuttoning and unzipping his pants.

'Louisa—'

She slid the leather belt out of his pants with a smooth movement and knelt over him on all fours, pinning him down beneath her. 'Andrew I want you so badly,' she panted. 'Please, don't ask questions. Just shut up and fuck me. I want you now and I want you hard in me. I want you nasty. And I don't want to talk about it.'

Through the gloom she could make out the contours of Andrew's face, and letting her body sink down onto his she could feel the mound of his erect phallus through his open jeans and against the satin panties she still had on. Silence gathered around them and then, through the shadows Andrew moved, reaching out for his belt where it lay discarded on the bed. He twisted from under Louisa and rolled her over, sitting up on his knees and drawing her up to face him. With one hand he grabbed her wrist, and twisted it behind her arched back, holding it there whilst he caught her free wrist and twisted it likewise behind her.

'Stay there,' he commanded as he slid the soft leather of his belt around her wrists and tied it in a crude but effective knot. Standing up, he stepped off the bed and out of his trousers, then reached down for her once again. Louisa shuddered with delight and from her helpless position she offered her lips up to his. Andrew ignored her gesture but picked her up as easily as though she was a child and then, quite unexpectedly, he turned her around and threw her face down on the bed. Leaning over her he reached down and brutally ripped her panties off in one vicious action, tearing them in two and cutting a weal into her thighs as he did so, bringing a hiss of pain to her lips. Then there was a pause and Louisa sensed Andrew move away from the bed and out of the room.

She knew he had returned when she heard a creak and felt his body straddle hers, but then she could hear nothing except for the short pants of her own breath. Ignoring her gasps Andrew leaned over her and with an icy coldness he stroked something metallic down her back. With chilling clarity she realised that the instrument was the edge of a knife, biting into the fabric of the cotton shirt she still had on.

She was immediately stilled into absolute immobility, whilst above her Andrew slid the knife down the length of her torso, the only noise the tearing of the fabric falling apart under the pressure of the blade as he cut her shirt into two parts using the length of her spine as a guide. Then Louisa felt his hands grasp a handful of her hair and he pulled it backwards to drag her roughly to her knees. She saw the flash of a knife appear from behind her and in one fluid movement Andrew stripped the buttons from the front of her shirt, the knife cutting through the barriers of thread with barely any discernible resistance.

'That's for tearing my shirt,' he whispered into her ear, as she kept her eyes fixed on the knife in front of her. A moment later Andrew cut through the fabric of her brassiere with the same aggressive fluidity of movement, the cups falling open and apart to reveal her swollen breasts. Louisa shuddered again, leaning backwards against Andrew's chest and away from the knife blade, the tatters of her shirt falling around her wrists as Andrew cupped her breasts in his hands, teasing the nipples with his thumbs. A moan of pleasure crept out from her lips, but was cut off as he pushed her face downwards once again, and covered her body with his, his penis pushing aggressively into the crack between her buttocks.

Her breath hissed out from her mouth and she attempted to shift her body away as he taunted her with his cock at the base of her butt. Andrew's hands slid over her back, pressing her head back down into the sheets and forcing her buttocks upwards, whilst a finger jabbed into her cunt, wetting itself in her. Finally Andrew spoke. 'Sorry, Lou, I only want your ass right now,' he informed her, removing his dampened finger, running it down the crack between her buttocks and easing it inside her. She cried out and gave an involuntary shudder, partly through surprise and partly through nerves, as her butt-hole tightened involuntarily around his finger. After a moment he laughed. 'You can relax. I've decided not to fuck you in the ass. Not right now anyway,' he added as an apparent afterthought. As her buttocks relaxed he extracted his finger and then, pulling Louisa to her feet, he guided her over to the chest of drawers at the side of the room, before bending her still silent and acquiescent body over the edge of the cabinet. 'Now I can really get at you,' he murmured.

Slowly and deliberately, Andrew slid his fingers deep inside her crack, reaching inside to touch the walls of her vagina and stroke the darkness inside. Then, equally slowly, he withdrew his finger from her and instead slid his hands around Louisa's front, across her belly and down towards her clit, spreading the moistness from inside her onto the softness of her clit, rubbing and caressing it as it swelled and grew beneath his touch. Simultaneously he took advantage of the wetness seeping out of her cunt to slide his cock straight inside her. Louisa's knees buckled involuntarily and she gasped as he pushed her harshly up against the cabinet, her face pressed against the cool plaster of the wall. Andrew split her thighs further apart and with her hands bound behind her in the small of her back she was utterly dependent on him to keep her upright. Despite the wetness within her his shaft grated against her flesh as it slid in and out of her, and as if to enhance his dominance he wrapped his arms around her waist and hoisted her further forward.

'Is this what you wanted?' he grated hoarsely into her ear. 'Tell me. I want to hear you tell me.'

'Yes,' she gasped against the thrusts pushing her against the wall. 'I want you to fuck me with your cock until I scream. I want you to do me until I beg you to stop . . .'

Andrew groaned and Louisa could feel his cock pulsing inside her in preparation for ejaculation. But even as she registered that fact in her brain his hands continued to viciously squeeze and assault her clit until she cried out and orgasmed, the tiny organ throbbing hungrily under Andrew's hands. A gasp rose to her throat as the spasms passed and her cunt contracted. Then she heard Andrew pant with satisfaction as his cock deposited its fluid into her, spurting hotly out of him as a series of shuddering spasms pushed her still further up against the wall.

Finally they were both silent and as Andrew lifted himself off her Louisa groaned with relief. She could feel bruises starting to grow on her thighs and her ass, not to mention the bindings around her wrists. She turned to Andrew and raised her eyebrows. 'Are these coming off any time tonight? Or is this still my punishment for ripping the buttons off your shirt?'

Louisa woke early the next morning and left Andrew still slumbering in bed whilst she went to shake out her muscles with a hot, invigorating shower. She strolled into the shower, a tiled room with huge shower heads hanging from the ceiling, and let hot water beat into her aching flesh.

Perhaps, she thought, the whole situation can be resolved. I am certainly not getting the FBI involved any more than I absolutely have to. And they can forget about having agents snooping around and keeping an eye on me.

Creamy lather ran down her body and around the curve of her breasts as she turned up the water, the vicious jets waking her up, clearing her mind and creating a sense of well being. In her mind she ran over her plan for the day's activities, trying unsuccessfully to push the thought of Tessario to the back of her mind. Right now, she wanted the business to carry on and if Andrew was correct then her best bet would be to ignore Tessario's presence and make life so dull and tedious that he would give up and move on. Surely if the Mafia really were planning to use her business to launder money they would need it to be viable for the time being, so they would just leave her to run things.

'And Agent Krysakow can just get stuffed,' she said, thinking out loud. In response there was a snuffle of restrained laughter and she opened her eyes to see Andrew standing behind her. 'Well,' she said archly, 'I would have thought you'd still be in bed, or practising reef knots somewhere.'

Andrew joined her under the shower and put his arms around her. 'Better than that,' he said. 'I've been practising moves in my mind and I was thinking we could try out the theory. Just to see if it works, you understand.'

He ran his fingers down her spine, and found the bruises on the tops of her thighs and her buttocks. Louisa winced as he ran his fingers over them.

'Oh,' he said with mock sincerity. 'Does that hurt?'

'Bastard,' laughed Louisa. 'You know it does.'

'So what else hurts?' asked Andrew, running exploratory hands over her tender flesh. 'How are your tits?' He slid his hands around the base of her breasts, cupping them to hold them away from her torso.

'My tits are just fine,' she retorted. 'And no thanks to you.'

'They look more than fine to me,' Andrew replied, as he observed her nipples crinkle into hard tight buds against his touch.

Louisa shook her head in disbelief. 'This isn't like you,' she teased. 'Don't you have an early meeting to go to?'

'And how is your pussy this morning?' he continued, ignoring her comments completely and continuing his systematic examination of her naked body, apparently oblivious to his swelling cock rising between them.

'My pussy is also just fine,' she replied. 'This isn't like you, Andrew. What's got into you?'

'Maybe it's my hidden side,' he retorted. 'Or maybe I'm starting to worry about that Italian stud you're going to be keeping at your office. What if he starts getting into you?'

'Thanks,' she said sourly. 'Just as I was managing to get him out of my mind.'

'So you do think he's a bit of a stud do you?' he asked.

Louisa bit her lip. Suddenly she was inexplicably wary of telling Andrew about Tessario's behaviour and his blatant attempt to seduce her in the limousine. With a guilty flush she realised that she also hadn't told Andrew anything about Tessario seeing the leather basque.

Andrew, however, mistook her silence for agreement. 'Oh,' he said testily, 'that's the way it is, is it?'

'No,' she scoffed. 'He's slimy and uncouth. An unsophisticated animal.'

'Well,' continued Andrew, 'in that case perhaps we should get you some practice.'

'At what?'

'At fucking like an animal,' he replied, casually sliding his fingers down and into her bush, pulling gently at the blonde hair. Louisa swallowed as a sensation of lust swelled inside her once again, threatening to make her knees buckle underneath her. 'Andrew, when you talk dirty to me . . .'

'What?'

'It makes me want to screw you senseless,' she whispered.

'Then get down on your knees and start working,' he whispered back to her, pressing down on her shoulders. Shakily Louisa slid to her knees to take Andrew's cock in her mouth. She put her lips around his member and slid her lips down the length of the phallus to the balls at the base. She held him there for a moment, then reversed her movements, increasing the pressure around his cock as she slid her pursed lips back up to the head. Andrew groaned as she began to move in a rhythm, sucking him aggressively and quickly twice then slowing down to a lingering pace on the third stroke. As she looked up she could see his face flush with desire and excitement and she put her hands around his buttocks to draw him closer to her mouth, greedily feeding off his hard penis and the control she had over him. She continued to fellate him until she felt and heard the warning signs that his control was weakening, then she slowly eased the pace down and looked up at Andrew's face, his eyes closed and his hips rocking slightly as a groan slipped from his lips.

'You give great head. Did anyone ever tell you that?'

'Only the guys who were paying for it,' she teased, slowly straightening up and putting her arms around his waist.

'So, what do I get if I pay?'

'Well,' she replied, 'there are levels. Level one gets you straight sex. Level two gets you a blow job. And level three . . .'

'Yes,' he asked, in a voice that was thick with imagination and desire.

'For that you get to do whatever you want.'

'Well then,' he continued 'it's a good thing I've got a great imagination.' He opened his eyes and reaching out to the wall unit behind him he retrieved a set of handcuffs. Louisa stared at them. 'When did you manage to sneak those in?' she asked.

'You'd be amazed at what I've "sneaked" into your apartment,' he replied, letting the handcuffs swing rakishly from one finger.

'So,' she said, hands on her hips, 'you're kinky. Who'd have guessed?'

'That's me,' Andrew replied. 'Mild mannered banker by day and sex beast by night.' Louisa laughed and with a swift movement Andrew pushed her back against the wall, then reached for her wrists and snapped the cuffs around one, pulling her arms up and swinging the chain over the cold water pipes before fastening her securely into the other handcuff. Louisa raised her eyebrows as he stood back to admire his work. Stretched out to its full extent her body was lithe and athletic and the water jetting from the showers above them ran down her skin, making sensual tracks across her breasts whilst a subtle shadow of the muscles she worked for in the gym was just evident beneath the feminine curves and soft luscious skin.

'Very nice,' said Andrew approvingly. 'I'd forgotten how nice it was just to look at you. Perhaps I should leave you there for a while.'

'Very funny,' said Louisa, 'but I've got a business to run.'

Andrew laughed. 'You've changed your tune.'

'Let me down now,' she instructed, writhing against the restraints.

'You're not exactly in a position to be bossy any more,' he murmured. Gazing down at her and reaching out for a bottle of bath oil, he dribbled it down her front and let his fingers trail the sensuous path of the oily droplets, stroking his way down the central groove between her breasts, down her belly and along the line of fine blonde hairs that led inexorably into the golden blonde bush at the apex of her thighs.

'Andrew,' Louisa began weakly, as his oiled hands stroked their way into the gap between her thighs and then around the labia, exploring the crevices as though they were new and virgin territory, whilst all the time he watched her impassively, the only signs of his own excitement the erect and solid penis tantalisingly out of touch. Despite any intentions Louisa may have had she heard herself draw in her breath sharply as Andrew began to masturbate her, sliding a single finger inside her to explore her sex, whilst the other hand began to stroke her clitoris; long caring strokes at first that rapidly became a harsher rubbing, exciting and stimulating Louisa's senses. She hung from the pipes, her eyes closed as she gave herself up to the erotic sensuality of his touch, her breasts thrust out in supplication and her legs spreading wide to enable him to penetrate her with ease. When she felt a fullness inside her she knew that he was testing her cunt for size, easing first two, then three fingers inside her and setting up a rhythmical motion that set her senses on fire.

The water was still cascading from both of them and Louisa could feel a tension in her belly and electricity running in bolts of excitement from her cunt through to her head as her first orgasm sparked its way through her. Reaching for the full degree of satisfaction her head hung back and she panted and moaned with animal sounds as Andrew thrust his fingers in and out of her. It was only after the sounds of her pleasure had completely faded away that he replaced his fingers with his manhood, driving into her with urgent strokes, forcing her back up against the tiles as he gave in to his own needs, finally matching her climatic moans with a long drawn-out groan of satisfaction.

Chapter 3

Louisa was already hard at work by the time Tessario turned up at the office the next morning. He strolled in without knocking at the door, dressed much as he had been the previous day in a beautifully cut suit, but looking, she thought, now that she knew the truth about him, very dark, brooding and threatening. She looked up and noted his presence and then, with a deliberate air and a very determined effort, she dropped her gaze and continued with her paperwork, leaving him standing and waiting in front of her.

'Please don't come in without checking next time,' she said without looking up again. 'I might have an important client in here.'

'Or even your boyfriend,' he retorted. 'But I guess you lock that door when he turns up. Right?'

Louisa looked up. 'If I didn't lock my door before, I certainly will from now on.' She paused. 'Anyway, I've been pulling out some files for you to review.' Tessario's eyebrows lifted in surprise. 'Well,' she continued, 'you gave a very convincing little speech last night, so I've got some work for you to do.' She pulled a box of files from behind her desk and sat back. 'You do want to do it, don't you?' she asked archly.

Tessario let a smile cross his features. 'Sure, partner,' he said and hoisted the box up. 'What is it that you want me to do with all this?'

'I need you to review these files so that we can use them as a systems backup. Check and make sure they conform to the information on the IT system. I assume you can use a computer?' He nodded. 'Fine, while you're doing that you can use the opportunity to familiarise yourself with the information that's held in the files. It should give you a clear idea of what the business is about. I've had an office put aside for you down the hall and if you get stuck you can ask me, or the admin department and the bookers.' He picked up the box and began to leave.

'Oh,' she said reluctantly, 'and I thought I should introduce you to the rest of the office staff.'

'I'm sure they can't wait,' he replied ironically.

Louisa shrugged. 'I'll take you round the office later. Maybe we can actually get some work done today,' she finished, looking back down at her notes.

Tessario smiled. 'I hadn't expected to settle in so quickly,' he said. 'This shouldn't take too long to get through.'

Louisa looked up once more from behind her desk. 'Good,' she said brightly. 'That's the last box. I've had the others put in your office already. That should keep you busy for a while.' She put her head back down and let him leave.

When the door clicked shut she lifted her head and gave a deep sigh of relief, trying to calm her nerves. If he did manage to stick with the files it would be a miracle. They were the most dull analyses, reviews and examinations of old accounts she had ever seen and updating the information on the system would try the patience of a saint. With a bit of luck he would get on with it and stay out of her hair for the next few days. Surprisingly there was no sound from Tessario over the next hour and slowly her apprehensions began to slip away. Maybe he was really working his way through the mound of papers. 'Fine,' thought Louisa and carried on with her own paperwork, trying to get as much done before her next appointment.

At twelve-thirty she was holding an open call, a chance for new hopefuls to get their faces and figures examined by professionals, who then had the dubious honour of either telling them they had no hope of a career in modelling, or that given time, effort and a lot of luck there was a slim

54

possibility that they may make some money, or even become supermodels. Louisa's last PA had arranged the event before she left, and the bookers would be playing a major role, but she would at least make an appearance and give a brief talk on the business. Plus, she always liked to spend some time at these events, on the off-chance that a new 'find' might walk through the door.

She checked the time; it was already midday, so she decided to give up on her desk chores and went into the bathroom to check her make-up. The open call was on the top floor, which was used and maintained as a bookable meeting hall by all of the leaseholders in the building. At the last moment she remembered Tessario. For a moment she toyed with the idea of excluding him from the session altogether, but then she reconsidered. After all, she thought, what harm could it do? At least he could see that they actually had work to do and it would give her a good opportunity to introduce him to the staff. She phoned through to his office, but to no avail and when she checked it was locked. As a last resort she called down to the reception desk.

'I'm sorry, Ms Dane,' was the reply. 'Mr Tessario left for lunch half an hour ago. He didn't say what time he'd be back.'

Louisa sighed inwardly. 'That's fine,' she said. 'When you see him just let him know I was looking for him. You can buzz me upstairs in the open call, or send him up to meet me there.'

'Great,' she thought turning away, 'that really sets the standard for the day. But never mind,' she consoled herself as she walked to the lift, 'at least this looks as though he won't be spending much time in the office, and that's all to the good.'

The lift deposited her on the fourth floor, where there were already a group of eager young girls and a fair scattering of mothers in attendance. They all looked up with interest as she arrived and went straight to where the Head Booker, Claudia, was sitting, smiling around at the hopeful faces as

55

she walked through the room. 'How's it going?' she asked quietly.

Claudia looked at her list of names and pursed her lips in contemplation. 'Not bad. There are a couple of possibles, and some interesting faces that may have potential. No-one totally outstanding.'

'Any particularly pushy mothers?'

Claudia raised her eyes to the heavens. 'Believe me, more than one. There's a girl over there whose mother won't let her out of her sight, and the poor kid looks like she's hating every minute.' Louisa followed Claudia's nod to where a streaky-blonde middle-aged woman was fiddling with the back of her daughter's hair. As she caught sight of Louisa's attention the woman twisted her sulky-looking teenager around. Louisa smiled in acknowledgement and turned her head back to Claudia.

'Oh-oh,' she said.

'I know. How are we going to let her down gently?'

Louisa shrugged. 'She won't believe us whatever we say, so try not to let it worry you too much. Try to have a chat with the girl and see how she feels about it. After all, we're not here to be the mother's therapist.'

Claudia nodded, checked the time, then looked back down at her list. 'I think we should give it another ten minutes or so, then give them a talk and line them up for interviews and photos as required.'

'Fine,' said Louisa. 'You've obviously got everything in hand. I'll stay on a bit longer then get down to the office. You know where I am if you want me.'

Claudia nodded. 'Louisa, on another note—'

'He's my new business partner,' Louisa advised her, accurately guessing the question before it was voiced.

Claudia looked surprised. 'I thought Alex Prince was coming on board.'

'A change of plan,' said Louisa cheerfully. 'Although this is a temporary measure, we're looking to add a different business perspective to things. Anyway, his name is Paolo

56

Tessario, but we don't yet know how long he'll be able to work with us. I think he's got a lot to offer the business. I've been looking for the right opportunity to introduce him to everyone, and I think it will be later today or tomorrow.' Claudia nodded, apparently satisfied, and Louisa stood up, relieved to have covered the issue successfully. Unlike the rest of the staff she would normally discuss anything important with Claudia. They had worked together since she had set up the business and were friends as well as colleagues; however, right now she wanted to keep everything to herself. Whether or not Claudia felt alienated was not the most important issue at present, the last thing she wanted at this time was to have anyone on her staff getting bad feelings about Tessario. 'God knows,' she thought, 'I've got enough of those myself.'

The hopeful teenagers and potential models continued to arrive until there were a group of around fifty, some with mothers or school-friends. Then, after a short welcoming speech, the bookers began the business of interviewing, photographing the ones with some potential and examining any portfolios of earlier work. It was then that Louisa's day started to take a turn for the worse.

Tessario finally appeared at the entrance to the hall with another man she didn't know, whose appearance, jewellery and swarthy complexion put Louisa in mind of a bad gangster movie. At least, she thought as the two approached her, Tessario looked semi-presentable. Aware that every move and word was being watched and recorded by her staff she greeted them with a broad smile on her face.

'Hi there,' Tessario called as they approached.

'Good lunch?' Louisa asked, although the answer was obvious from his friend's slightly weaving walk. Thankfully Tessario himself seemed in control of his actions.

'You should have joined us,' Tessario said, nodding a greeting.

'Next time, perhaps,' Louisa agreed in a slightly frosty tone.

'Meet my second cousin, Anthony,' Tessario went on.

'How do you do?' she said formally. Anthony nodded absent-mindedly, looking around the room with interest.

'Great babes,' he murmured appreciatively.

'I beg your pardon?'

'Great babes. Young babes.' He flicked a glance at Louisa with a lascivious smile. 'Anyone available? I could do with one right now, if y'know what I mean.'

'I imagine I do,' Louisa said, her voice dropping to an undertone as she saw Claudia register the visitor's question with a look of surprise. She fixed Tessario with a stern glance, and he gave Anthony a good-natured push on the shoulder. 'Just Tony's little joke,' he assured her. 'Hey, mind your mouth, Tony. These aren't babes, they're ladies. Right, Lou?' Tony just snickered and gazed around the room, his eyes slightly defocused from drink as he examined the girls in front of them.

Louisa drew in a deep breath. 'Why don't you take your cousin down to your office to relax. We all have work to do and you're probably distracting the models.'

Tessario nodded, apparently taking her suggestion to heart, and turning to Anthony slapped him enthusiastically on the back. 'She's right, Tony, let's go downstairs. I've got a bar and the cable channel. C'mon.' Anthony shrugged and they ambled off, Tessario giving a final cheerful wave to Louisa as he went, to which she gave a tight little smile. Turning away, and ignoring Claudia's curious but surreptitious look at the departing men, Louisa gave an inward sigh of relief and tried to set her attention on the business at hand.

As soon as they identified her as the owner of the business, the hopefuls began to swarm around her and she was soon swamped with questions and requests for information. She joined Claudia and the others in the unpleasant business of letting people down gently. When she finally left the hall the group had been trimmed down to a more manageable and potentially successful group of around ten, of which perhaps one or two might be signed up for the agency or, in the case of the very young girls, asked to come back in a year or two.

Louisa went down to her office, planning to get back to work. The door opened under her touch and she walked in to see Anthony directly in front of her, sitting on the sofa with his trousers around his ankles. A half-naked girl with badly dyed red hair was crouched at his feet sucking enthusiastically at his crotch, her head bobbing up and down while he lay back groaning and murmuring to himself. Neither had heard Louisa enter and for a few more seconds the tableau continued in front of her stunned and horrified gaze until she exploded with rage.

'What the hell is going on here?' she demanded, her voice ringing down the corridor behind her. 'How dare you? Get up! Now!' Anthony opened his eyes in surprise and almost simultaneously the girl swivelled and stared up at Louisa with wide, shocked eyes. Louisa strode towards her and picked up a discarded bra and T-shirt. 'Get these on. Now!' The girl grabbed them and disappeared into the bathroom, following Louisa's pointing finger, the beginning of shameful tears starting to drizzle down her face.

'Hey, what are you doing?' Anthony protested, pulling up his pants as the door swung open to reveal a small crowd of staff members who had responded to Louisa's angry bellowing. Behind them Tessario's head could be seen as he tried to push his way through them and into the office. 'What the fuck are you doing?' Anthony said again, then turned to address the onlookers. 'Hey, you lot. Get out of here.'

Reaching the front of the crowd Tessario's more commanding voice echoed Anthony's instructions. 'The show's over. There's nothing to see. Everybody get back to work,' and he began to shepherd the gawking viewers and giggling women out of the doorway. Louisa stood in the centre of the room with her hands on her hips, unable to speak for fear of what she might say whilst Anthony stood arguing with Tessario.

'What the fuck were you doing in here, Tony?' asked Tessario.

'Enjoying myself. You said, go amuse myself. What the

fuck's she doing here?' he asked belligerently, stabbing a finger in Louisa's direction.

'This is my office,' she snarled back.

Anthony shrugged. 'So? I thought you were upstairs with your babe parade.'

Before Louisa could issue a retort the bathroom door opened and the girl emerged, looking young, tearstained and bedraggled. 'And who are you,' snapped Louisa, as Tessario shepherded Anthony into a corner of the room.

The girl looked up with a quivering lip. 'It's not my fault,' she whinged. 'I was upstairs at the interviews.' She shrugged. 'I saw him with you and I thought he was a boss. He said he was. He said he could put my portfolio into the agency.' The final sentence tailed away into a wail and more tears.

'You said what?' demanded Louisa, turning on Anthony and ignoring the girl sobbing beside her.

'So?' he snarled back. 'What? Like I can't use my influence?'

'What influence?' she demanded as Anthony drew himself up to answer, advancing on her with a threatening expression on his face.

'Hold on,' shouted Tessario, standing between the two and splitting them up. 'OK. Let's all calm down.' He looked around him as Louisa held her temper in check on one side and Anthony simmered on the other. 'You,' he beckoned to the girl and opened the door. 'Sorry, but things have got all out of shape. You just go down the corridor and wait in that office there. I'll come and talk to you in a moment.' She nodded and sloped off, sniffing plaintively into a tissue.

Tessario shut the door and looked at Louisa. 'I'll handle this,' he said.

'You can't handle anything,' she hissed dismissively. 'You couldn't even keep this . . . this animal on a leash for ten minutes. Now God knows how many phone lines are ringing this information around the city. This isn't something to be handled; it's a disaster!'

'Well, if you'd kept your big trap shut instead of shooting

your mouth off then there wouldn't have been any "disaster",' jeered Anthony.

'It's a good thing I walked in when I did,' Louisa snapped back. 'Do you have any idea what trouble we could be in? Do you even have any idea how old that girl is?'

'Don't you talk to me like that, you slut,' Anthony snarled back as Tessario again moved between the two of them. 'And don't you question me either.' He paused, puce with rage. 'She was old enough to know what she was doing all right. And she would have finished the job if you hadn't walked in here and started squawking.'

'Enough already,' Tessario shouted across the hubbub as Louisa began to answer back. Then on a lower and calmer tone, he repeated himself. 'Enough.' Getting some silence he turned to his cousin and jerked his head towards the door. 'Anthony. Wait for me outside.' Anthony gave Louisa one last snarling look. 'Go!' Tessario repeated. 'And, Anthony,' he added as an afterthought, 'don't go into my office.'

The door shut behind him and Louisa faced Tessario again. 'So,' she said. 'You're in charge. What are you going to do now?'

'What do you expect me to do?'

'I expect you and your friend to get out of my office and stay out.'

Tessario gave a mirthless chuckle. 'No, Louisa, that's what you want, but it's not going to happen. Now this mess is over and done. It can't be the worst thing that's ever happened in here.'

'This is my office and my company,' she said. 'Who do you think you are to talk to me like that?'

'The man with the money,' he retorted. 'Now grow up. I'll go and sort those two out.' Then he was gone, shutting the door quietly behind him.

Louisa let him go without another word and stood alone in her office. Suddenly she couldn't bear to be there. She called her PA. 'I've got to go out. Cancel any meetings and tell Claudia to call me at home if there are any problems.' She

61

grabbed her handbag and rushed for the door, a feeling of oppression almost overwhelming her. Trying to retain some semblance of dignity she walked slowly and calmly through the offices and flagged down a cab outside. Fortunately, as the rush-hour traffic hadn't yet started she was on the way home in just a few minutes.

The apartment felt chilly and empty, and she felt very alone as she sat in the lounge, isolated and vulnerable for the second time in a week. This time, however, there was no Andrew to talk things over with. He had had to leave town for an emergency meeting in Washington and he wouldn't be back or contactable until morning. There were no tears at first, but she sat, angrily beating her fists into the damask material of the sofa beneath her.

'Why?' she cried out. 'What did I ever do? Bastards . . .' She shuddered as sobs overtook her until eventually she lay stretched out on the sofa, exhausted and overwrought from the strain of holding in her feelings. 'What am I going to do?' she asked herself. 'What on earth am I going to do? And this is only the second day he's been here,' she thought.

What if this happened again and again, each time a variation on the theme? How the hell was she going to function and run the business, let alone keep it all from becoming general knowledge? She sighed. The FBI had been right. Tessario was a mobster and so were all his family and she simply wasn't suitably prepared to deal with this. 'Damn them,' she thought impotently, 'this is my business, no-one else's and I don't want it like this.'

As she lay there miserably contemplating the future the phone rang. 'Ms Dane?' The well-modulated voice at the other end of the line was familiar.

'Agent Krysakow,' she replied with a sigh. 'And how are you today? Still dispensing good news to all and sundry?' There was a pause before he answered.

'You don't sound very happy, Ms Dane. I might even say resentful.'

'Very astute,' she agreed.

'Perhaps you have reconsidered my suggestion in the light of the past twenty-four hours,' he continued. Louisa bit her lip and let out a deep sigh. 'I imagine things have been a little . . . disrupted?'

'You could say that,' she agreed.

'Perhaps then you would prefer that we become more involved?'

Louisa hesitated. 'What use would it do?' she asked.

'We could keep you safe, for a start,' he replied. 'And you could help us put these animals away.'

'Look, I know I should want to help,' she continued, 'but I can't say that I think I can make a big difference to anyone.'

'Trust me,' Krysakow went on, 'you don't know yet how much help you could be.' He paused. 'Apart from anything else, you must know by now that this could be the only way for you to keep your business.'

'You've changed your tune from the other day,' she said. 'Then it was "the only way to stay alive".'

Louisa heard a brief chortle from the other end of the phone line.

'Maybe it's just that your business seems to be the most important thing to you,' he replied.

'You're wrong there,' she replied wearily. 'It's all important to me. And I want everything, my business and my life, just the way it's been up until now.'

'Then your best chance is to work with us,' Krysakow continued smoothly.

'What do you suggest?' she asked, hearing a rush of confidence in his voice.

'You need a new PA. Tomorrow, one of your regular business associates will suggest an unemployed model with excellent PA skills. You can employ him straight away.'

'He'll be one of yours?' she asked incredulously. 'And you really think he'll pass for a PA in a model agency? I don't think so.'

'Trust me,' he replied, and she could hear the easing of

63

tension in his voice as he became more certain that she would agree to his proposal.

'OK,' she replied, somewhat reluctantly even now. 'I don't have any other options, do I? But I'm warning you right now, Mr Krysakow. If this agent of yours messes me around I'm getting rid of him without question. OK?'

'With respect, Ms Dane,' came the chilling reply, 'I think my agent is the least of your problems,' and the phone was disconnected.

Louisa was in the office the next morning when a call came in from her friend and business rival Suzanne Muller. 'Hey, Suzy,' she called out, with a false cheerfulness she didn't really feel. 'How's it going?'

'Exhausting,' came the response, 'but very profitable,' and she gave her trademark giggle. Louisa smiled in an automatic response.

'What can I do for you, Suzy?'

'Darling, it's more what I can do for you. I know Yve went back to Europe, but I think I've got the perfect replacement for you.'

'A PA?' asked Louisa. 'I'm sorry, Suzy, but I heard about one last night and I'm expecting a call today.'

'Darling, what a shame, and this chap comes with simply glowing references.'

Louisa stared down the phone. 'A man?'

'Well, I wouldn't have thought you were that old-fashioned.'

'No,' she said, 'I'm not. Well, tell me about him if he's that impressive.'

'He's a model really but you know how it is. Anyway he comes highly recommended with organisational skills to die for. Plus I believe he's very easy on the eye, although not interested in girls at all, so no worries there.'

'He sounds great,' Louisa muttered into the phone.

'Nonsense, he sounds divine. And the wonderful thing is, he's available right now. I can give you his number if you want to see him.'

'Absolutely,' Louisa answered. 'He sounds too good to miss. How did you hear about him?'

'An old friend rang me and told me. Of course I told her that I would die rather than let Janine leave me, but I immediately thought of you and your predicament . . .'

By four o'clock that evening Louisa had a new replacement secretary with excellent references and apparently all the skills to match. To her surprise it was Agent Scott.

She shut the door on her office. 'Isn't this taking things a little too far?'

'Paolo Tessario has never met me,' Scott replied. 'There's an acceptable degree of risk.'

'Thanks a lot,' she said with a withering look. 'That's very reassuring.' Unable to sit still, Louisa sprang from behind her desk and started pacing about the office whilst Scott remained seated on the sofa in front of her. 'I'm not sure about this. Are you sure you can do it?' she asked, pausing for a moment.

He shrugged. 'There's a lot to my training. Filing, answering phones and word-processing were among the easier skills to master.'

'I don't think I want to know any more,' she said, resuming her pacing.

'I wasn't planning to go into details,' he replied.

'And you're gay?' she asked nervously, looking him up and down.

'Temporarily. For this assignment.'

'That's fine, just don't camp it up too much.'

Scott smiled. 'No problem.'

Louisa continued pacing restlessly around the room. 'It's just that he's so unpredictable,' she explained.

'I gathered,' he replied.

'I mean, sometimes he's nice as pie and pleasant and, well, intelligent. He made some really good suggestions in a note to me today, and he's gone through lots of files whilst he's been here. Then all of a sudden he'll turn around and be a complete pig.'

65

'I know,' said Scott patiently.

'Then he just seems to say or do the most offensive things that it's possible to imagine,' Louisa went on.

'Ms Dane,' Scott interrupted, 'please understand something. We appreciate what you're going through, and you have done the right thing in deciding to work with us.'

'I didn't have much choice,' Louisa retorted. 'And don't forget, you're on probation right now. If things don't work out, Agent Scott, you're straight out of that door.'

'Of course,' he agreed. 'But from now on it's just Scott, OK? Anyway, now that I'm here I'll be able to keep an eye on him.'

'But you can't stop his behaviour, can you?' she retorted, throwing herself back into her chair. 'Maybe I shouldn't have agreed to this.'

'I'm sure that when you've had a chance to think things through again that you'll be pleased you did,' he said as there was a tap at the door. Louisa looked across the room at Scott who smiled at her reassuringly. 'Would you like me to open the door, Ms Dane?' he asked.

She shook her head. 'Come in,' she called. The door opened to reveal Tessario, carrying a bundle of files and with his jacket slung over one shoulder.

'I was just going home . . .' he began, and stopped when he saw the stranger on the sofa.

'Ah, Paolo,' Louisa, said nervously. 'Please, come in and meet my new PA.'

'You mean you've actually hired someone?' Tessario said in mock surprise.

Scott stood up and held out his hand to Tessario. 'Semi-permanently. And on trial,' he explained. 'Scott Stephenson.'

Tessario nodded pleasantly. 'Paolo Tessario, Louisa's partner.'

'Business partner,' Louisa interrupted.

'Whatever,' replied Tessario, looking Scott up and down. 'So how did you get through the gate? Apparently she's been looking for ages.'

Scott shrugged. 'I'm good at organising things. And Ms Dane liked my references.'

'I didn't see them,' Tessario said, looking across at Louisa.

'He's my PA, not yours,' she replied.

'True,' he said. 'OK, see you tomorrow,' and with a nod at Scott he left the room.

There was a moment of silence after he left and Louisa let out a sigh of relief. Scott smiled. 'I told you. Why would anyone pay much attention to your new PA?'

'Yeah,' she agreed, 'I guess you were right after all.'

The door rattled and Tessario put his head into the office again. He looked at Scott. 'Who did you say were your referees?'

'I didn't,' Scott replied evenly.

'So. Do you have the details there, Louisa?' She passed the sheets of paper over to Tessario. 'And you've checked them out?' She nodded. 'Mmm. Then I guess if I call them as well it won't be a problem.'

Louisa shrugged.

'None at all,' replied Scott. 'Is there something specific you want to know about?'

'No, but you can never be too careful,' Tessario replied and with a flash of a smile he left once again.

Louisa looked at Scott.

'It seems that you were right,' he said. 'Not the most trusting of people, but it's not a problem.' He stood. 'The references are kosher. I think the best thing now would be for me to make a quick tour of the offices and meet some of my new co-workers. No,' he went on as she began to get out of her seat, 'I'd prefer to do this myself and alone. I'll see you first thing in the morning and in the meantime if there's a problem, you've got my number.' He paused. 'But trust me, there won't be a problem.'

She nodded. 'If you say so.'

'I do.'

Louisa spent the first part of the evening wandering about

her apartment trying to decide what to do. Andrew was still in Washington and he wouldn't be back until morning. She could call up some friends but, she thought, they would probably already have plans and, anyway, she wasn't really in a party mood. Plus, they would be bound to want to know how the relationship with her new partner was working out and she wasn't really in the mood to discuss anything at present. No, she decided, she would stay in and settle down.

She took a long, hot shower and returned to the lounge, pink but relaxed, in a night shift and matching dressing-gown of indigo satin. She looked inside the fridge but although there was plenty of wine there was little in the way of food. She shrugged and pulled out a tub of ice cream. She wasn't hungry for a proper meal anyway. After she had eaten the ice cream she returned to the fridge for a bottle of Chablis and poured herself a large glass, as her thoughts inevitably turned back towards work and the business.

She went back into the lounge and lay restlessly on the sofa: a black mood was settling over her again and although she knew it wouldn't do any good, and that there was no-one to see her sitting there sulking, the feeling wouldn't go away. As she stomped into the kitchen to replenish her glass there was a buzz on the inner door. 'Get stuffed,' she thought, ignoring it at first, and returning to the sofa she turned on the television to drown out the noise. Whoever the caller might be, they had been convincing enough to make it past the reception area. They must be exceptionally persistent. The buzzer kept on ringing relentlessly until Louisa finally gave in, went over to the front door and flung it open. Agent Scott was standing facing the entrance with his finger still on the button. They looked at each other for a long moment, each taking in the other's appearance.

Scott had forsaken his earlier uniform of a softly deconstructed Armani suit, crisp white shirt and expensive-looking tie and replaced it with well-worn, faded jeans and a soft crew neck cotton jumper with a leather thong necklace at his throat. In casual clothes he looked very different; younger, slim and rangy, with dark hair and hazel eyes set in a lean face, and high Slavic cheekbones that gave his expression a look of intensity.

Louisa was suddenly very conscious of her own minimal attire. The satin slip stretched only as far as mid-thigh and the matching satin dressing-gown was designed to drape, unfastened, down to the floor, revealing the full extent of her bare legs. She switched the gown around her just as she realised that Scott was covertly examining her legs. He looked up.

'You're the last person I expected to see,' she said.

'I was passing. So I thought I'd drop by. Can I come in?' Scott asked. Pursing her lips she gestured indoors. 'Thanks,' he said, striding inside.

'You look different out of a suit,' Louisa said, awkwardly and unnecessarily.

'I could say the same about you,' he replied, looking somewhat pointedly at her ankles. Suddenly flustered she pulled the robe further around her.

'Wine?' He nodded and she pointed at the sofa. 'Sit down and I'll get the bottle.' She went back to the fridge and retrieved a new bottle of Chablis. On her return she found Scott examining the artwork on the walls.

'I didn't realise how nice this place was, last time I was here,' he commented. 'You have great taste.'

'Thanks a lot,' Louisa said somewhat sarcastically, returning to the sofa.

'No, I mean it,' he insisted.

'Well, thanks,' she said, slightly shamefacedly. 'Sorry, I'm not in a very good mood.' Rather shakily she poured a glass of wine for Scott. 'Cheers.' He raised his glass silently. 'So, to what do I owe this pleasure?'

He sat down at the far end of the sofa. 'I just wanted to be sure you were OK.'

'Why wouldn't I be OK?'

'After I left you this afternoon I went off and had that chat with your staff. They told me all about the problem in your office the other day.'

69

Louisa reached for the bottle and poured herself another glass, ignoring the buzzing effect that the rapidly consumed wine was starting to have on her. 'That's putting it delicately,' she said staring down into the wine. 'Does everyone know?'

'At the office? Well yes. It seems there were a lot of people around and, well apparently you were all shouting pretty hard.'

Louisa sighed. 'Do they all know what it was about?'

Scott nodded. 'Not the specifics necessarily, but they're gossiping pretty wildly.'

'Oh God,' she said. 'What a mess.'

'Well it's not that bad,' he said.

Louisa looked at him. 'How could it be worse? I'm the boss. I'm supposed to set the standard. It doesn't exactly inspire confidence in me or my partner.'

He considered then shrugged again. 'A bit of gossip . . . big deal. It'll be old news by the end of the week.'

There was a pause. 'Anyway,' she added, 'thanks for coming by.'

'Have you eaten?' asked Scott, looking at her closely.

'Just a tub of cookie-dough ice cream.'

He made a face. 'Very nutritious. Right then, Agent Scott to the rescue.' He stood up. 'The kitchen's through there, right?'

Louisa looked up from the sofa. 'What do you think you're doing?'

'Making some dinner.'

'Thanks, I appreciate the offer,' she began, 'but I'm really not very hungry.'

'You will be,' he said ignoring her protestations and striding towards the kitchen, leaving her gaping at his retreating figure. 'Just stay there and relax,' he called. 'It's all part of the service. It's called seeing your tax dollar at work.'

'There's almost nothing in the kitchen,' she said weakly, following him in.

He turned from the refrigerator. 'You're right,' he said, retrieving some eggs. 'Never mind, it's nearly time for supper

70

anyway. Now,' he repeated, 'go and sit down and I'll be as quick as possible.'

'OK,' said Louisa compliantly. 'Can I do anything?'

'No,' he repeated. 'I told you, just go and put your feet up. Relax.'

Louisa sat down at the dining table, which Scott had laid with linen, silver cutlery and candles. 'You're obviously much better at this sort of thing than me.'

'I enjoy cooking,' he explained emerging from the kitchen with a steaming tray of bagels, and creamy scrambled eggs with smoked salmon. 'Mind you, this is pretty basic stuff. I can do better but, to be honest, you haven't got much food in your kitchen.'

She shrugged. 'I'm not that interested in cooking myself,' she explained. 'I like good food, but I order in or get caterers—'

'Right, here we go,' said Scott standing behind her and helping her to a toasted bagel, heaping the scrambled eggs on top. 'Now for the final touch,' he said, sprinkling on a little caviar. 'You may not have much in the way of spices and basics,' he continued, 'but at least you have the essentials in your kitchen – wine, smoked salmon, the end of a pot of caviar and some rather ageing bagels. Who could ask for more?'

Louisa laughed ruefully. 'Sorry. I'm being very ungrateful,' she said. She reached for her glass, twisting in her seat to face him. 'Here's to you and your supper. With thanks.'

Scott smiled. 'Better eat it whilst it's hot,' he advised and sat down beside her.

The supper was delicious, the scrambled eggs light and fluffy with the tangy saltiness of the fish biting across the lighter flavours. 'That was great,' agreed Louisa with a smile as she finished. 'Just what I needed.'

'I told you so,' said Scott, returning from clearing the plates into the kitchen.

'I mean it,' Louisa repeated. 'Thanks.'

There was a pause. 'Right,' said Scott, 'I'd better go.'

'Are you sure?' asked Louisa, suddenly reluctant to see him leave. 'Wouldn't you like to stay for a while?'

'Sorry, I should go. It wouldn't be a good idea for me to stay any longer.'

Louisa's hand reached out to his. 'Why not?'

Scott smiled ruefully. 'Because you're my boss, and what if Tessario popped by to see your gay PA snuggled up with you.'

Louisa smiled flirtatiously upwards at him. 'So we'd be snuggled up, would we?'

Scott inhaled and stood. 'I must go.'

She shrugged her shoulders. 'OK. I won't beg.'

Scott smiled. 'I shouldn't think you've ever had to do that.' He leaned down and kissed her on the cheek. 'Goodnight. Get some sleep and I'll see you in the morning.' She nodded and watched him leave, wishing Andrew would turn up unexpectedly. No chance of that.

Reluctantly she drifted into the bedroom. She threw herself on the bed and was flicking through the TV channels when the phone rang.

'Hello?'

'Louisa?'

'Andrew?' she asked. 'Oh Andrew, I'm so pleased to hear from you.'

'Why? Are you missing me?' he asked.

'That's for sure. I was just thinking about you.'

'What? Not about work?'

She laughed. 'You'll be pleased to know I wasn't thinking about the office for a change.'

'Is everything alright?' he asked.

She lay back on the bed. 'No, but I'm fed up of talking about the business. When are you coming back?'

'Tomorrow,' he said. She sighed, plaintively. 'Why?'

'I was just feeling really horny. I was about to have to look for a dirty movie on cable to satisfy me.'

There was a pause, then she heard Andrew sit down. 'Where are you now?' he asked.

'In bed.'

'What are you wearing?'

She lay back. 'A very short satin shift.'

'That's all?'

'Yes,' she breathed down the phone. 'Why?'

'I left something for you,' he said. 'For when I was away. It's in the bottom drawer of your bureau.'

'Hold on,' she said, suddenly excited, and putting on the speakerphone she went to the bureau. In the bottom drawer was a box containing a large rubber vibrator. She ran an exploratory hand up and down the shaft and returned to the phone. 'I've got it.'

'I want you to do something for me,' he said. 'First of all I want you to slide your hand down into your shift and touch your nipples. Now I want you to turn the vibrator on and start to touch your nipples, and I want you to pull them, so they're really hard.' She breathed out deeply as she followed his instructions, the vibrator buzzing audibly as she ran it across her chest and belly. 'Now I want you to slide the vibrator down and start to use it on yourself, and I want you to leave the speakerphone on,' Andrew commanded. 'I want to hear you tell me how you feel as you bring yourself off.'

Louisa slid the buzzing dildo down towards her clit, and gasped as the machine set off tingling sparks of desire inside her sex with its constant vibrations against her soft flesh. 'What do you want me to do now?' she whispered. 'I'll do whatever you tell me so long as you tell me what you're doing too.' She could hear the excitement in Andrew's voice as he answered her.

'I'm stroking my cock, Louisa. It's big and hard and hungry for your cunt. I'm rubbing it harder, and thinking of sliding it into your hot wet hole.'

She whimpered as he spoke. 'I'm putting it inside me now,' she murmured as she slowly eased the vibrator inside her. 'Can you hear it as it goes into me? I'm watching it go inside me and my cunt is eating it up. It's a big thick cock and I'm taking it into my hole.' She began to work the vibrator into her

73

sex, enjoying the constant shuddering sensations inside her as she moved it up and down, her other hand playing with her clitoris as the moistness grew around it. She groaned. 'Andrew. Can you hear me? I'm fucking myself hard. Really hard. I'm pounding it into my hole.'

From the phone came a sudden curt instruction. 'I want you to stop, Louisa. Wait. I want you to slow down and listen to me.' She paused. 'Are you going to be a good girl, Louisa?'

'Yes,' she whispered.

'Then I want you to do what I tell you. Get down on the floor and on your knees. I want to hear you fucking yourself. Stroke your tits again and slowly let that cock out to stroke your clit instead. I want to hear it buzzing as it covers you with your juices.'

'I'm doing it,' she murmured, stepping down from the bed and settling on her knees.

'Tell me what you're feeling.'

Louisa groaned. 'I'm stroking my tits and my nipples are hard.' She slid her hands down her shift, the satin whispering as it rippled under her touch. 'But my cunt is still wet and dripping.' She spread her legs apart and leaned back on her heels, letting her hips jut up towards the ceiling, running one hand up and down her thigh. With the other hand she grasped the dildo and set it vibrating again.

'Run it over your clit,' instructed Andrew again, his voice sounding fainter against the sound of the vibrator. 'But don't put it back inside yourself again until I give you permission. Remember that, Louisa, you're not to come without my permission.'

Louisa nodded wordlessly and her breath hissed through her teeth as she ran the vibrator across the length of her clitoris. 'Ahhh.'

'Tell me,' demanded Andrew.

'Ahh, it's burning into me,' she whispered as her clit throbbed with frustration and desire. 'I'm running it up and down my slit and over my clit. I'm itching for it but I haven't put it back in me. Please, don't make me stop again,' she groaned as her hands ran downwards to her hole. 'Please,' she begged, 'I just want to fuck myself. Let me do it now.'

'No,' said Andrew, ignoring her pleas.

Louisa obediently leaned forward on her knees, balanced on one elbow but keeping one hand free to run the vibrator up and down the length of her sex. 'I'm on my knees. I'm keeping it out.'

'How do you feel?'

'I feel hot,' she whispered back. 'Hot and hungry for a cock. I've got to do it soon, Andrew . . . Please let me do it to myself,' she begged.

'Stay on your hands and knees,' he ordered. 'And slowly put the cock in your hole.' Louisa shuddered with relief as she slid the buzzing dildo inside her.

'Ohhh,' she gasped. 'Yes, yes it's hot in me. And it's so big inside me. I'm squeezing it; grinding it into me.'

'Push it in harder.' Andrew's voice came over the phone and she leaned forward, beating the dildo as far as it would go inside her, hearing his laboured breathing growing louder and louder and knowing he was abusing himself as she was abusing her cunt.

Suddenly and unexpectedly her orgasm washed over her in a wave of shuddering pleasure, her cunt clutching and grasping at the slippery dildo as she cried out, 'God yes, yes.' Then she heard Andrew give a harsh cry from the other end of the phone line and his own masturbation reached a climax as she groaned and fell forward on the floor, exhausted, relieved and infinitely more relaxed.

Chapter 4

'What's this about a trip?'

Louisa's head shot up from the paperwork scattered across her desk as Paulo threw the door open, demanding an answer from the edge of the office.

'I beg your pardon?' she asked in icy tones that belied her surprise and alarm.

'This foreign trip you're doing,' he continued, his frame filling the doorway. 'First of all, why didn't I know about it and second, when are we going?'

Louisa gritted her teeth and looked Paulo straight in the eyes. 'I assume you're referring to the fashion photo shoot for LaVeile magazine?' she asked. He sneered back at her from his advantage of distance and height.

'Yeah, that's right,' he drawled. 'That'll be the one. Unless you've got any other little holiday plans set up.'

'This is a fashion shoot,' she repeated. 'It will be work, not a holiday, although that's something I don't expect you to understand. Anyway,' she continued archly, 'after Tuesday's little fiasco I would have thought your cousin would have lined up enough models to keep you "entertained" for a week or two.'

Paolo crossed the expanse of carpet from the door to her desk in three long strides and, planting his hands menacingly on the edge of the desk, he leaned across it so that his face was only inches away from hers. 'Don't test my patience, lady,' he growled. 'And don't try to get smart. You're not up to it.' Then suddenly the air of overt menace was gone. He straightened up and continued in a voice laced with sarcasm. 'I'm just dying to get out there and learn more about the tough life you lead. After all, I need to know a lot more about the business if we're going to be partners, don't I? And we are going to be partners, Louisa, for a long, long time. Anyway,' he concluded, 'I'm sure there's always room for one more on a junket like this.'

Louisa stuck her chin up and, hiding the sinking feeling inside her as best she could, answered him as nonchalantly as possible. 'If that's what you want, then fine,' she said shrugging. 'But,' she added as he turned to leave the office, 'remember that it's work and we'll be there on sufferance. No-one will be interested in you, it's the models that are important. That means you'll be getting up early, making sure the models are ready to hit their marks on time, working with the photographer and the stylist as and when necessary – everything. This time just remember that your behaviour and mine reflects on the Dane Agency and I won't have this business's name ruined just because you fancy a quick screw. Is that clear?'

'My my, princess,' Paolo smiled from the doorway. 'You do have a way with words when you're in the mood. I wonder what you'd say if I got you really excited?' He turned to leave. 'I'll expect the tickets later on, and I don't plan to travel coach, so I wouldn't make a mistake with the booking if I were you.' Then he was gone, letting the door slam noisily behind him as he went.

Louisa slumped back into her chair with a sigh. At least he'd gone away with a smile on his face, even if it was at her expense. 'Damn the man,' she thought. Of course it had occurred to her that he'd want to go on the shoot, but she had just wanted to get away from him and have a breathing space whilst she thought about what to do with him. Well, she thought, on reflection perhaps getting away would give her an opportunity to make some sort of connection with him. If she couldn't get rid of him, perhaps she could kill him with kindness – or at least politeness. And after all, what trouble could he cause if she was there to watch every move? With an inward shiver she reached for the phone to call in Scott just as he materialised at her door.

'You heard?' she asked needlessly. He nodded, walking across the carpet to her desk, so that she could not fail to compare the two men, so different in style, attitude and most of all, profession. Not for the first time in the last few days she found her mind on a worrying track, considering the attributes of Scott's body lying dormant beneath the crisp shirt and tie. As on every other occasion his matter-of-fact attitude brought her back to earth.

'I think you made a mistake in attempting to exclude him.' He fixed her with a stern look and continued. 'I wasn't aware about the trip until I began to review your appointments this morning, and obviously that put me in a difficult position in trying to deflect Tessario from barging in to see you.'

'Sorry,' she replied guiltily. 'I didn't think.'

'That, Ms Dane is what could get you into big trouble,' he replied. 'However, I think you should take him along and use this as an opportunity to make friends with him. Well, if not friends, use the opportunity to get on better terms with him,' he added, catching sight of Louisa's outraged face.

'Look, let's not lose sight of what's at stake here,' she said. 'My business. What good will being chummy with Paolo Tessario do?'

With a sigh Scott explained again, as if to a child. 'We need to get access to information on any aspect of the mob dealings, so we need to get into his records.'

'But why would he hold the records here?' she asked. For a moment Scott looked distinctly uneasy. Then he shrugged. 'Well, they might be here, or,' he paused, '. . . they might be at his home.'

Louisa fixed him with a chilly look. 'This is the first time I've heard about bringing his "home" into things,' she said.

'You don't need to worry about anything except following the plan and letting him accept you into his circle.'

'His "circle"?' she said incredulously. 'So when did being in his "circle" become part of the great plan?'

'Look, Ms Dane,' Scott snapped, suddenly losing the facade of camp dizziness that he carried around as his persona in the office, his demeanour becoming harder, more direct and more authoritative as she looked at him. He came behind the desk, leant over her and swivelled her chair so that she was facing him. 'The issue here is to get the information we need and get you out of this loop that connects you with the mob so that you can go back to running your business on your own, just the way you used to. If you want to do that then you'll have to follow my lead. Remember, things change and you will need to adapt just to survive,' he finished, releasing the chair and retreating away from her. 'I know this isn't what you're used to but just trust me and do what I say and you'll be fine. Remember, I'm here because you realised you had no other reasonable option. Don't let a few days of Tessario's inactivity fool you into thinking that the reality has changed at all.' Louisa sucked in her breath as Scott turned on his heel and walked to the door. 'Remember,' he said, his hand on the door handle, 'he's a nasty piece of work who's slipped through the net so far. It's up to us to reel him in.'

Louisa gazed at his departing back with a sick feeling. Ignoring all of Scott's machismo she was afraid that the basic message was correct. He was right, she had been guilty of wondering whether to let Tessario just do his thing in one half of the building whilst she went about business as usual. But now that he was insisting on coming to Spain it looked like there was no alternative. She was going to have to get close to him and find out some information to get him off her back and get the FBI out of her hair at the same time. Well, that was the plan anyway.

She sighed, suddenly feeling very tired and weary. And what would happen if Tessario got wind of this involvement with the FBI? One thing was for certain, she would be more scared of him than the FBI every time.

Andrew turned on his heel to face Louisa as she sat on the edge of the sofa. 'Are you mad?' he asked in dangerously calm tones. 'Are you completely out of your mind? Going off with this, this thug . . . alone?'

'Hardly alone,' replied Louisa, stung into a response. 'For God's sake, Andrew, I'm going with an entire crew. The editorial assistants, the photographer, his assistants, the models, the hairdressers, the stylists, the make-up artists . . . you know what these things are like. There'll be dozens of us.' He continued to glare at her. 'OK, well maybe not dozens but you know what I mean.'

Louisa reached out to pour herself a glass of Cabernet Sauvignon. They were in Andrew's lounge, attempting to have a romantic evening together before she went away for the week to Spain. So far, romance was nowhere in evidence, and Louisa could see it slipping further away from her as she watched Andrew's face harden and get more and more cross.

'I just don't want you to get hurt,' he muttered, grabbing his glass and turning to face the window, simmering with rage as he looked out over the city.

'Oh Andrew,' she sighed, exasperated by his reactions. 'What could possibly happen? We're all in different villas and I'll hardly be alone with him. And anyway, exactly what do you think he's going to do? Lure me into his web of vice? Ravish me during siesta time?'

Andrew turned back to speak and then thought better of it. Instead, he sat down at Louisa's side, gently picking the glass from her hands and placing it on the coffee table in front of them.

'I don't know what might happen, and I don't like to think about it,' he said. 'But you must know he's dangerous. The FBI—'

'The FBI,' she replied scornfully. 'I don't see them actually doing anything to help me. Agent Scott just sits there, messing up my diary and watching everything that's going on around him, scaring the hell out of me to make me fall into line. And it works,' she said ruefully. 'Oh,' she continued, warming to her theme, 'he thinks this trip is a terrific idea. He can see

81

me and Tessario getting along like little chums on a holiday outing.' She paused for breath. 'At least Tessario says what he thinks straight up. He doesn't hang about thinking how to slime his way into my good books, he just gets on with it and doesn't give a damn about the consequences . . .'

'Come on, Louisa,' Andrew snapped, leaping to his feet. 'He's playing with you, and you should be able to see it. What is it about him that you can't tell what he's like?'

She arched her eyebrows. 'And exactly what does that mean?'

'Maybe you like him more than you're willing to admit. Or maybe you just like the feel of a bit of rough,' he snarled, jerking his head back as her palm cracked against his cheek.

'How dare you?' Louisa gasped. Breathing heavily Andrew eyed her angrily, his chest heaving as he tried to hold his temper in check. Then, convulsively, he wrapped his hands around her head and drew her roughly towards him, kissing her aggressively on her lips, bruising them with the harshness of his actions. In a seamless movement he took his hands from around her head and slid them down her sides, pulling her closer towards him and letting his hands run down to cup her buttocks and draw them closer towards his groin, so that she could feel his erection through the short silk shift dress that she wore.

Andrew slid his hands beneath the flimsy material and moved them slowly up her thighs, lifting and holding the fabric as he went so that he could use it as a sling with which to cradle her buttocks, pulling her even closer into him. Allowing the silk to fall back into place Andrew slid his fingers around the tight lycra of Louisa's G-string, using it to guide his fingers to the mound of golden hair that formed her bush. He ran his fingers across the tiny cotton front of the panties as his lips pressed against hers once again, and his tongue slid into her mouth. Louisa groaned deep in her throat and wrapping her arms around his shoulders ran her fingers down his back.

Andrew responded to her eagerness by sliding his fingers

inside her G-string and running them along the groove of wetness, the slickness of her hidden flesh swelling up as his movements stimulated her and increased her need for him. Wordlessly he backed her up to the sofa behind them and gently lowered her onto the cushions, following her down so that he was on his knees on the floor in front of her. As Louisa lay back and closed her eyes in ecstasy Andrew released her buttocks from his grasp and with an organised air he pulled her shift up and her G-string down, splitting her thighs apart to inhale her feminine perfume.

Louisa let out a sigh of pleasure as, unasked, Andrew's head slid between her thighs and she felt his tongue slide between the walls of flesh and into the warm cleft. Rivers of her sticky moisture combined with his saliva as she shifted in her seat, aware of his fingers running through her pussy hair and his tongue flicking in and out of her and roaming across her clit, stimulating the tiny bud to continue to grow and swell beneath him. Then, as the probing of his tongue continued she could feel beads of sweat breaking out across her flesh and the need for climax became irresistible. Her body moved with the pressure of his fingers and tongue and the growing sensations combined in an erotic cocktail of delicacy and aggression. Louisa felt the tensions in her body pulling upwards from her thighs and gathering at the base of her stomach; then they grew and swelled within her clitoris and her vagina into a brief, intense explosion that ran upwards from the base of her groin and sent her inner body into contractions of pleasure. As Louisa's body pulsated beneath Andrew's touch she could almost sense the satisfaction that he derived from his ability to do this to her, and through the haze of pleasure she felt, rather than heard him pull off his shirt and trousers and mount her body, pushing her further back into the mound of cushions.

Andrew climbed onto her and pushed his swollen member inside Louisa, holding her legs apart to increase the depth of his penetration into her. She could feel him pumping into her, fighting a losing battle in his attempt to hold back his own orgasm, excited by the ease with which he had removed her senses from the world and reduced her to a creature that begged and groaned for his touch. As the pounding of his thighs increased in pace, Louisa took control of her senses and swung her legs around his waist and her arms around his shoulders. She pulled him closer towards her so that with each movement he rocked himself against her clit, painfully grinding himself against her until, with a final pumping action, he shuddered and groaned and fell against her.

The editor-in-chief of LaVeile magazine had been a great supporter of Louisa's developing business – particularly in encouraging Louisa to make contact with her up-market relatives and friends and use her access to wealthy European families to advantage. After an initial reluctance Louisa had cast her reservations aside and become shameless in using both distant relatives and old school-friends to advance her profile in the fashion world. She also discovered that there were very few occasions when the prospect of a set of glossy photos in an international magazine would be turned down, be they pictures of the family in its entirety, the daughters of marriageable age or simply the gracious family residence in the Hamptons, Paris or Gstaad, and the phrase 'everybody wins' seemed particularly appropriate.

Recently LaVeile had been running a series of cover stories and editorial fashion shoots using new models, and the editor had decided to run a profile on Louisa and her business, and to use a group of her newest models for the next shoot. In the light of Louisa's European connections the editor had chosen to use a group of Spanish islands lying just off the African coast as the background: primarily famous for having a rugged coastline, outstanding windsurfing and miles of glistening dunes to which nudists flocked, the plan was to photograph the models amongst the surroundings of Las Canarias that made the resorts look both isolated and beautiful, but promoted the island as a desirable spot for yet more tourists to visit.

The group would comprise one of the LaVeile editors,

Venetia Hall, who was nominally in charge of the whole affair, although the style editor had already set and confirmed the ideas, clothes and colour plan for the shoot. The stylist on location would be Serena Calder, a gaunt American of an uncertain age, who was notorious for going on location, seducing the locals and taking them home for the night. The make-up artist, Alan Vale, would also be in attendance. He was many models' current favourite 'make-up man', primarily due to his uncanny ability to make them look more incandescent than normal and this, at least, might ensure some reasonable behaviour and minimise tantrums. In any case, thought Louisa cynically, most of these girls had been deliberately chosen as being new to the business and that also should limit some of the problems that usually arose in keeping them in check. Alan would, of course, be bringing his ever-present assistant and boyfriend, Leo, with him.

The final member of the La Veile group was the photographer, André Stevens, who had been commissioned for the full series of shoots around the world. He would be bringing his assistant, the assistant's sidekick and also his wife, a beautiful but quiet and retiring woman who never failed to travel with him, just in case he should become a little too interested in one of his subjects and decide that his spouse no longer had quite the right style to continue as his muse.

Finally, there were the models, five of them, similar in that they were tall, thin and attractive, but with very different characters and temperaments. Louisa pulled out their cards and studied them, trying to anticipate any specific needs or problems that might arise.

Nadine's photo showed a big-boned blonde with a wide luscious mouth and an air of vitality. Coming from the mid-west she initially impressed people as being calm and pleasant with a clear, rational view of the world; but she had an unpredictable nature that meant she was just as likely to take a swipe at a photographer as to pose for him if he crossed some indefinable boundary. Despite, or perhaps because of this, Nadine had rapidly become a minor celebrity on the model circuit, and was tipped for great things in the business. Assuming, Louisa thought, that in the meantime she didn't get sent to jail for roughing up or offending one of the powerful magazine editors. Although she was less self-absorbed than many models Louisa had met in the past and could be lots of fun, Nadine was a 'loose cannon' and on a trip like this she might play up to that reputation. Louisa sighed; the prospect of keeping both Nadine and Tessario out of trouble was dreadful.

The others were a motley crew, she thought, but less difficult to handle. Eila – a bald, tattooed and emaciated New Yorker with a face like an angel that was thrown into relief by her lack of hair, but whose command of bad language placed her firmly on the wrong side of the tracks; Tirrin – a quietly spoken brunette who was already contemplating a boob job at the advanced age of twenty-two, having come to modelling late in life after a teenage marriage and a messy divorce; Sarah – who was an English aristocrat and probably the most reliable of the four. She was also the newest and therefore easiest to keep in control

Finally there was Corin Dale. Attractive was an understatement here, she thought as the face of a god with pecs to match gazed back at her. He was also highly heterosexual and his libido was becoming legendary around the business. He had only been on the circuit a few months, having ambled into the office to please a now-deserted girlfriend and unlike some members of the modelling fraternity he didn't seem to have trouble getting along with anyone; editors, both male and female, loved him because he constantly flirted with them and was adept at implying he might go to bed with them to further his exposure; the stylists and photographers adored his looks and the way the camera loved him, and even most of the female models liked him because not only was he straight, but he also made them look good whenever he took them to parties, which he did on a strictly rotational basis, his level of commitment to anyone other than himself being almost zero.

Completing the party, there was Louisa herself. It was clearly understood that Louisa had been invited along as a special dispensation from the editor for some shots with the models. However she was not to get involved in the business of the shoot, simply to be available for some photos should she be needed, and to look after the girls. Now, she thought with a sigh, she would be looking after Tessario as well.

The party flew into the island airport in Fuerteventura and immediately caused a fuss. The fabulously gangling, attractive and youthful models caused the police and security guards to lose sight of their job and stare at the girls, whilst the make-up artist, Alan, and his boyfriend couldn't take their eyes off a trio of windsurfing Australian tourists in coach class, and kept changing their positions in the passport queue in order to try and get their address. Meanwhile Louisa had her hands full trying to keep the models together, since they were showing a remarkably unprofessional tendency to want to go walkabout, see the sights and have a holiday. She sighed and gritted her teeth as once again she repeated her advice and instructions.

'No, Tirrin, there are aren't any shops here. It's fairly primitive and it's not the tourist season . . . Yes, there is a nightclub but it's in Puerto Rosado and that's about fifteen miles from where we'll be staying . . . No, I don't think you should go out for a walk tonight, Eila, you have a shoot at dawn tomorrow and you need to rest—' The only one who didn't fuss about the surroundings, the locals or the sun was Corin, who wafted through the airport with a lazy smile on his face, apparently oblivious to the lascivious expressions on the faces of the females that he passed on the way to the cars.

In the mêlée at the customs desk Louisa lost Paolo and when she finally looked around he was nowhere to be seen. In irritation she walked about searching for him until, inevitably, she supposed, she spied him talking to Serena. He seemed to be deep in a meaningful conversation, whilst Serena maintained the habitual air of bored élan of someone who has been everywhere and done everything. Adopting her own facade of casual non-interest Louisa strolled up to the couple, but the warning expression on Paolo's face as she approached them was enough to make her smile brightly and keep walking past them, hoping against hope that he was not suggesting anything too appalling. However, the glimmer of a smile on Serena's face when she finally joined the party in the limousines was an indication that, for the time being at least, Paolo was restraining himself and managing not to offend anyone. Finally then, they were all through customs, their bags and equipment had been collected and they were travelling northwards to their chosen villas in a set of somewhat ageing limousines, the best that the travel company had been able to arrange. The villas were set at the edge of a small village on a rocky outcrop facing the sea and separated by the main road from the miles of sand dunes that stretched out into the distance; an undulating sea of silver crystals that had been swept in from the Sahara over the thousands of years of the island's development.

The group decamped from the limousines, which for many of them had been the final straw in the long trip from New York, walked inside and looked about them.

'God,' Venetia said, to no-one in particular, running a manicured fingernail across the surface of the dining table. 'Why do I let myself in for these things?'

Paolo looked across the room at the elegantly coifed brunette, her clothes layers of black linen. 'You've got a problem with this?' he queried.

'Of course I do darling,' she drawled. 'It's so primitive. Imagine! Some people come here for a holiday.' Her lip curled in distaste at the very idea, and Louisa, coming into the room, could virtually see Paolo's hackles rise with irritation. For once she felt she could be in agreement with him, but her main priority was to keep everyone happy – without any input from Paolo if she could manage that.

She leapt into the fray before Paolo could speak. 'You're so right, darling,' she agreed with Venetia, shooting a warning glance at Paolo as he reluctantly sank back into a seat, 'but we're only here for a few days and as you told me this is the best they could offer.'

'True,' yawned Venetia. 'God I am so-o-o exhausted. I'm going for a rest. Toodles . . .' and she drifted from the room with veils of black linen floating behind her.

Louisa raised a warning finger as Paolo rose from his seat once again. 'Don't.'

'Don't what?'

'Don't start with me – just listen for a change. This is an important job for the future of the business. We need this job,' she continued, deliberately emphasising the 'we' although she could see the signs of irritation across Tessario's face as he listened to her lecture. 'You cannot stuff this up. Is that clear? Just stay out of trouble, watch, take care and try to learn something.'

'Like what?' he sneered, his temper as always just a little out of control. 'Like how to prance about like those queens upstairs? Or to be a spoilt bitch? I don't think you and your friends can teach me anything I need to know.'

'For God's sake,' she hissed 'will you just let us all get on with our jobs.' She turned to leave, 'And keep your homophobia to yourself, you jerk.'

Suddenly she felt his powerful hands grasp her shoulders and hold her in place, as his lips came very close to her ear. 'And you just remember one thing,' he whispered gently into her ear. 'I've put up with you so far, but no more. Don't ever take that tone with me again.'

Louisa gazed across the beach and down towards the surf; it was still only six-thirty and the sun was just breaking through the clouds, but in the distance a group of windsurfers were already scudding across the morning waves. Turning her back to the sea the villa complex was about one hundred yards to the left and the group of models and assistants were in front of the buildings, whilst the photographer was in consultation with his assistants and Venetia. For the time being she wasn't needed. In front of her the sand dunes stretched into the distance and further away the rugged character of the island was evident from the craggy mountains. After they had finished the seaside and beach shots they would all decamp to the village of San Antoine in the highlands in order to complete the shoot. In the meantime the only people they had disturbed whilst examining the dunes for optimal locations were a few nudists lingering in the fading sun. This had hardly caused a flurry among the more exhibitionist models, but had sent Venetia into a mild tail spin, since the sight of ugly bodies was anathema to her 'refined' New York sensibilities. Frankly, thought Louisa, she thought Tessario had the right idea when she caught him blatantly laughing at Venetia's display of excessive emotion.

She glanced around to see where Tessario was, and was horrified to see him once again sidling up to Serena. Before she could move he had slipped his arm around her waist as she was bending down to twitch a piece of fabric into place. To Louisa's surprise she made no sign of being annoyed or even alarmed, instead she half turned with an indulgent laugh and shrugged him gently off, clearly sending him elsewhere whilst she completed her job.

'I don't believe it,' thought Louisa, as she caught Tessario's eye and instantly looked the other way. 'That son of a bitch is at it with Serena – and she's enjoying it.' She stomped off in the other direction, uncomfortably aware that Serena had also observed her reaction and was no doubt putting her own interpretation on them – an interpretation that she could do nothing about!

By lunchtime the first set of shots were completed and the photographer deemed the sun to be too hot to continue working. Venetia called a temporary halt to proceedings and the group sauntered back to the villas, supposedly for a rest and a siesta. Anton and Leo clearly had more than rest on their minds and raced each other upstairs into their room, pausing only to collect a bottle of wine from the bar. Tessario had also disappeared from sight and she assumed he had gone back to his room as well. Suddenly restless, Louisa pulled open the shutters in her bedroom and looked out into the dunes, silver and glistening in the sunshine. On an impulse she grabbed a robe, sun lotions and a huge brimmed hat and went out into the sunshine. She walked into the dunes, looking for a quiet and sheltered spot away from the rest of the world where she could relax and work on her tan, however unfashionable that might be to the rest of the group. In the sixties visiting hippies and nudists had started a trend for creating little round turrets, built from stones thrown up by the sea, large enough for one or two people to sunbathe in and high enough to cut out any of the stiff sea breeze that could arise. Finding a vacant turret Louisa looked around: there appeared to be no-one else nearby, and she set about applying her sun lotion. She pulled off her bikini top and rolled onto her back, luxuriating in the warmth of the sun above her and the feel of the sand beneath her skin as she rubbed lotion carefully around her body. The sensuous feel of her curved breasts beneath her touch, combined with the heat and the almost hypnotic silence, broken only by the light sound of the breeze catching the top of the stones that surrounded her, was desperately relaxing and, feeling distinctly naughty, she slowly allowed herself to spin a fantasy in her mind.

Draping one hand above her head Louisa slid the other inside her bikini bottoms, stroking at her clitoris with delicate fingers. She closed her eyes and imagined the arrival of another sun-worshipper. She would see a muscular and very masculine body and, feeling a little voyeuristic, she would be unable to resist the opportunity to examine her fellow sunbather more closely. He would be tanned and naked with powerfully muscled buttocks that glistened in the sun from a liberal application of oil. As she was watching him from within her hide-away he would become aware of her presence, sit up and spy her watching him. Silently he would move and join her, his naked and glistening body just touching hers as he sat down on the sand beside her inside the little turret of stones that protected them from the gaze of the outside world. Louisa heard her breath rush out from her body as she increased the pace of the sensual strokes that were turning her body into liquid metal, and increased the pressure on her sensitive flesh, enjoying the shivers of pleasure that sparked inside her, but refusing to allow them to reach a climax before she had completed her fantasy.

The man reached out to touch her nipples, which crinkled instantly beneath his touch, whilst the feel of her breasts caused his veins to expand and his immensely endowed cock to stand erect. Louisa breathed in, a shuddering deep inhalation, as he slipped his hands inside her bikini bottoms, the hot oil on his fingers making his exploration of her clit warm and easy. With no warning he ripped her bikini off and pushed her back onto the sand, shadowing her with his massive body. Then, kneeling astride her, he began to rub sun-warmed oil into her breasts, kneading them and grazing the sensitive areolae with rough callused fingers as he worked. The whole time she lay supine beneath him, her only sounds the occasional mew of pleasure, and her only movements being to stroke his distended cock where it lay upon her belly.

Finally, he responded to her groans and turning his back on her he straddled her once again, and took the oil, this time rubbing it into her spread thighs and the tangle of bleached blonde hair at the apex of her legs. Then, as she begged him with sighs and groans and thrusting movements from her pelvis, he finally allowed his oiled fingers to probe her sex, splitting the labia and examining each crease and crevice so that he had an intimate knowledge of her. Finally one finger penetrated her and she squirmed and gasped with the pleasure of finally having a part of him inside her. Her body closed around his finger and he inserted a second then a third, so that she was swollen with him, whilst his thumb worked at her clitoris, playing her sensually, yet refusing to let her clit heat up to the point of orgasm. When she thought she would die from longing and desire he stood and turned to go, leaving her writhing on the floor, forced into begging for sex, offering herself up to him on any terms. Only then did he turn back to her, covering her with his shadow as he studied her face. Seeing only desire he threw himself on top of her, thrusting his oily cock into her hot, wet sex and she climaxed immediately.

Louisa groaned and exhaled deeply as the shudders of her orgasm subsided, and dragged herself back from her fantasy. She rolled onto her side and opened her eyes to see Paolo Tessario – stark naked except for a pair of Ray Bans – looking straight back at her from the entrance to the turret. She gasped with shock and sat up, immediately averting her gaze from where it had inevitably settled on his groin. Apparently unperturbed by her presence, or her reaction, Tessario sat down on the sand with a small, wicked smile playing across his features.

'You look like you were enjoying yourself,' he commented casually, staring pointedly at her swollen hard nipples. 'But you should get that off,' he continued, waving his hand in the general direction of Louisa's bikini bottom. 'You'd get a better tan and we could all get a chance to see what you've been hiding.'

'Don't be disgusting,' hissed Louisa, blushing furiously as she pulled her robe around her shoulders and sat upright. She grabbed her bottle of lotion and her hat as Tessario's hand whipped out and around her thigh, running down the full extent of her leg as she rose and finally pausing to grasp her ankle. She looked down at his wrist, now securing her firmly in place, and then into his sunglasses where her angry reflection was mirrored back at her. 'Let go of me please,' she demanded haughtily. Instead he ran his fingers back up and around her thighs, softly stroking the smooth flesh of her inner thighs in a movement so unexpectedly sensuous that she caught her breath. Then he abruptly let go his hold on her and stood up to face her. Louisa caught her breath once again, forcing her eyes away from his groin, although she had already noted that his phallus was large and erect,

93

standing proudly out of the thick mass of dark curly pubic hair. Instead she looked him straight in the eyes.

'Would you like to cover yourself up?' she asked, finally regaining her normal chilly tones. 'You seem to have forgotten your towel.'

Again, apparently unperturbed Tessario smiled at her and took the proffered towel. 'You know,' he commented as he draped it casually around his waist, 'if you didn't have such a stick up your ass you'd be quite attractive.' He paused. 'You'd still be a real hard-ass bitch, but you might be a reasonably fuckable chick.'

'Not with you!' Louisa spat back, all her former caution gone.

'Only if you got real lucky,' he snapped back, quick as a flash of lightening.

Furiously Louisa turned to leave, only to find herself held by a pair of strong hands and swivelled back to face him. Before she could move or argue he had pulled her towards him, holding her arms against her sides so that she was left almost helpless and unable to struggle as, without any sensitivity or delicacy, Paolo forced his lips over hers and kissed her. After a momentary surprise she spat back her response, shaking her head to leverage herself free, and twisting helplessly within his grasp.

'Let go of me!' she demanded. Laughing he released her, and she made to slap his face, but with a swift movement he parried her stroke and once again took possession of her hands.

'Well,' he said with a smile. 'You're quite the little vixen, aren't you.' Then the smile was gone as he held her arm. 'I warned you before,' he said, suddenly dangerously quiet. 'Don't try stuff like that.'

'You're a pig,' stormed Lousa. 'I suppose manhandling women was normal where you grew up, but it's just not good enough around civilised people.'

'What would you know about the way I grew up, you spoilt little bitch?' Paolo hissed back. 'You know nothing about me.'

'You give yourself away with every move you make,' she snarled back, equally furious.

'Hah,' he sneered, openly contemptuous now. 'Maybe you just see what you're looking for to confirm your own prejudices. Anyway, it's only your exaggerated sensibilities that seem to be offended by me.'

'Well, well,' she sneered back. 'Wonders will never cease. I didn't know you could put all those syllables together, although I still don't imagine you could spell them.'

Paolo dropped her arm, which he had held to prevent her slapping him. 'You really are a nasty piece of work,' he said. 'For all your fancy education and superficial charm, you aren't warm or attractive in any real way.' As soon as his sober turn of phrase had arrived, it had gone again. He smiled, shaking off their conversation, and tipped his head towards hers confidentially. 'Not to worry, babe, there are plenty of other hot little slits just begging me to fill them.'

'You're disgusting,' said Louisa as she turned to leave, half expecting him to prevent her departure once again.

'Just living up to your expectations,' Paolo called out as she left. This time however, he didn't try to stop her, but when she looked back from the next rise of sand dunes he was standing there, with his arms crossed across his chest and the towel still draped around his waist, watching her hasty retreat.

The afternoon photographic session was on the beach and marked the final session on the coast. The clothes were bikinis and sarongs, draped around the models so that they looked like a flock of birds of paradise, perched incongruously around the edge of the beach. In the distance other islands could be seem through a misty haze, and closer to shore a flotilla of windsurfers raced each other across the waves. Half way through the afternoon the stylists had a brainwave and after some rapid negotiations the group relocated at a windsurfing school further up the beach. At first there was nothing to be seen apart from the large, rather dilapidated wooden building, set in acres of golden sand running down to craggy black rocks, rockpools and the intense green-blue of the sea. However, the models immediately perked up their slightly flagging spirits as windsurfers came out to meet them, living props for the girls to adorn themselves around. The arrival of these gorgeous specimens of manhood also proved almost too much for Alan and Leo to bear, particularly when several were found to be more interested in them than in the girls. They were immediately in their element and disappeared into the club-house to review the latest styles in windsurfing accoutrements, much to Venetia and Serena's chagrin.

As the sun began to sink into the ocean the backdrop of crimson and orange provided a fitting end to the day's shoot and finally André called a halt to work and they wrapped it up. Everyone, it seemed was in a good mood. 'Everyone except me,' thought Louisa moodily as she joined the rest of the group for dinner in the main dining room of the largest villa. There was salad for those who wanted it, but the non-modelling members of the group were tucking into *zarzuela*, a speciality fish dish, and soaking up the garlic sauce with hunks of crusty white bread, drinking the Rioja wine imported from the mainland and generally relaxing and enjoying themselves.

Everyone seemed to be laughing and chatting and some people were definitely getting a lot more friendly as the supplies of white and red wine were beginning to dwindle. Louisa looked across the room where once again Tessario was sitting next to Serena. The older woman was laughing like a teenager at something he had said, copying his body language and catching his eyes with flirtatious little glances. 'God,' thought Louisa, 'she's old enough to know better.' In response, Tessario was leaning closer to Serena and blocking out his next-door neighbour from the conversation. As his neighbour was Nadine this wasn't a terribly sensible move, but just as Louisa was sure Nadine would blow up and throw a tantrum Tessario leaned back, threw his arm around her shoulders and whispered in her ear. Whatever he said it was certainly went down well, judging by the expression on

Nadine's face. Louisa sighed; short of making a major scene there was nothing she could do about Tessario's dalliances with these grown up women, all of whom were used to having their own way. She sighed again. She would kill him if he caused trouble for her, Mafia or not.

She was roused from her irritable stupor as she realised Corin Dale was leaning solicitously over her shoulder, waiting for an answer to a question that she had completely failed to hear. 'Sorry,' she blustered. 'I was miles away, what was that?'

'I just wondered, are you OK?' he asked placidly. 'You seemed a bit out of things over here and you were giving some awful heavy sighs just then.'

Louisa looked. 'Did I? Sorry, I didn't realise. I'm fine, just a bit out of sorts. I guess I'll have an early night and sleep it off.' He smiled and nodded agreement, then as she rose from the table he squeezed her hand and kissed her goodnight before returning to talk to André and his quiet wife, sitting like a beautiful statue at her husband's side. Louisa walked over to the stairs, and took one last look back to where she could see Tessario, still flirting outrageously with Serena, but casting a sly knowing smile in Nadine's direction. He looked up and catching sight of Louisa gazing over at him he gave her a brief, mocking salute. Louisa's jaw hardened in irritation. 'That man,' she thought, 'he never misses an opportunity to annoy me,' and stomped up the stairs.

Chapter 5

Louisa went up the creaking stairs and down the hallway and let herself into her room without meeting anyone else. Once in bed she let her mind drift, trying to put herself in a better mood and look on the bright side of things. At least the pictures were clearly going well, she thought, so the magazine would be happy and that meant more work for everyone. That was all to the good. The only fly in the ointment was Tessario and at least, as he had been so eager to point out, he was keeping people amused rather than annoying them. She ground her teeth with irritation and made a deliberate attempt to relax herself and forget the frustrations of the day.

However, time ticked by and Louisa still couldn't get to sleep, her worries about the business, Tessario and the FBI growing as the night continued until she was almost rigid with anxiety. To make matters worse the bed was incredibly hard and she ended up tossing and turning in an attempt to find a comfortable spot. Gradually the rest of the group in her villa came up the stairs to bed; she could hear drunken whispers as they wandered along the corridor to their room whilst she tried to persuade her body to relax and let herself drift into unconsciousness. Around one o'clock she decided she would never be able to stop obsessing about work and was reaching for the light switch when she distinctly heard a floorboard creak and a very feminine giggle from the next room – Serena's. Suddenly all her nerves were on edge and she could not avoid hearing the creak of a bed as a second body joined the first. From behind the thin wall of the villa's bedrooms a woman groaned with pleasure and she distinctly heard a man's voice whisper; although she couldn't hear the words she knew instantly who it was and even in the cool darkness of the night she felt herself flush with rage. 'The bastard!' she thought, 'he's fucking Serena.'

From behind the wall the woman groaned again, and Louisa could almost share the sensations as the man's response was to crush his partner into the bed beneath him. Louisa shivered and she rolled over, unable to avoid hearing the movements in the next room intensify as their lovemaking progressed and the bed began to make a gentle, regular thud against the wall. In desperation she bit her lip as the noises grew, only to slowly realise with horror that the couple were now pressed right up against the wall next to her bed. Through the thin plaster she could hear the sound of flesh slapping against the wall and with each movement of the man's body the woman whimpered and moaned with increasing vigour. As they were clearly approaching a crescendo of lust Louisa put her head under the pillow in an attempt to block them out. Finally they reached a point of mutual release and both cried out in unison before collapsing back onto the bed, exhausted if the complete cessation of any noise was an indication. Louisa breathed a sigh of relief, and silently prayed that she would be asleep before, or if, they managed to get round to more sex and desperately ignoring the lascivious sensations that had caused her own hands to stray downwards as the coupling had progressed. However, her relief was short-lived and she soon heard the creaking sound of someone opening the door to Serena's room. For a moment she entertained the idea that Tessario was leaving, but she was soon dissuaded from that notion as a second whispering female voice joined the first two, and the greetings were soon followed by a creaking noise and more giggles as a third person joined the couple in bed.

There was silence, and however much she might have wanted to go to sleep Louisa was now stiff with tension, an initially unwilling voyeur who could no longer bear to miss any sound. She guiltily found that she was unable to prevent ~rself picturing the scene in the next room, and as she heard ~g mid-West accent she realised it must be Nadine who had joined Serena's bedroom romp. Nadine, like the two other members of the ménage, clearly had no qualms about anyone overhearing them.

'Give me your pussy, baby,' Louisa heard her croon in uncharacteristically soft tones, and then a feminine chuckle was followed by the sound of a slap. Nadine squealed in apparent surprise and pouted, 'I want you to suck me, not her.' Apparently the contretemps was quickly resolved and Louisa heard a thud as someone threw themselves on the bed, followed by a groan. Then Nadine's voice could be heard again. 'Come on, baby,' she encouraged. 'Come to Nadine. I'll make you all hard again for my pussy.'

There was a sucking noise and the sound of a man's deep-throated groan was immediately and unnervingly recognisable to Louisa as Tessario. After a moment's silence he murmured to himself or Nadine, 'Yeah, suck me, you bad little slut,' and there was another sound of a strong, firm slap on buttocks. Louisa swallowed, unaccountably turned on at the sound, and she slowly let her hands slide downwards to her clit and her cunt. In the other room the noises of three-way oral sex were getting louder and more abandoned. But now Louisa was lost in her own fantasy of sexual abandon, where she was the one sucking at Tessario's thick hard cock, whilst his hands were around her head, dragging her towards him and crooning at her as she moved. Almost subconsciously she heard more talking from Serena's room. This time Tessario was speaking to one of the women. 'Ahh, yeah,' he groaned. 'Suck me, suck me harder. Now let me fuck your mouth, yeah like that,' and she shivered as she worked at her clit, imagining him pumping at her mouth, pushing gently but firmly in and out. Now Louisa's imagination took over and she hardly heard the noises and muffled groans from the next room.

In her mind's eye she could see herself lying flat, sucking Tessario's cock as he knelt over her. Her hands had grasped his ass and as she drew him closer towards her she realised some-one else had lain down between her legs and was inserting their tongue into her, fucking her orally as she was sucking

Tessario. Louisa groaned, and her hands moved more and more rapidly against her clit, drawing the sex juices from her cunt to stimulate her. She grabbed at her breasts and her imagination roamed again to place her in the threesome next door, the man fucking one woman whilst she in turn sucked at the other woman's sex, her clitoris swelling to its full extent and finishing in a burst of orgasmic delight as they all came together.

From outside the haze of her imagination Louisa could clearly hear a combination of full-throated squeals from Nadine, a deep growl from Tessario and delicate, almost inaudible sighs from Serena as they also reached the pinnacle of their orgy. Groaning with need Louisa's clit filled and swelled and her orgasm also stabbed at her from within, giving her a gasping release from the tensions of the day, and finally she was able to sleep, temporarily released from her worries and immune to any further noises from Serena's room.

As she got up for breakfast the next morning she was treated to the sight of Serena emerging from her room, attractively crumpled in a silk robe, escorting Tessario to the door and kissing him goodbye with an air of satisfaction. Nadine, it seemed had already left. As she saw Louisa Serena smiled and, turning on her elegant slippered heels, she retreated back into her room on her own, leaving Paolo to observe the expression on Louisa's face with a sardonic air about him.

'Good morning, partner,' he greeted her as he strolled past her room and towards the stairs. 'How are you today?' She simmered with rage.

'Get in here. I want to speak to you . . .' her voice tailed off as he twitched an eyebrow in her direction, but only paused briefly in his exit down the stairs.

'Hey, I'm sorry,' he replied with exaggerated politeness. 'Any other time I'd love to take you up on an invitation to join you in your bedroom, but right now I'm on my way to breakfast. If you want to talk you could join me, or perhaps we could chat later. I'm rather tired right now and I need a cup of coffee to get back on my feet. You know how it is . . .' He paused again for effect. 'Then again, maybe you don't,' and with a chuckle he continued on down the stairs. Apoplectic with rage Louisa was left with two alternatives – to run down the stairs and have it out with him right there, or to do as he suggested and leave their discussion until later. She turned back into her room, slamming the door as she went, still able to see Paolo's little smirk as he continued down the stairs knowing he had needled her into yet another rash reaction. She threw her clothes into her suitcase, furious with herself far beyond the embarrassment of the situation, and peeved that an under-educated, unsophisticated, sex-obsessed pig like Tessario should have got the better of her.

At eleven the cars rolled up outside the villa, ready to transport them further inland to the mountain village of San Antoine. The chauffeurs toiled up and down the stairs collecting what seemed to be an unending supply of suitcases, personal effects and clothes racks to go in the cars and the van that followed.

Louisa gritted her teeth and descended to the front of the house where the group was gathering. Venetia had taken over the organisation, putting the models into different cars and sending them on their way with severe admonishments about their behaviour and not making unexpected stops for refreshments.

'Good morning,' she called out, spying Louisa making her way to the last remaining limousine. 'You're with Paolo in the Jeep.' She pointed to where Tessario was standing, leaning against the side of an open-topped Jeep. He waggled his fingers in a perfect copy of Serena's usual farewell and Venetia giggled girlishly, waggling her fingers back before turning to Louisa. 'He's so cute,' she murmured. 'And Serena tells me he's very well built. Where did you find him?'

Louisa shook her head, successfully ignoring both the comments and the question. 'Venetia,' she demanded, 'what's going on? Why am I with Paolo in that, that thing?'

Venetia sighed. 'Darling, I thought you knew. There's been

a complete balls-up with the cars. We came up one short on the limousines and now they're all full.' She looked down at her list. 'I mean, there was no way any of the girls or stylists could go up the mountains in the Jeep, and as for Alan—' She paused and raised her eyebrows as if the truth of her statements was self-evident. 'And then Paulo said he was sure that you and he could make the trip together. After all, you're a little more,' she paused again. 'Well, let's say more rugged than some of the rest of us.' She finished, running slightly disapproving eyes over Louisa's chosen outfit, a pair of khaki shorts and a crisp white cotton shirt knotted at the waist, matched up with a pair of fake, and therefore rather stylish, hiking boots. In contrast Venetia herself was wearing a black raw silk trouser suit, and a matching wide-brimmed hat to protect her from any intrusive elements. 'You don't mind do you, darling?' she finished, her tone of voice leaving no room for debate. 'I'm sure you'll be fine with Paolo, but,' she lowered her tone, 'do take care of your skin. The sun can be so-o-o ageing. Here, I've got a spare hat,' she continued, reaching into the back of the limousine where Serena was sitting looking smug, and withdrawing an enormous straw hat with a dipped brim. 'If you want one, that is.'

'Thanks, Venetia,' said Louisa in somewhat stilted tones. 'Rather foolishly I packed mine. I didn't imagine I'd be needing a hat for this trip.' Turning towards the Jeep where Tessario was clearly enjoying every moment of her discomfort she gritted her teeth. 'I'll see you in San Antoine.'

Tessario watched her approach and opened the passenger door as Louisa neared the car. 'What do you think you're doing?' she asked.

'Being a gentleman?' he suggested, laughter bubbling from his throat.

'Thanks,' Louisa said firmly, 'but I'll drive.'

To her surprise he didn't argue. 'Great,' he replied. 'I need the sleep,' and climbing into the car he tipped the seat back as far as it would go, stretched his legs out over the dashboard and tipped his hat over his face, looking like a misplaced cowboy.

Louisa pursed her lips and trudged around to the other side of the car. She pushed roughly at his legs. 'Cut that out. You can't lie like that when I'm driving.'

With an exaggerated sigh but without any argument Tessario withdrew his legs, sat back in the chair and re-tilted the hat to cover his face. 'So exactly how long is it since you drove a stick shift?' he asked from beneath his hat as she started up the car. Startled, Louisa looked down and realised he was right: it wasn't an automatic.

'I've had plenty of practice,' she announced simultaneously with a vicious grind of the gears as she attempted to put the car into motion, cursing beneath her breath as she saw a slow smile spread over the lower half of his face. She tried again and after what seemed to be a humiliating eternity she got the car into gear and they set off down the dusty road.

Fuertevenura's roads were somewhat limited and their route took them back down along the coastline, following the single straight new motorway which had been built to service the tourist trade. Neither said a word as they drove along, the breeze blowing off the sea as a freshening change to the hot sun that was rapidly climbing in the sky above them. Shortly, they turned off the main highway and headed into the mountains and quite quickly after that the roads became far less well repaired and more dusty, and they drove through barren, desert-like hills populated by groups of cacti but little other plant life. They saw no-one and no other cars once Venetia's limousine had swept past them on the main carriageway, and then only Tessario had given them a cheery wave, while Louisa scowled to herself and continued her mental tally of the insults he had given her to date.

After about an hour they were well away from the coast and came to a small village. Tessario, who had apparently been asleep, tilted his hat back on his head and sat up. 'Let's stop,' he said. 'I'll buy you a beer.'

'No thanks,' Louisa said, taking the car round the next

bend. 'I just want to get to San Antoine as quickly as possible.'

'Look,' said Tessario, 'be sensible. It's hot. It's not going to get any cooler and we should at least get a bottle of water. You must be completely dried out.'

Louisa paused for a moment, and drew the car over to the side of the road. 'You're right,' she said. 'I'll wait here, you can go find a shop.'

Tessario shook his head in despair. 'Come on, Louisa,' he said, 'can't we just leave this out for a while. Let's go, sit down and have a chat.' He hopped out of the car and came around to her side to hold her door open. 'What do you say?'

Louisa reached for her bag. 'Alright, but don't read anything into this.'

Tessario closed the door behind her and followed in her wake. 'Would I?' he asked.

In the village they found a little café in a deserted market square where Louisa ordered coffee and Tessario ordered beer and a sandwich. Looking about him Tessario breathed in the air. 'Lovely, isn't it?' Louisa nodded. Casting her a glance Tessario continued. 'I've been looking for a chance to have a word with you. A little chat to clear the air. And it seems you want the same.' He paused. 'OK?'

Louisa fixed him with a stare. 'OK. I told you to steer clear of causing trouble. Instead, as far as I can tell you have slept with anyone who didn't walk fast enough to get away from you. So you tell me, why would I think anything was OK? While you're screwing them you could be screwing up my business at the same time.'

Tessario laughed. '*Our* business, don't forget. Anyway, I don't think it's any of your business who I screw. And,' he continued, 'you seem to be the only one who has a problem. I'm getting on with everyone else on the shoot.'

'That's because they don't know who you are or what you do.'

'And what does that mean?' he said sharply, with a dangerous tone in his voice.

'You're a thug and a mobster,' Louisa spat out, unable to stop herself, the suppressed anger and irritation at his behaviour, her anger at everyone else's blindness, all bubbling to the surface in an unstoppable torrent of indignation. 'Why the hell did you ever get involved in my business? You obviously know nothing about it . . .' She would have carried on in a stream of invective, if she hadn't caught sight of his darkening features. With an effort she reigned herself in, and with an equally obvious effort Tessario calmed himself and the expression on his face slowly cleared. There was a long pause whilst they sipped their respective drinks. Finally Tessario broke the silence.

'Louisa, I don't know what information you think you have and I'm not sure I want to talk about it.' Louisa opened her mouth to disagree but he held up a warning hand. 'No. Listen to me. You obviously resent me being around, but I'm here and it's a job I've got to do. You'll just have to put up with it.'

'Fine. You know how I feel,' Louisa replied, feeling slightly cheated of her opportunity to hurl insults at him. 'Any more problems and maybe I'll just get out and get on with my life somewhere else.'

'I don't think you want to do that,' Tessario said gently. 'Look at what you've built up and what you would be losing if you left without giving things a chance to settle.'

'Maybe I'll just take that chance.'

They stared into the distance, deadlocked.

'Sometimes I can't make you out,' she said. 'You change all the time. And how come you've been turning on the charm for all the other women. What is this? Some big macho-trip?'

Before her eyes Tessario relaxed back into his seat and the atmosphere changed. 'Maybe they just like the feel of my cock. Want to try it?'

'Oh God, you're disgusting.'

107

Tessario laughed. 'You can't admit it, can you?' he said, rising to his feet.

'What can't I admit?'

'You want it so bad and you can't admit to it. What is it? Are you frigid? Does that stuffed-shirt boyfriend of yours ever do anything for you or do you just help him jerk himself off?'

Instinctively Louisa stretched out and slapped him. 'Don't you dare talk to me like that.'

Tessario looked down at her. 'I told you never to do that again,' he said quietly. 'This is your last warning.' Quite suddenly he reached out and kissed her, his tongue sliding between her open and shocked lips, tenderly exploring the inner recess of her mouth. As he did so Louisa felt a sudden rush of guilt mixed with desire as the memory of the previous night's erotic fantasy swept over her and her body contracted inside, threatening to leave her helpless. With a force of will she didn't know she still had, Louisa pushed Tessario away. 'I told you never to touch me again.'

'Then we're quits,' he said, serious for a moment. Reaching out to collect the keys lying on the table he straightened up and turned away from her. 'Come on, you'd better get a move on. I might go without you,' and he began to walk to the car, leaving Louisa to pull her wits together and follow him.

There was very little conversation until they got to San Antoine. Each was absorbed in their own thoughts, and Louisa was struggling against the guilty notion that she had somehow exposed herself in enjoying the imaginary sensations of Tessario's lovemaking. The feelings had been intense and pleasurable, but, she reasoned, unreal. They were just her own mind playing tricks on her. But as they arrived at the local hotel where the rest of the group were already ensconced and completing the shoot, she was left with the uncomfortable thought that she had never had a fantasy that included Andrew.

Louisa turned around from the bar to see Paolo slide the fingers of one hand along the back of Venetia's dress, whilst

108

he ran his other arm around Serena's waist and drew them both towards him at the same time. The sulky expression on Serena's face was everything that Louisa had dreaded but, she thought, at least Venetia was looking pleased.

'Well,' she thought sourly, 'he obviously gets a lot of practice in running a string of women. Why should this lot be any different?'

She turned away to avoid looking at the threesome any longer, partly to avoid the feelings of tension and partly because the very sight of them together made her remember the previous night and feel very uncomfortable. She found herself facing Corin, Alan and Leo who were strolling up to the bar together. Alan waved enthusiastically at her as they approached.

'Sweetie,' he called out as they got closer, 'isn't this place simply adorable?'

'Lovely,' she agreed, with a fixed smile, as they sat down. 'But I'm always glad to get home and see a taxi. Even if the driver doesn't know where to go.'

They chuckled and Alan ordered sangria, smiling winningly at the handsome young man behind the bar, but with absolutely no effect. Groaning about the effect that the potent combination of fruit, spirits and red wine would have on his head, Corin opted for a beer.

'Don't you have to watch that beer gut?' teased Alan, leaning forward to pat Corin's flat, muscular six-pack stomach.

The model smiled. 'Never have so far,' he commented. 'I guess I think it'll take care of itself, but I do work out most days as well.'

'You should drink more water,' snapped Louisa, 'and he's right, you shouldn't be drinking beer.' Corin just smiled and sipped at his drink, and as music began to filter through the sound system he raised his eyebrows and looked across at Louisa. 'Shall we?' he asked. Not waiting for a reply he grabbed Louisa's hand and dragged her along behind him, past where Paolo who was still chatting with Venetia. Corin rocked in time to the music in the centre of the dance floor. Beautiful he might be, thought Louisa, but a dancer he certainly was not. Flailing arms and legs threatened to decapitate anyone who came within range, and within minutes a large space had formed around the two of them. With a surprising abruptness the music was replaced by gentler, romantic songs, immediately drawing a larger crowd of couples back onto the dance floor. Louisa smiled at Corin and turned to leave, but instead he caught her hand and, giving her his trademark wide smile, he drew her back towards him. After a moment's consideration she let herself be drawn into a closer embrace suitable for the music, her mind on other things.

She leaned against Corin's shoulder, watching the people around them. Alan and Leo were departing from the party, clearly deeply entranced by each other, whilst in the corner Nadine was having a deep and possibly violent conversation with one of Serena's assistants, punctuating any points in her argument by waving her fist in the air and occasionally leaping from her seat in the heat of the moment. Louisa sighed and made to extract herself from Corin's arms, but was surprised when he held tight, and wound his arms around her body.

'Relax, boss,' his lazy voice murmured in her ear. 'She'll be fine.'

'I'd better check,' began Louisa. 'You don't know what she might do and I don't want a lawsuit.'

'You're not responsible for everything she gets up to,' said Corin. 'She's a big girl and anyway,' he went on, 'she's not going to do anything. She's got a big mouth, that's all. Look.' As they turned slowly round Louisa could see that Nadine and her companion were now roaring with laughter. 'You worry too much,' continued Corin, looking down at her. 'I like that about you.'

'Right now I have a lot to worry about,' sighed Louisa, giving in to the strength in his arms and relaxing against his body, enjoying the simple sensations and the aroma of heterosexual maleness. He laughed gently, a rumble moving around his chest and easing slowly out through his mouth. 'God,' she thought, 'he's all so male. It's almost too much masculinity to handle.' Shivering slightly Louisa realised both that she was becoming aroused, and that her breasts were betraying that arousal as her nipples hardened and brushed against Corin's chest through the fine fabric of her top. With a start Louisa realised she had been daydreaming and that she was looking straight at Corin, who had a knowing smile flitting across his face. Suddenly flustered, she attempted to move back from him a little but was hampered both by the fact that the dance floor was now crowded with smooching couples and by Corin's refusal to give in to her attempts to release herself. Instead, he took hold of Louisa's arms and guided them around his back and onto his hard, tight ass, holding her wrists captive behind him whilst he leant down to kiss her. It was only as his lips covered hers that Louisa realised with equal measures of pleasure and alarm that Corin was also deeply aroused.

For a moment she fully intended to fend him off, telling him that she never got involved with her clients, until that thought disappeared as her innate sensuality betrayed her good intentions. A rush of excitement again swept through her, making her body quiver and ache to be released from her pent-up feelings of frustration and desire. Then Corin released her wrists and as she opened her eyes and met his gaze she knew that she would not be abandoning this opportunity.

'Are you tired, boss?' Corin queried, still slowly sliding her around the dance floor.

'Exhausted,' Louisa replied.

'The we'd better get you to bed, hadn't we?' Without any further ado he drew her easily to the edge of the dance floor and guided her steps across the grassy bank that led back to the villas. The sounds of the music rapidly disappeared and as they went Louisa felt an explosion of lust for this god-like body next to hers. Abruptly she pulled up, and drew him back towards her, using her puny strength to draw his groin towards hers. They fell to their knees on the grass and in a sudden frenzy of sexual heat Corin began to tear at her shirt and at the shoulder straps with his teeth whilst Louisa tussled with the belt on his jeans.

Ripping her shirt away, Corin tipped her backwards to lie flat, simultaneously pulling her skirt above her knees in order to gain access to her sex, and tore off her panties, giving Louisa a pre-orgasmic shudder as she anticipated the pleasure that would follow. Desperately she reached out and pulled the remains of his shirt off him, wrapping her legs around him and drawing him towards her sex. Her obvious desire only served to excite Corin even further, and he tore off his pants and flung them away. As the distant light from the villa windows filtered over them she realised that Corin's exposed cock was big, circumcised, thick and very hard, the head shining and swollen purple. Then he blotted out the light completely, covering her with the full length of his body and whilst his tongue slipped inside her mouth, his cock butted up against and then inside her slit, made slippery and easily accessible by the juices that were welling from inside with her increasing anticipation and desire. Suddenly he was thrusting against the walls of her sex, stretching her flesh around his member as he forced his way in and out of her, thrusting violently against her, his whole body grinding her slight form into the ground beneath them.

Louisa lay back, gasping for breath as Corin continued to thrust against her, then the lips of her vagina were spread further apart as he reached beneath her and roughly split the flesh open with his fingers to give himself greater access to her. Neither spoke as he continued to pleasure himself inside Louisa's cunt; there was just a primeval grunting from Corin as he worked towards his orgasm, apparently oblivious to any of Louisa's needs.

As he continued to fuck her Louisa became sure that his orgasm was very close and in a desperate attempt to slow him up she began to push at him, trying to attract his attention and murmuring his name to ask him to slow down. To her distracted amazement he ignored her motions, and instead gathered her wrists together in one huge hand and pinioned her hands above her head. Then, pausing his thrusting for one movement he ripped at the straps of her top, tearing them away from their stitching to expose one luscious and swollen breast. Roughly he reached for her nipple with his mouth, sucking viciously on the tight, stimulated bud until Louisa squealed in pain. Only then did he pause for a moment to lick around the areolae, calming the flesh before repeating his actions and attacking her nipple once again. Louisa shuddered, feeling her clit throbbing afresh, and drew her knees upwards, wrapping her thighs around Corin's back as he resumed his rhythmical penetration, maintaining his painful hold on her nipples. As he climaxed his cock throbbed into her and he shuddered, snarling obscenities whilst Louisa finally signalled her orgasm with a whimpering moan that grew into a cry as her body also shuddered with waves of pleasure, matching her partner's in their intensity.

Somehow they managed to pick themselves up, pull on their clothes and sneak back to the main hotel building without anyone noticing. At the door to her room Louisa turned to Corin who was standing expectantly behind her. 'Well,' she said awkwardly, 'um, goodnight, I suppose.' Corin looked down at her with an amused expression across his perfect, craggy features. 'Do you really want me to trot along to my room and sleep there?' he asked.

'I just thought . . .' her voice tailed away.

'Don't think,' he advised and pushed the door open. Louisa swallowed and went inside, feeling strangely gauche and unworldly.

'I think I'll just have a quick shower,' she said nervously. 'OK?'

'Fine,' Corin agreed, walking over to the windows and pulling open the shutters, so that the sounds of the party drifted in on the breeze.

'Right,' she said again, 'I'll just go on in then.'

Corin turned towards her, completely at ease and apparently enjoying her discomfort. 'I'll be waiting for you,' he said, pulling open the top button of his denim shirt.

Louisa fled to the bathroom and threw herself under the shower. Thoughts raced around her head. Half of them berated her for her behaviour, whilst the other half pointed out that she was a grown woman and a free agent; that she could do what she wanted; that at least it wasn't Tessario and that it had been so good, raw and harsh and unexpected . . .

By that time she had showered and pulled a large fluffy bathrobe around her. 'Right,' she said to herself as she looked in the mirror and straightened her hair. 'You're going to go out there and let him know that this is unprofessional behaviour and you really shouldn't have done it. Now that you have there's no way this can happen again.' She straightened her shoulders again. 'Fine. He'll just have to leave and go back to his room.'

She emerged from the bathroom to find Corin lying on his side in bed, propping his head up with one hand whilst he waited for her. The crisp white sheet was draped around his waist so that his golden tanned chest and the light covering of dark gold hair glinted in the subdued lighting. Louisa took a deep breath and tried to ignore the stabbing flicker of lust that shot through her.

'Corin,' she began.

He raised his eyebrows. 'Nice shower?'

'Yes, yes, fine,' she blustered.

'Good,' he continued. 'Come and join me,' and he patted the bed beside him. Taking another deep breath Louisa moved forward to his side, with her nerves on edge and an almost overwhelming desire to lift the sheet and examine him.

'I'm not sure about this, Corin,' she continued, as she arrived to stand at the side of the bed. He crinkled his eyes in a query. 'After all, I do represent you. I mean this is rather unprofessional after all.'

114

'If that's all that's bothering you I can always change agencies,' he replied.

'No way,' she snapped automatically, and he laughed.

'I don't want to do that,' he went on. 'But I might need to be convinced that you really want me to stay with you. I might need some active persuasion to make me stay.' He paused meaningfully, looking at her with large blue eyes whilst his hand slid through the split at the front of her robe and crept around her to gently massage her buttocks. 'Do you know how many girls would like to be in your position?' he asked.

'You are so vain,' Louisa replied vaguely, her senses distracted by the gentle pressure of his palms, as he reached up to stroke her ass and the tops of her thighs.

'No, I just know my worth,' he answered, sitting up in the bed and swinging his legs over the side, drawing her forwards to stand between them. 'After all, everyone's always telling me how much I mean to them and how they don't want me to leave.'

'You know if you're not happy with the representation from my agency you can always move on,' Louisa stated firmly, trying to keep her mind away from the feeling of their combined sex juices welling up inside her and starting to dribble out of her cunt, just inches away from Corin's fingers. 'Right now you're getting good work, and we're busy working on developing your long-term career . . .'

'God, Louisa, loosen up will you?' he said, stopping his massage and clearly exasperated. 'I must be losing my touch.'

She paused. 'Am I really such a pain in the ass?'

Corin nodded. 'Right now, yes. Sometimes I wonder if you ever think about anything else but work. You've obviously never noticed me checking you out.'

'Me? I don't believe that for a minute,' Louisa laughed. 'You've got all these gorgeous women fawning over you all day.'

'So maybe I don't like making love to women more gorgeous than I am.'

'Oh thanks,' she replied.

115

He laughed as well. 'You know models. They're all self-obsessed and anyway, you're up here and they're not. Now,' he went on, his hands once again taking up their sensuous exploration, 'am I going to have to blackmail you into sex, or are you going to do it willingly?'

'Blackmail's a dirty word,' said Louisa, feeling all her previous intentions slipping away.

'OK, let's use "encourage",' he said, reaching out to loosen the belt at her waist.

'"Persuade" is even better,' Louisa murmured as the robe slipped from her shoulders and Corin pushed her away from the bed, and knelt on the floor in front of her. Gently he ran a hand up the silky soft skin of her inner thigh, then leaned forward to bury his head in the damp tendrils of her pubic hair. She shuddered beneath his touch. 'Ahh,' she cried out softly, as his tongue stroked the folds of flesh, lapping at the sex juices mingled with the remains of her shower, enjoying her cleansed softness.

Gently at first he sucked her clit, then, satisfied with its responses and the stiffening of her muscles against his touch he returned to the fold of her sex and explored further. Sending quivering pulses up Louisa's spine his tongue delved deeper into her, exploring her flesh in a calm, methodical manner, whilst his hands drew her ever closer towards him. Louisa breathed deeply as she played with his hair, finding great satisfaction in the slow relaxed nature of Corin's touch, in total contrast to the wild frenetic sex they had experienced before. Slowly he withdrew himself from her and she gazed down at him with drugged eyes. 'Your turn I think,' she stated, and with his willing assistance she pushed him firmly back to lie across the bed, exposing once again the enormous manhood, swollen and ready for her mouth. Louisa took it between her lips and ran her tongue up and down, testing for signs of sensitivity, and as she did so Corin ran his fingers distractedly across her head. He gathered her hair into his hands and pulled her face up to meet his, kissing her gently so that she could taste her own juices. Then, before he sent her back down to his cock, his hands fondled her breasts, hanging from her body, heavy and aroused. As he caught sight of her amused expression he smiled.

'I guess you could say I'm a major tit man,' he explained. 'Now suck my cock again. Please.' Leaning over him she eased downwards to take his phallus into her mouth, licking away the droplets of fluid that sat quivering at its head. Corin gave a quiet rumbling sigh of pleasure, his muscles tensed once and then he relaxed as he gave himself up to her. He gave a last exhalation of breath as she ran her tongue around the base of his penis and then teased him with upwards licks and movements, before sucking down on him, taking as much as possible in her mouth and testing his threshold for pain by grating her teeth gently along the shaft. However, her aggression only seemed to excite him further, and his chin lifted as he gritted his teeth with a light moan at her mistreatment of him, begging her to continue.

As the early morning light streamed in through the open windows Louisa crawled from her bed and crept into the bathroom where she stared at herself in the mirror. She looked well and truly fucked, as though she had been up half the night; which of course she had. She stared deep into her reflection and gave an involuntary shiver at the recollection. Corin had left at dawn and now she could hear the sound of the morning preparations from around the hotel. She could imagine the cases being filled and packing completed, ready for the final run back to the airport in time for them all to get the flight back to Madrid and then on to their different destinations. She and Tessario were booked to go back to New York, as were the hair and make-up artists, but the models, Venetia, Serena and the photographer's group were all going on to Paris and London for different pieces of work. She was going to have to make sure she sat next to Alan and Leo, she thought, contemplating a ten-hour flight to New York stuck next to Tessario, and it was a real pity that Corin wasn't going back to New York.

Louisa scrambled back into bed for the last few precious minutes before her wake-up call and lay flat on the top of the sheets. She stretched her hands above her head, draping her body across the bed and slowly let her hands stroke her breasts, replaying the scenario from the previous night, and regretfully wishing she could have Corin just one more time. Then the maid service knocked at the door to wake her up. With a rapid movement Louisa slid under the covers, pulling the sheet up to her neck. The maid knocked again. 'Si,' she called out. There was no reply, just another knocking. 'Si,' she called again, louder this time, but there was just another rustle and a further knock at the door. 'Si,' shouted Louisa in exasperation, sitting up in bed with the sheet clutched around her. Instead of the maid, however, Corin opened the door, dressed only in a pair of his tight, but faded jeans. Before she could speak he was followed in by the dark-eyed, young Spaniard who had been working as the barman the previous night. Louisa raised her eyebrows in surprise.

'Good morning, Corin,' she said archly. 'Who's your friend?'

Corin smiled and turning around he closed and locked the door. 'This is Miguel,' he said.

'Good morning, Miguel,' she said. 'So why is he here?' she asked, looking back at Corin.

'Miguel and I were wondering how tired you were feeling?' he continued, approaching the bed. Louisa's stomach lurched. 'Corin,' she said in a shocked whisper. 'Are you suggesting what I think you're suggesting?'

Corin sat down on the bed next to her as Miguel circled to the other side of the bed and leaned against the window frame, before pulling the shutters across, and darkening the room. 'Is that a problem?' Louisa spluttered incoherently as Corin leaned over her to kiss her, his chest warm against her flesh. Miguel looked on with interest. 'He's very well endowed,' Corin whispered into her ear.

'How do you know?' she whispered back disbelievingly. In answer Corin looked up at Miguel, who took the glance as encouragement and came to the other side of the bed. Slowly, he took one of her hands away from where it had been holding the sheet against her bosom and reached out to caress her right breast.

Louisa swallowed in surprise at the delicate motions stimulating every nerve she possessed and as her eyes fluttered shut Corin removed her other hand and put his lips over her remaining free nipple, biting it with just enough force to make her shudder with desire.

'Corin . . .' she began weakly.

'Shh,' he admonished her and slowly, with no further protestations but a growing sense of inevitability she lay back onto the bed, allowing the men on either side of her to caress her breasts. Eventually Miguel rose and, leaving Corin to continue to tease her, he stripped the sheet back to expose her body in its luscious entirety. With an approving look he disposed of his trousers and split Louisa's thighs apart to make room for him, attending to her sex with a deep long exploration of her hole and playing her clit into a frenzy of swollen ecstasy with his fingers, until she was gasping for release.

Submissive and acquiescent now, she was moved to lay across the bed, then Corin knelt at her head, feeding her mouth with his massive cock whilst Miguel opened up her thighs and fed his own solid cock into her equally eager, wet cunt. Louisa sucked at Corin's cock, knowing from practice the strokes that would please him, and pushed into a regular motion by Miguel's determined thrusting from between her thighs. There was no sound in the room other than the creak of the bed, the heavy breaths of the sweating men and Louisa's panting moans. Sensations flickered through her body, their intensity moving around to different parts of her depending on whether Miguel had paused in his actions, or Corin had reached out to electrify her nipples with another touch.

Louisa ran her tongue around Corin's penis, sucking aggressively at him and bringing him to a climax. He groaned loudly and panted, and Louisa felt a pulsing of his organ just as the salty fluid jetted out of his cock and hit the back of her throat. She swallowed rapidly and eagerly, hearing his grunts and feeling the stronger pulsing of his hips as he pushed himself still further into her mouth until he was drained. That done, he eased himself out of her, the bed creaking as he withdrew to its far end to observe the remaining pair, sprawled across the bed.

Miguel paused. 'You go on,' Corin said, settling himself and waving them into action. Miguel nodded and, pushing Louisa further back onto the bed, he scrambled on top of her, hooking her ankles over his shoulders so that his shaft now went straight and deep inside her. Louisa instinctively gasped with the motion and then let her breath drain slowly away as intensely pleasurable sensations began to flood through her body. Now that Corin had come she was able to focus all her attentions on the one remaining orifice and although Miguel's penis was not as big as Corin's, it was solid and wide, and his technique provided a combination of sensations that raced through her body. She grasped each wave of sexual pleasure as another was already starting to course through her, until finally she reached the crest of her orgasm and almost screamed from its intensity, clutching at the crumpled sheet beneath her and almost unaware of Miguel's body above her, convulsing in its own frenzy of ecstatic fulfilment.

Chapter 6

Louisa emerged from the plane journey at JFK Airport feeling both exhausted and bad-tempered. She had spent most of the last leg of the trip avoiding talking to Tessario and trying to get some sleep. It was eight-thirty in the morning and the plane was two hours late, so now she thought, they would inevitably get stuck in traffic and delayed even further. Walking towards customs she found she was shoulder to shoulder with Tessario.

He smiled brightly. 'Good morning.'

'Hi.'

'Sleep well?'

'No, not very,' she snapped.

'Oh dear,' he said with mock sympathy. 'We need our blood-sugar level raising, do we?' He leaned closer. 'Not a morning person I guess.'

Louisa shot him a filthy look. 'No,' she said firmly.

He laughed. 'Never mind, Lou, soon be back to normal.' She groaned inwardly and stalked ahead, but Tessario hadn't finished. As they came into the main arrivals hall they were still side by side, her walking along and answering monosylabically, he chatting about the day and the need to get back into a routine to avoid jet lag. Without warning he wrapped an arm around her. 'Don't worry, Louisa,' he said with no relevance to anything. 'You'll feel fine by tomorrow morning.'

She unlatched herself roughly and looked up at him. 'I know,' she said firmly. 'I have travelled abroad a great deal and I know how to get over jet lag. So you don't need to touch me again. Thank you.' She looked out across the crowd and saw with relief that Andrew was at the barrier waiting for her. She waved at him.

'Hey,' said Tessario, 'isn't that your boyfriend?'

'Yes,' she replied sharply. 'How do you know?'

'You'd be surprised at what I know,' Tessario replied with a little smile.

Gritting her teeth Louisa diverted her course towards Andrew, Tessario following along behind her. 'Hi, darling,' she said, reaching out to kiss his cheek.

'Hi.'

'Hi,' went an echo behind her. Louisa looked around. 'Andrew,' she said stiffly. 'Have you met my business associate, Paolo Tessario?' Andrew's jaw stiffened as Tessario cheerfully reached out a hand to his and pumped it enthusiastically.

'Hey, Andrew,' he said with a broad, knowing grin. 'Great to meet you. Lou's told me so much about you.' Andrew's eyes swivelled to Louisa, who shot a sideways look at Tessario.

'I take it you brought a car?' she said, ignoring Tessario's comments.

'Of course,' Andrew replied in guarded tones. 'Where do you want to go? Home or to the office?'

'I'd better get to the office,' she decided. 'I'd much rather go home and get some sleep, but there are some calls I need to make and there are bound to be some papers that require my attention.'

He nodded. 'I thought so. I'll come with you. I've got some notes for you to look over.'

'Anything I should know about?' butted in Tessario.

'No,' said Andrew evenly. 'Nothing at all.'

'OK then,' replied Tessario with an inane smile, all the time maintaining Andrew's increasingly irritated gaze.

'Look, do you want a lift to the office?' asked Louisa reluctantly.

'Hey, that would be great,' said Tessario. 'I had a relaxing flight, and I'm ready to review a few papers of my own.' He winked lasciviously at Louisa. 'If you know what I mean.' He walked away and she rolled her eyes upwards.

'What did you do that for?' hissed Andrew.

'What did you expect me to do?' she asked angrily. 'I could

hardly leave him here and meet up with him at the office in an hour, could I?'

'Why not?' he hissed back, equally irritably.

'Well I couldn't,' she snarled.

Tessario turned back. 'Are you guys coming along?' he asked, apparently oblivious to the black looks he was getting from both Andrew and Louisa.

'Yes,' she snapped. 'Right, where's the car?'

The journey back into the office was long and tedious, and the atmosphere in the car made conversation strained and difficult. Tessario, however, seemed oblivious to any tension. He chatted and commented on the trip, relating interesting anecdotes about the islands and talking about the models and the photo shoots. Although everything he said was technically true, it made them all sound like a happy little band of troupers, Louisa thought, and it was clearly getting under Andrew's skin.

Andrew sat at the opposite side of the limo staring at the floor, glowering at Louisa as each new story was related to him. In response to any of her direct questions he would only answer in clipped monosyllables, and eventually he gave up speaking altogether. Ignoring them both, he pulled some papers out of his briefcase and studied them instead. Finally they reached the office. However, by now Louisa was truly furious at Andrew's childish behaviour and stormed into her office, all but ignoring Scott who was sitting at his desk. Andrew strode in after her and slammed the door behind him.

'Right,' she said turning to face him across her desk. 'What's all this about, because I am dog tired and I can do without any histrionics from you.'

Andrew slammed a fist on the table. 'Histrionics? You've got some nerve. What the hell's been going on?'

'What are you talking about?'

'You. And me. And whatever's been going on in Spain. And don't give me any lies. I saw you and Tessario coming off the plane together, chatting on your way down the corridor. It must have been quite a nasty surprise to see me. And all the way back in to town it was "Louisa and me" . . . "me and Louisa" . . . "we did this, we did that" . . . Were you two apart at all?'

'Good God,' exclaimed Louisa. 'You mean you were listening to all that drivel. Is that what this is about? A bout of jealousy? Are you completely mad?' Andrew, already furious, went crimson with rage.

'You could at least be honest,' he hissed. 'What were you planning to do? Carry on behind my back? Or just start working for the mob as a sideline?'

'Don't be so bloody stupid,' Louisa yelled back at him. 'In case you hadn't noticed I am a grown up and I don't have to answer to anyone, including you.'

'That's the way it is, is it?' he stormed.

'Look, Andrew,' she said, attempting to calm the situation. 'This is ridiculous. Tessario means nothing to me . . .'

'Don't lie to me,' he yelled, infuriated beyond belief.

Equally angrily Louisa yelled back. 'I am not lying. I was not fucking Paolo Tessario.'

'Then who were you fucking?' he shouted, losing his temper completely.

'Corin Dale,' she screamed back across the desk. As soon as the words were spoken she bit her lip, folded her arms and stood with her chin in the air as she waited for Andrew's reaction. There was a moment's icy silence, then Andrew spoke. 'Well, at least that's cleared the air,' he said quietly, and turning on his heel he walked out of the office, slamming the door behind him.

Louisa stared after him and then sat down in her chair with a thump, the adrenaline rushing around her body eliminating any remaining tiredness. The room suddenly seemed very silent and empty. She stared into the middle distance, for a long time. Then, in an attempt to freshen up and relax she showered in her bathroom, but again found herself thinking about the row and getting angry with Andrew once more.

'Son of a bitch,' she thought, letting the water beat off her back and shoulders. 'How dare Andrew lecture me? And

124

where does he get off implying I'd sleep with that bastard Tessario? How did he even think of it?' Even as she was telling herself this she was reminded of her fantasies, which seemed to revolve around Tessario. 'Well that's natural,' she told herself. 'Dreams allow you to explore the things you wouldn't normally do,' all the time resolutely ignoring the fact that unlike her dreams she was in full control of the content of her fantasies.

She tilted her head back to get the full effect of the cascading water, feeling unaccountably horny and yet unable to stop replaying both the row and her fantasies through her mind. 'God,' she thought, 'Get a grip on yourself. You've just blown away a relationship, so why the hell are you thinking about sex?' Pushing any libidinous thoughts to the back of her mind she pulled herself back to the real world and left the shower to dry and re-dress. Back in her office she tried to decide what to do. She grabbed her diary to review the day. To her irritation Scott had filled in some appointments; nothing major, just a few calls and an interview with a prospective PA, another reminder that Scott's presence was supposed to be a temporary one. There was a knock at the door and Scott put his head around the door, clearly planning to ignore the fact that Andrew had only recently stormed out.

'Your appointment is here,' he said mildly.

'Fine,' Louisa replied, determined to maintain some minimal dignity. 'Send her in.' Scott gave her a quizzical look. 'What?' she snapped.

He shrugged. 'Nothing, but I thought you knew, it's not a she,' and he opened the door to reveal the shape of a good-looking young man, with intense blue eyes and a smile creasing the edges of a full mouth. He was casually dressed in chinos and a dark green jacket and his shoulder length hair was tucked behind his ears. For a prospective employee he seemed both casual and very relaxed.

He held out his hand. 'Chris Dennison. Nice to meet you.'

'Right,' she said with a tight smile. 'Well, let's see your résumé.'

He stopped and dropped his hand. 'I'm sorry, I didn't realise you wanted one.'

Louisa sighed in exasperation. 'That's hardly a good start is it?'

Dennison looked puzzled. 'Isn't it? I thought you knew why I was here.'

'Of course I do,' she said in a patronising tone, 'but it would help if we had something to discuss, wouldn't it?'

He tilted his head to one side, looking confused. 'I thought we could discuss the changes to your business.'

Louisa glared at him. 'I'm sorry but I think you've got this all wrong,' she snapped. 'Being cute and appealing isn't enough around here. Tell me, why would I be the one answering the questions?'

There was a pause then Dennison gave her a big, relaxed smile. 'Can we start again please? I'm from NYU Talk magazine. I've got an interview with you for the college business magazine.'

Louisa's clapped a hand over her mouth. 'I am so sorry,' she said. 'I completely forgot, and it was me who arranged it. It just didn't get into my diary.'

Dennison shrugged. 'That's OK,' he said. 'I was pleased to get the interview. I would have put up with just about anything.' He paused. 'And I'm also pleased you think I'm cute and appealing. Even if it isn't enough to work here.'

Louisa blushed. 'Sorry,' she said. 'Perhaps I was a bit sharp there.'

'That's OK,' he said, 'as long as we've got it cleared up.' He paused again. 'I'm a big fan of yours, Ms Dane.'

'Louisa, please.'

He smiled. 'I'm a big fan of yours, Louisa.' He stood up and held out his hand once again. 'It's a pleasure to meet you.' She laughed and came out from behind her desk to take his hand.

'Likewise,' she agreed shaking his hand. Dennison looked down at her, his hand lingering in hers far too long for a casual handshake. Louisa cleared her throat and looked down at their hands, clasped together, as Dennison reluctantly released her.

She showed him over to the sofa and went to order coffee, when a sudden thought stopped her.

She turned to face him. 'Do you know what time it is?'

'About eleven-thirty,' he replied easing up his sleeve to reveal strong tanned wrists.

'It's five in the afternoon in Spain and I'm still on Spanish time,' she replied. 'I think we deserve a drink after all that confusion, don't you?'

'Great,' he replied with a smile.

Louisa turned to her drinks cabinet to retrieve a bottle of champagne and two long stemmed champagne flutes. 'So,' she said, returning to the sofa, 'tell me about yourself.'

He shrugged. 'Not much to say really. I'm doing a master's in journalism and ultimately I want to get into one of the men's style and fashion magazines. That's why I was hoping you'd give me an interview.'

'And are you going to sell it on?' she asked with a smile.

'If I can,' he replied, turning to face her. 'Would that be a problem?'

'Not necessarily,' Louisa replied holding out a drink.

Dennison put down his pad onto the mahogany table in front of them and took the proffered glass from her hand, the air crackling with suppressed sexual tension. He looked up at her. 'So what would I need to do to make sure there wasn't a problem?'

'I'm not sure,' she said slowly, feeling an unexpected throb of sexual desire overwhelming her still simmering feelings of anger at Andrew. 'What were you thinking of?'

He thought before replying. 'You know,' he replied, 'in a position like yours, you could take advantage of someone like me.'

'Oh,' Louisa murmured. 'How exactly?'

'You might refuse to give me an interview.'

'Unless . . . ?'

'Unless I met all the necessary criteria.' Dennison's hands trailed lightly down her arm and the attraction flew between them like an electric charge. Louisa gave him a sidewards glance.

'Would you be coming on to me, Mr Dennison?' she asked in mock surprise.

He shrugged. 'You're a very sexy lady,' he explained. 'I wouldn't want to upset you.' There was a pause. 'So . . .'

'So, there could be quite a few important criteria for you to fill,' she agreed, and with that approval his hands slid across the neck of her blouse and outlined the slender 'V' of her exposed skin. 'However,' she went on, 'I have very exacting standards. You might fail and then where would I be?'

'Failure isn't in my vocabulary,' he murmured back. 'Satisfaction is guaranteed.'

The leather of the sofa rustled as Louisa stood. 'Really?' she asked. 'Well, first of all I think I should see exactly what your credentials are.' She ran a finger under his chin. 'Just remember who's boss and we'll get on fine.' She walked to the door and leant her back against it, turning the key in the lock whilst the younger man watched her intently from the sofa. She walked back to her desk, sat down and leaned back in the chair. 'Now, why don't you show me what you've got,' she said, slowly and deliberately removing the phone from its cradle and swinging her feet up onto the desk in front of her so that Dennison could see the full extent of her legs. 'I get bored easily and I need to be entertained.'

He arched one eyebrow and stood, facing her with a half smile of expectation across his face. 'Where would you like to start?'

Louisa pondered for a moment and pointed at his shoulders. 'Let's go from the top down.'

He shrugged his jacket from his shoulders and unbuttoned the top buttons of his shirt. 'What would you like to see?'

'All of you.' He walked over to her, slowly releasing the buttons of his shirt, until it was open to the waist and he was standing in front of her. 'Not bad,' she said, and reaching out she grasped the waistband of his pants and roughly pulled him closer to her. 'But I think you could do better.'

'You're probably right,' he agreed, letting his shirt slip from his shoulders. 'But I might need the right motivation.' With

128

a calculating air Louisa placed one hand on the crotch of his trousers, where his penis was already noticeably solid. She slipped her other hand inside her blouse and reached for her nipple, beginning to manipulate it, stroking it within the confines of the lace cup of her bra and maintaining his gaze as her pupils slowly dilated with desire, stimulated both by the sensations that grew with the increasing hardness of her nipple and by her intimate knowledge of his growing desire.

Dennison stood motionless, his erection hardening beneath her immobile fingers. When Louisa finally deigned to release the buttons on her blouse and expose the cleavage and lace cups of her bra, his cock was solid beneath her touch, and his eyes were drawn inexorably to her full breasts.

'Do the right things and I might give you a reward,' she murmured. 'But fail and I might dispose of you in a moment.' She released him and leaned back in her chair, undoing the front fastening catch on her bra so that in an instant the heavy mounds of flesh were within his reach. Dennsion smiled and then, leaning forward, he tilted her chin and kissed her gently on the cheek. She looked up in surprise and they stayed motionless for a moment, as he ran a hand down the length of her arm, the silk crawling sensuously beneath his fingers as he finally reached into the open blouse to cup her breast. He slid strong and powerful fingers gently over her shoulders and across her skin, then kissing her lips he finally allowed himself to press both palms against her breasts, gently kneading at her.

Louisa lay back, her excitement betraying itself in the light flush of desire across her cheeks as Dennison's hands continued down towards her thighs, stroking her skirt upwards. She reached out to encircle him with her arms, and allowed him to crush into her with a kiss that became more intense with each moment, their lips seemingly locked together whilst their tongues explored the wetness of each other's mouth. She reached up and stroked a finger down Dennison's cheek. 'I want you to fuck me,' she said gently. Then her tone changed. 'Now,' she hissed. 'Do what you're told. Now!'

Her words acted on Dennison like an electric jolt. Immediately, he reached out behind her and swept the desk clean of files and phones, reaching down to pick Louisa up and carefully tip her back onto the table top. With a sigh Dennison pressed himself on top of her, one hand releasing her from the remaining minimal restraints of her blouse, the other running up and down her thigh, stroking the smooth flesh but not yet daring to explore above and beyond the immediate area. She bent one knee enticingly, and lay there watching and eagerly reaching out for him again. His reticence finally ended and he reached beyond her thighs, groaning with desire as he pushed up the silk of her skirt and pulled down her panties whilst Louisa lay back and let him perform for her, her eyes closed and her lips parted with pleasure at the sensations.

Carefully, almost tentatively, Dennison reached into her bush with long fingers, stroking at the soft hair within his grasp. He stood between her thighs and loomed over her, placing his hands on either side of her body and reaching down to kiss her gently on the mouth once again. She groaned, wanting more, and wrapped her legs around his waist, drawing his groin closer and suggestively grinding her hips against his. Dennison gasped and reached down with one hand, stroking her pubic hair before once again reaching beyond and into the moistness of her cunt as Louisa thrust her hips forwards and engulfed his fingers, desperate for more, for as much as he could give her.

Dennison reached further inside with deep rhythmical strokes, stimulating Louisa's sex and watching her closely as her eyes glazed over and closed. Louisa ran her tongue over suddenly dry lips as Dennison continued to masturbate her; his thumb gently creased across her clit whilst his forefingers explored deeper into her hole, teasing the moist fleshy sides of her until her clit swelled further and her orgasm broke like a fever, her back arching off the desk beneath him, so that he had to hold her down whilst her vagina throbbed and clutched for him. A line of sweat broke out across Louisa's forehead and she gasped as she reached the peak of sensation, then suddenly she relaxed and a throaty gasp of satisfaction broke from her lips. 'Good,' she groaned, and opened her eyes as she felt Dennison pull her hips to the edge of the table. She looked up to meet his slate-blue stare.

'So,' he said, 'is my performance up to acceptable levels?'

'Not if you've finished already,' she replied harshly. 'I told you, I can be very demanding and I'm not easily satisfied.'

He straightened and she heard the zipper of his chinos ease back. 'Is this what you wanted?' he asked. Then with a swift movement he was inside her, leaning over her once again as he reached down on either side of her breasts and began to drive his cock into the entrance to her sex, breathing hard with his exertions as he did so.

'Yes,' Louisa hissed triumphantly, as Dennison increased the pace of his powerful rhythm, dominating her with his size. Louisa instinctively squeezed his shaft with her vaginal muscles, watching to see him pause with surprise at the unexpected sensation, then she let herself relax and closing her eyes once more she leant back onto the table top and lifted her knees up to fully enjoy Dennison's vigorous thrusting as he enthusiastically filled her hole with his cock. 'Yes,' she approved in silky tones. 'That's good. That's very good.'

After those first gentle kisses he didn't attempt to touch her face again, but restricted himself to pleasuring her sex alone, his only caresses an increasingly aggressive grasping at her buttocks. She gasped as his fingers bit into her hard, then suddenly he withdrew his cock from her and studied her reaction, breathing heavily as he watched her. On a sexual power trip Louisa eyed him carefully, then drew her lips back. 'More,' she ordered. For the first time Dennison answered back.

'Are you sure you can take it?'

She laughed. 'Are you sure you can do it?'

'Oh yeah,' he replied. Drawing her back to the edge of her desk and easing her into a sitting position, he pushed the straight tight skirt back up to the top of her legs so that he could spread her thighs apart with ease. Louisa's blouse slithered from her shoulders and fell onto the desk and she sat half naked in front of Dennison's naked body. With a look of determined concentration he tilted her slightly backwards so that she had to balance herself against the desk with both hands, then he pushed her thighs apart and they both watched as his penis slid inside her cunt, the pink folds of her sex swollen around his member as it moved in and out of her. Suddenly he lost all restraint and pushed her down onto her back once again, pounding into her with increasing vigour, but maintaining his resolve and resisting his climax until he heard Louisa's high pitched whimpers of pleasure, at which point he reached for his own pulsating orgasm.

Fully satisfied they lay gasping on the desk until Louisa became aware of a knocking at the door. Pressing a finger against Dennison's open lips she separated herself from him and stood up, leaning unsteadily against the desk, pulling her blouse back on and tucking it into the waistband of her skirt.

'Yes?'

'It's your partner.'

She paused. 'I'm in a meeting.'

There was a pause. 'Then I suppose I'll see you later.'

She looked at Dennison who was trying to suppress a grin, and heaved a sigh of relief as he reached out for her. 'Good thing you locked the door,' he said.

It was six-thirty. Louisa got up from her desk and helped herself to a glass of wine from the fridge. As she sat down again there was a knock on the office door.

'Yes?' she called out.

'Can I come in?' Scott appeared around the door. Pursing her lips she gestured indoors. 'Thanks,' he said, striding inside.

'Wine?' He nodded. Louisa stood up. 'You sit down and I'll get another bottle.' She went back to the fridge and retrieved a bottle of Colombard. On her return she found Scott examining the montage of family photos on the wall behind her desk. She poured a glass of wine and handed it to him.

'It looks like a lovely childhood,' he said. 'Ponies, skiing, swimming.'

'Don't you start,' she snapped unnecessarily. 'I've had

132

enough of the "you spoilt bitch syndrome" from Tessario to last me for the rest of the year.'

Scott didn't reply, but sipped his wine, letting the silence grow as she stalked back over to the sofa. 'Sorry,' she said. 'I'm tired from the journey.' She finished the contents of her glass. 'What can I do for you this evening?'

He sat down on the far end of the sofa. 'I just wanted to be sure you were OK.'

'Why wouldn't I be OK?'

'I heard about your bust-up with Andrew,' he explained. 'To be honest, I heard the bust-up through the walls.'

'I'm OK,' she said. 'Andrew was very possessive sometimes. And there was something about Tessario that drove him crazy.'

'So you won't be patching things up.'

'No,' she said firmly. 'Once Andrew's made his mind up that's usually it.'

'And you don't mind,' he said cautiously.

'No,' Louisa said. 'If anything it's a relief. I feel free. Well,' she added with a smile, 'I suppose I am.' Then she sobered. 'Listen, Scott,' she said. 'I don't know how long this can go on.'

'In what way?' he asked, in his usual clipped tones.

She looked at him with exasperation. 'With Tessario of course. He's already embarrassed me once . . .'

'But you said he got on with most people in Spain,' he interjected.

'Yes,' she went on, 'but his behaviour is unpredictable. He knew what he was doing this morning. He deliberately went on and on about me and the group in Spain to wind Andrew up. Anyway,' she continued, 'that's not something I want to talk about. Tell me, what have you found out while I've been away?'

Scott shook his head. 'Nothing. He hasn't had time to do very much, but this is clearly a long-term operation.'

'He must have done something,' she said in exasperation. 'I've given him every file under the sun and he appears to have read them all. He's not as stupid as you made out you know. He's absorbed a load of information.'

Scott shrugged. 'We just have to watch and wait. I don't like it any more than you do,' he added. 'But that's the way the Bureau want to play things.'

Louisa pursed her lips. 'I don't like this, this lack of action,' she said. 'It's driving me mad.'

'There is something you should be aware of,' Scott went on uncomfortably. 'It's really why I wanted to talk to you.'

Immediately Louisa's antennae twitched. 'Tell me.'

'There's been some talk.'

'What sort of talk?'

'Gossip. In the industry. I wouldn't have known but the models are full of it and people have started to ring in.'

'About Tessario?'

'Yes. I don't know exactly what set it off . . .'

'Oh I can imagine,' Louisa muttered.

'. . . But someone's got the wind up and I've had a few calls from worried people disguising their reasons, but clearly checking out the state of the business. Your working with LaVeile helped with credibility, but you do need to do something to quieten things down.' Louisa leaned back in her chair, thinking hard. 'I'm sorry,' said Scott. 'Perhaps I should have told you earlier, but I thought you needed to re-orientate yourself first.' She nodded absent-mindedly.

'Thanks,' she said. 'I need to think.'

He nodded and rose from the sofa. 'I'll be in here first thing in the morning.'

Louisa watched the door close behind him and spun her chair around to face the window. 'Damn,' she thought. And just as things were looking a bit brighter. She sighed. 'This I could do without,' she said out loud.

'What?' asked a familiar voice behind her.

She spun about. 'You,' she said bluntly. Tessario didn't move at this unfavourable start, but waited with one eyebrow raised inquisitively.

'The behaviour of you and your chum has raised some

134

"questions" in the industry. Questions I'll need to address if I want the business to survive.'

Tessario looked puzzled, but sat down on the opposite side of the desk. 'Tell me,' he said.

'You don't know what this industry is like,' she explained. 'People come and go, and a bad rumour can destroy everything.'

'And there's a rumour? What about?'

'About my new partners,' she said flatly.

'Ah,' he said. 'Anthony's little indiscretion before we left for Spain?'

'I imagine so,' Louisa replied.

'So you want to do – what?'

She shrugged. 'I need to raise the profile of the business and let everyone know that the agency is here to stay. I need to convince them everything is fine. I need faces; faces the industry knows.'

He shrugged. 'No problem.'

'I beg your pardon?'

He shrugged again. 'Easy. Big party, lots of faces, plenty of champagne and lots of girls. No problem.' He reached for the phone and Louisa slapped her hand down over his.

'This isn't some little nightclub promo,' she snapped. Tessario stared meaningfully at her hand and she let him go, forcing down the temptation to slap him, wary of his reaction. 'Anyway,' she went on, 'we need something right now, not two months down the line.'

'Trust me,' he said smoothly. 'I'll arrange everything you need.'

She pursed her lips, almost convinced by his bravado. 'I'll need to know and approve your plans,' she said cautiously.

Once again he shrugged. 'No problem. I'll put a deal together and get back to you.' At the door he turned back to her. 'Relax. I'll talk to you in the morning.'

'One chance,' she called out. 'That's all we have with this.'

He nodded and waved, and she watched him walk confidently down the corridor, too tired to argue any more. It could wait until tomorrow, and anyway, she thought, since when had she been able to stop him doing anything.

She stretched her arms and legs, called the downstairs reception desk for a car and pulled her bags together. Right now she was more concerned about the FBI's continued failure to make any move or actual investigation of Tessario's work. 'I'm getting tired of all this,' she thought. 'It just seems they want to leave everything up to me.' The reception desk rang up to announce her car's arrival and she locked her office and left.

Passing Tessario's office she noticed that the door had been left open. She tapped cautiously against it, and poked her head around. Tessario was nowhere to be seen, but a tall and extremely well dressed brunette was rising from an armchair in one corner of the room. Louisa was struck first by her long sensual limbs as she unwound her legs and stood by the chair, then by the glossy hair cascading half way down her back and her appraising hazel eyes, as she waited for Louisa to speak.

'Is Paolo still here?' she asked, suddenly aware that she had been staring.

The woman nodded. 'He's just along the corridor if you want me to call him.'

'No, that's not necessary,' Louisa replied, fumbling for words. 'Just tell him I said goodnight,' and feeling strangely flustered she backed out of the room. It was only when she got into the lift that she realised she hadn't asked any questions and hadn't even introduced herself to the stranger. 'I must be more tired than I thought,' she told herself on the ride home, as an excuse for her sudden attack of nerves. 'Nerves?' she thought irritably. 'In my own office?' She gave a mental shrug and attempted to put the moment to the back of her mind. The car dropped her off at her apartment, and she let herself in, flopping exhaustedly down on the sofa.

When the phone rang she felt she was too tired to face talking, and let the answerphone screen the call. The machine bleeped and Chris Dennison's voice came over the loud-speaker. 'Hi, I was wondering if we could finish our, ah, interview. But you're not there so it doesn't matter . . .' She reached out and grabbed the handset.

'Hi,' she said. 'Sorry, I just couldn't face moving.'

'How are you?' he asked.

'I'm fine. Tired, though. I can't imagine why.'

Dennison gave a little laugh. 'I wondered if you'd like to do something tonight, but if you're too tired . . .' Louisa lay back on the sofa and contemplated her options. It was still early, and the prospect of an early night that had looked so tempting a moment ago now looked a bit dreary, if she was on her own.

'Look, Chris,' she said. 'I really am jet-lagged, but if you can handle it we could share a bottle of wine.' She could almost hear Dennison's smile crease his face in reply.

'Great,' he said. 'I'll be right over. Um, exactly where are you?'

Louisa opened the door on Dennison's warm smile about an hour later, by which time she was seriously questioning her sanity. Every muscle she possessed ached from a combination of her flight, the stress of her row with Andrew and her subsequent physical wrestling with Dennison in her office. However, just thinking of that session made her brush off her tiredness in anticipation of more.

Dennison walked in and kissed her extravagantly on the lips, swinging a bottle of champagne in her direction. 'You know, you do look a bit tired,' he said.

'Thanks,' said Louisa sarcastically, not particularly pleased at this overt honesty.

'Sorry,' he replied. 'But I was thinking, you know a bath might do you some good.' He popped the cork on the champagne and poured her a glass. 'A long, hot, relaxing bath.'

'With you?' she asked.

'With me,' he agreed.

'You know,' said Louisa, 'I think a bath was one of the criteria I meant to list for you.'

'Excellent,' he replied. 'So where's the bathroom?'

137

Louisa waved him down the corridor. 'What?' he said, 'All the way down there?'

'Don't be cheeky,' she admonished him. 'I have a shower room next to my bedroom, but the bath is separate.'

Dennison stood. 'Give me five minutes, and finish your champagne, then come along and join me.'

'OK,' she said. 'Are you going to run it for me?'

'Well, maybe,' he replied. 'But first of all where's the kitchen?'

She pointed the way and he left, carrying the champagne bottle, and going via the kitchen where clangs and the sound of unit doors being opened and shut betrayed the fact that he was searching for something. Louisa decided to give him the benefit of the doubt and settled back into the sofa to finish sipping her champagne. She was still in her suit, so it seemed sensible to go and change into a dressing gown, her favourite burgundy silk robe. That done, she wandered along the corridor to the bathroom.

She opened the door on a mass of steam and to see that the entire room was filled with a mass of candles; all shapes and sizes, from tall church candles to stubby old red candles that she kept in case of an emergency blackout, all illuminating the bathroom with a low, subtle, sexy light.

Chris was waiting for her in the centre of the room with a tiny towel wrapped around his hips. 'Quick work,' she commented as she approached him. He smiled and shrugged.

'A little hackneyed perhaps, but attractive all the same,' he admitted. 'At least it should get even the most tired executive into the mood.'

'You're probably right,' murmured Louisa as she let her robe drop to the floor and reached out for his towel.

138

Chapter 7

When Louisa finally arrived at the office the next day she found that for a change she was the last to arrive. She ignored Scott and walked past him, straight into her office. However, he immediately leapt to his feet and followed her in to give her the morning's mail.

She looked up as she realised he was still standing there.

'Problem?' she asked.

'Information.'

'Oh?'

'Tessario has been in for hours.'

'How do you know?' she scoffed. 'Have you got a bug in his office?'

'Reception told me,' he said with an indulgent expression on his face.

She nodded and returned to sifting though her mail. 'So?'

Scott looked puzzled. 'I thought you would want to know,' he explained. 'He's been on the phone pretty much the whole time. His line is constantly engaged but no-one has any idea who he's talking to.' He paused. 'Do you know?' Louisa shrugged but didn't answer. 'This could be important,' Scott pointed out.

'Why?' she retorted. 'Who do you think he's calling? His uncle the Godfather?' Scott pursed his lips and glared at her. 'You know,' Louisa said, throwing her letters back down onto the desk, 'I am getting very tired of that expression. Anyway,' she admitted, 'he's probably involved in organising a PR event for the agency.'

Scott stared at her. Then his face cleared. 'You wanted to keep him busy,' he said nodding. 'Good idea.'

Louisa shook her head in irritation. 'No,' she explained. 'He offered to take over the job, and I let him. He thinks he can come up with the result and I'm going to let him have a try.'

'Are you mad?' Scott exclaimed.

'Who's talking now?' asked Louisa. 'The FBI agent, or my ever-so-concerned PA?'

'Your PA,' Scott replied. 'I'm sorry you had to ask. You should know by now that the FBI would be very happy for you to ingratiate yourself with Tessario and his family by allowing him to get some real or apparent influence over the business. But you must realise what this will mean.'

'What exactly?'

'Louisa,' he said, pausing for a moment, and failing to answer the question directly. 'When will this event take place?'

She shrugged once again. 'I'm leaving it up to Paolo,' she replied slightly defiantly. 'As soon as possible I suppose.'

'Paolo, as you've taken to calling him, will use all of his Mafia contacts and then he will fill the place with his Mafia friends. Everyone else will recognise that and you will only succeed in achieving the exact opposite of what you wanted. You will compound all of the rumours and you will ruin the image of your business.'

He stopped and waited for her response. Instead Louisa lay back in her chair and let it swing about. Tilting her head to one side she looked Scott in the eyes. 'So what?' she said. 'The only person who really cares about all this is me and it's my call. Anyway,' she went on, 'I can always start up again somewhere else. I've got a new policy: I'm going to relax and see what happens and if the business goes belly up then *c'est la vie*, I'm out of here.'

Scott stared at her once again. 'You've flipped,' he said with an air of confidence. 'You must have.'

'Well,' Louisa replied. 'It's my choice. But right now I'm still in charge, and I'd like to get on and write some letters if you don't mind.'

Scott retreated out of the door, but instead of getting down to work Louisa rested her head on the back of her chair and stared out of the window. It was, she thought, really quite satisfying to throw Scott off guard for a change. Truthfully, she had been planning to use this morning to have a meeting with Tessario and then take over the project herself. It was too important to be left to chance. However, it looked as though things had moved on and she had certainly not expected Tessario's input to be so whole-hearted, effective or immediate.

Walking into his office she was greeted with a cheery smile as he replaced the phone in its cradle and leant back in his chair, waving her to the other chair as he did so.

'I gather you've been busy this morning,' she said cautiously. He nodded. 'On what project?'

'On your party of course,' he replied.

'And how have you been progressing?' Louisa asked in the same cautious tone.

He nodded with satisfaction. 'How does next Thursday night suit you?'

'That's very sudden.'

'You wanted it organised quickly,' he replied. 'Anyway, there's nothing else on in town that night, I've checked. So that means the social set will be looking for somewhere to go.'

She nodded with approval. 'What about location?'

'The Middleton Tower on the Park.'

'Interesting,' she replied. 'Very expensive, very exclusive and an apartment block not a club or a hotel. So, any particular reason why?'

'Its got character, it's central, it's opulent so it will impress everybody and it was free. A friend has leant me an apartment.'

She nodded again. 'Fair enough. Clearly everything is well advanced. And is any of this confirmed yet?'

Tessario looked shifty. 'All of it is.'

Louisa stared at him in shock and surprise. 'Everything?' she repeated incredulously. 'I thought we agreed you would discuss this with me first.'

Tessario shrugged. 'It needed doing, so I did it.'

'What about the invitations?' she asked.

'Sorted.'

'I see.' There was a pause as she mustered her thoughts and quelled her sudden desire to panic. 'Might I see the invitations?'

'Sorry,' he replied. 'I subcontracted the work and approved the design. I could get you a copy if you wanted.'

Louisa shrugged. 'No matter. I suppose if its all been done then there isn't a lot of point is there? Do you have a copy of the guest list?'

Silently, Tessario handed her a set of papers, which she flicked through. As far as she could tell from her first glance everyone that she would have considered appropriate appeared to be on the list; magazine editors, competitors, photographers, society hostesses, eligible bachelors, marriageable heiresses, some New York-based actors, a few politicians and some models . . . basically everyone that she would have wanted to be there. She put the paper down and stood. 'Well, you seem to have everything in hand,' she said briskly.

Tessario looked up at her in surprise. 'Don't you want to know more about the event?' he asked. 'Entertainment, food . . .'

Louisa paused at the door. 'There doesn't really seem to be a lot of point, does there? I mean, you've already made the decisions, so I'll let you get on with it. It's your baby, let's see what happens.'

'You didn't think I'd do it did you?' Tessario's voice cut across her final words. 'And now you're expecting it to be a disaster.'

'You're paranoid,' replied Louisa. 'Just let's get on with it,' and she left, shutting the door quietly behind her.

She saw very little of Tessario over the next few days and spent the time working as normally as possible, at the same time fielding questions both from the media, who wanted to know about the party, and from people hunting for an invitation. In the meantime she decided to take Chris Dennison along as her escort in order to avoid feeling obliged to accept when, or if, Tessario asked her to join him. The whole time she suppressed her worries as well as possible and tried to keep her concern about the party to a minimum, if only to avoid another confrontation with Scott.

The evening finally arrived, to the obvious excitement of the staff, and even Tessario was ruffled, staying on the phone barking orders and receiving faxes all day. At four o'clock Louisa closed the office and went home to change and prepare for the evening. The staff, in contrast, were changing at the office and going out for drinks beforehand, and for a moment she felt a sense of regret that she couldn't join in the fun. This evening however, was not for fun, she reminded herself. It was for promoting the agency and convincing the people that mattered that the business was in good shape and looking forward to a prosperous future, and that magazines and advertisers should feel confident in placing her models in their assignments, advertisements and promotions.

With no sense of enthusiasm, but a definite feeling of trepidation Louisa reviewed the contents of her wardrobe. Eventually, with time running out before Chris arrived at the flat, she decided on a short silk dress in ice blue, with sapphire and diamond earrings and a necklet to match. Identically coloured shoes and a tiny jewelled bag completed her outfit. She looked at her reflection; OK she thought, very restrained but rich, elegant and still sexy. It would do.

The doorbell went and she walked through the lounge to check the video phone: it was Chris Dennison. He came bounding into the apartment, full of tireless enthusiasm as always. 'You look great,' he assured her, wrapping his arms around her. 'And you smell really good, good enough to eat—'

Louisa pushed him off. 'Please, Chris,' she said. 'I'm not in the mood and we have to get to the party.' Unperturbed he threw his arms around her again, leaning over her to nuzzle at her earlobe. 'You are incorrigible.'

'I know,' he replied. 'It's one of my most endearing qualities.'

'But timekeeping is one of mine,' she went on. 'We have to go.'

Chris released her reluctantly. 'OK,' he said, 'but I want it on record that I tried. And I expect to get my rations later tonight.'

Louisa shook her head, exasperated. 'You'll get a kick in the ass if you don't behave,' she replied. 'This is important and you'd better be handsome, charming and quiet,' she finished.

'I'll be the perfect escort,' he promised her. 'You'll be proud of me.'

'Hmm,' she finished, leading the way out of the door. 'I'd better be.'

As they drove from her apartment to the Middleton Building Louisa found herself grinding her teeth nervously. Chris looked across at her in amazement. 'What on earth's the matter? You were nervy in the apartment, but now you're wound up like a spring.'

'I'm just worried in case this is a complete disaster.'

'Why would it be a disaster?' he asked reasonably.

She waved her hands dismissively. 'Lots of reasons: my partner is organising it; I haven't been involved; I don't like to give up control and, I just don't know if he's up to it. It could be a disaster,' she repeated.

Chris looked out of the window. 'Well he's certainly arranged a major welcome for you,' he commented. 'It looks like an Oscar party out there.'

Louisa looked out of the car window towards the building where a crowd of guests was being ushered inside beneath a huge banner comprising vast photographs of Dane Agency models together with one of Louisa, gathered into Corin Dale's arms and surrounded by Nadine, Tirris and Sarah, taken on the beach in the Islas Canarias. Lights were flashing and a long train of cars were pulling up at the entrance and stacking back up to the corner of the block, delaying their arrival.

Chris looked over at her. 'I don't think you need to worry. It

144

looks to me like your partner really knows how to make a party go with a bang.'

The car finally drew up at the entrance and they walked inside into the huge foyer, crowded with models, actors and celebrities, posing for photographers and talking to journalists. Tessario was standing at the top of a wide, sweeping marble staircase, greeting people, directing waiters laden with glasses and bottles of champagne – and clearly looking out for Louisa's arrival.

'Are we late?' muttered Chris, as they walked in.

'No,' she hissed back. 'We're the guests of honour.'

A fanfare started up as they walked through the foyer and the crowd, assisted by the quantities of champagne they had already consumed, began to applaud their entrance. Louisa looked around, acknowledging people she knew, and smiling broadly as Tessario came down the steps to greet her, even though her stomach was still turning cartwheels.

'Ladies and Gentlemen,' he said, 'the founder and creator of the new Dane Agency, Ms Louisa Dane.' The crowd burst into applause again and taking Tessario's outstretched hand Louisa walked up the steps and turned to face them all.

'I'm so glad to see you here tonight,' she began. 'And like you I am looking forward to this evening, and to the future of a new and re-invigorated Dane Agency. I am sure that there will be many more years of working with my wonderful models and staff, and I hope there will be just as many years when I can look forward to working with those of you here tonight. Thank you. I will also look forward to talking to you individually throughout the evening. But for now, please enjoy yourselves.'

Tessario stood forward as she finished to a final round of applause. 'Thank you, Louisa,' he said. 'And now, the party, dinner and entertainment is all awaiting us upstairs on the first floor of this fabulous building, where we can celebrate the new dawn of the Dane Agency right through until dawn tomorrow.' There was a subtle titter of amusement and a murmur of interest at the prospect of the party. Then, as he drew Louisa to one side of the staircase, the guests began

145

to flow upwards and towards their destination, guided by the waiters to a huge corner apartment on the first floor.

'Well,' said Louisa. 'This is excellent.'

Tessario grinned, the most natural smile he had ever given her. 'Thank you. I'm glad to have pleased you at last. But don't speak now, you haven't seen anything yet. There's the party floor to go to first.'

She smiled. 'On the evidence so far you've certainly fulfilled all your promises. How? No,' she reconsidered. 'I don't think I want to know how you managed anything.'

'Oh, Paolo has lots of contacts,' came a deep, smoky, but unmistakably feminine voice from behind her. 'And those that he doesn't have, I supplied, didn't I, darling?' Louisa turned to find herself facing the brunette she had met in Tessario's office just the other day, as Tessario held out his hand and reached behind her to draw the woman forward.

'Gabriella, meet my business partner, Louisa Dane.'

'We've met. I told you,' Gabriella admonished him.

'Ah, really,' he said. 'I didn't realise who we were talking about. Well then, Louisa, please let me introduce my cousin, Gabriella Tessario.'

Louisa stared at him, and at the glamorous woman who was observing her reaction with an interested, if enigmatic air. 'How do you do?' Louisa said formally. 'It's a pleasure to meet you.'

'Likewise,' replied Gabriella. There was a pause as the two women studied each other and then Chris Dennison appeared from the base of the foyer and caught Louisa's hand. 'We should go on up,' he said. 'Come on, people will be wondering where you are.' Reluctantly she agreed and the group split and followed the last of the guests towards the party.

The Dane Agency party had taken over a huge apartment on the corner of the Middleton Building, a luxury apartment block built on the edge of Central Park. The theme on the invitations described the party as 'the new world of the Dane Agency'. Tessario had apparently interpreted this as Springtime and the apartment had been transformed into a woodland dell.

146

Any original contents had been removed and the flooring had been replaced with a carpet of grass; wide drifts of daffodils, snowdrops, crocus and other brightly coloured spring flowers were growing throughout the lawn and around the bases of trees; cherry blossoms, willows and woodland saplings could be seen planted and 'growing' around the apartment; the guests wandered along narrow country paths and paused to chat over ivy-covered tree trunks that served as occasional tables, whilst at the far corner of the apartment a river bank covered in bluebells ran up to a wooden bridge, which led across a stream and on to the door of a country cottage, in which the guests could dance or listen to music. Everywhere, waitresses, dressed like wood nymphs in silk slip dresses in shades of green and lemon, floated around the room carrying trays of champagne and canapés, whilst all around small fountains and springs bubbled with champagne and wine for the guests to help themselves. 'What,' said Tessario, appearing at Louisa's elbow and taking a look at her face. 'Why the surprise? You've been to parties before.'

'Yes,' she replied,' of course. But I'm stunned at how you managed to pull this off so quickly.'

'You did say you didn't want to know,' he reminded her. 'Anyway,' he went on, 'let's not worry about that right now. Let's enjoy ourselves.' He reached out and grabbed a couple of glasses of champagne from a passing waitress, and held one out to Louisa. 'It looks like congratulations to me.'

Louisa had sent Chris off to check out the interior of the cottage and had just finished a chat with Venetia Hall from LaVeile when she felt an arm around her waist and Corin Dale materialised behind her.

'Where have you been all evening?' he asked, leaning down to kiss her on the cheek, both of them smiling once again as another photographer recorded their meeting.

'Me?' she queried, with a laugh. 'What about you?'

'I've been checking out the talent,' he said, looking around the room. 'Plenty of it about.'

'Corin, you're dreadful,' she teased him, getting a big, slightly inebriated smile in return.

He slid his other arm around her, 'So what do you think?' he asked, looking around the room at the revelling crowds. 'It's a big success.'

Louisa smiled. 'I was really worried, but you're right, it's a success. Paolo has really pulled it off.' She cast another look around. Many guests were making their way into the 'cottage' for dancing, although all around the woodland the entertainment – individual strolling players of mediaeval jugglers, fire-eaters, magicians and in some far corners, erotic dancers – were still amusing groups of people. Meanwhile the original classical quartet in the 'cottage' had been replaced with a rock band and when the door was opened a growing group of people could be seen dancing although many were still sitting in the 'woodlands' area drinking champagne from the ever-bubbling alcoholic springs.

'So,' Corin said, 'how about a dance?'

Louisa raised her eyebrows. 'The last time I danced with you I ended up getting grass stains all over my dress,' she replied. Corin laughed in recollection and taking her hand he led her down the path, across the bridge and into the cottage. Once inside they made their way through masses of the fashion elite; magazine editors, publishers and photographers, plus a wide mix of young and old society hostesses. A large number of this group had homes which had been photographed, reviewed and approved of in the magazines, and many had known Louisa for years. Indeed it seemed that whilst not everyone knew everyone else, they all knew Louisa.

Within the cottage enormous photos of models, and also of Louisa at her home and at the office adorned many of the walls, and as they walked through the crowd people surged forward, shaking her hand, dropping bon mots and suggestions in her ear, generally being friendly. Everyone was eager to be associated with a success, whether it was real or not, she thought wryly, acknowledging the smiles and hellos as she moved forward, letting Corin's frame and well known face clear a path as they went. Finally they reached the dance floor and Corin dragged her onto it, swinging her around in his usual hopelessly inept style. Louisa stuck with it nobly for a few minutes, but was relieved when Chris appeared at her shoulder to cut in. Corin instantly waved them on and away, and moved to take over the care of a pair of nubile, youthful socialites who had been surreptitiously examining his physique from a distance. They were clearly delighted to accommodate him and the three swept away from the dancers and towards the bar.

As the music changed Chris drew Louisa towards him. 'Do you fancy a change,' he shouted into her ear above the noise of the music.

'Fine,' she called back, 'I could do with a rest.' Chris stopped dancing and holding hands they eased their way through to the side of the dance floor.

'Hold on,' he said and disappeared for a moment. On his return he took hold of her hand and led her towards the furthest corner of the room, then they slipped through the kitchen, out of the apartment and into the hall. Once there they got into the elevator and Chris pressed for the top floor.

'Where are we going?' asked Louisa curiously.

'The roof,' replied Chris. 'There's a garden up there and I thought we could relax for a while.' He paused and opened up his jacket to reveal a magnum of Veuve Cliquot champagne and glasses tucked inside his pocket.

'And you came well prepared I see,' said Louisa.

'Absolutely,' Chris replied. 'In every way.' The elevator doors opened and they went through a door marked as a fire exit and up a flight of stairs. 'This is the back way in,' he explained.

'How did you know about this?' Louisa asked, laughing.

Chris smiled. 'I did a little reconnaissance when you were dancing with the famous Corin Dale.'

'I should probably be downstairs being the hostess,' Louisa fretted as they climbed the stairs and turned the final corner. 'People will notice that I've gone.'

'Don't be ridiculous,' he laughed. 'It's past midnight, the party's in full swing, and right now half of them won't even remember why they're here.'

'Oh thanks,' she said. 'That makes me very happy.'

'No, seriously,' Chris replied. 'The magazine and newspaper columnists have all gone off to write or sleep, and the party people are settled in for the duration; end of story. You can relax, it's a big success. The business is safe.'

Louisa sobered for a moment. 'Not exactly,' she thought, but she gave Chris a big cheerful smile and took his hand. He took off again, pulling her along behind him, drawing her up the last flight of stairs and out through a large door into the cool night air.

The roof had a garden that had been moulded and designed to make the most of its position next to Central Park. On one side of the building the view of the Park was very accessible, whilst the remaining sides were surrounded by high, solid buildings, and around these there was a curtain of living plants; trees, shrubs and flowers that screened the garden from the adjacent buildings, and provided a break against the noise of the traffic. In the centre of the garden was a thick, soft, camomile lawn that scented the night air, with a variety of wooden benches and chairs around its edge. Further away from the centre small arbours of privet and bay trees surrounded carved stone benches, proving quiet and private oases even within the peace and stillness of the garden.

At this time of night there was relatively little noise from traffic and the only really noticeable sound was carried up from the party; laughter, a clinking of glasses and the sound of music, all evidence of a party in full flow. As Louisa walked forward, breathing in the scent of camomile and lavender, Chris went back to the staircase and pressed a button inside the door and suddenly the garden was illuminated by a series of hidden lamps, set behind shrubs and hedges, giving an ethereal glow throughout the garden that did nothing to take away the sense of mystery and stillness.

They strolled in the garden for a while and had stopped in one of the arbours when Chris suddenly tapped on Louisa's arm and drew her to one side. Louisa looked up in a silent query, and he pointed towards the door which was slowly opening. He drew Louisa further into the shadows. 'What's the matter?' she whispered, suddenly overwhelmed with a desperate desire to giggle. 'Aren't we supposed to be here?'

He whispered back. 'No of course we're not, and I don't want us to be disturbed.'

'Oh and why not?'

'Because I've got to have you and I don't want an audience.'

'Oh for goodness sake,' she whispered back, still laughing.

'Shh,' he replied again, pointing as Corin Dale appeared through the doorway.

'Oh my God,' she whispered. 'It's Corin and his nymphets.'

In answer, Chris simply put his hand over her mouth, as Corin looked suspiciously around the area, trying to locate the source of the noise. Apparently concluding that he had been mistaken, he turned and held the door open for the two girls whom she had seen him with on the dance floor. With many giggles of their own the girls approached the lawn, armed with a bottle of champagne and Corin's jacket, which they used as a rug to kneel on.

'Come on, Corin,' one encouraged him. 'Let's see what you've got.'

'Very romantic, Davina. Not,' the other commented sarcastically, and the two fell into more fits of giggles. Their mirth grew as Corin approached and stood in front of them, running his fingers over the increasingly obvious bulge in his trousers.

'If you want to find out, then you're going to have to do some work,' he said tauntingly.

'Very sure of himself, isn't he, Alicia?' said Davina.

'Very,' replied her friend. 'And he's got a reputation as well.'

'Well let's find out if he's got a good reason for it,' Davina replied and simultaneously they reached out eagerly for his groin, making him leap back in surprise, to their obvious and drunken amusement.

Louisa turned to Chris. 'We should go,' she hissed.

'How can we?' he hissed back. 'We'd have to walk right back across the lawn. Anyway,' he continued, 'don't you want to see? I know I do.' Louisa shot him a glare and made to move away, but Chris held her around the shoulders and put his hands gently back across her mouth. 'Wait,' he whispered in her ear. 'Let's just see what happens.'

On the grass the two girls were kneeling in front of Corin's massive frame. They had slid the zipper of his pants down and Davina was caressing the bulge in his underwear. 'Looks like it's all true,' she said to her friend, who took a turn stroking the solid mass with increasingly vigorous strokes. For his part, Corin stood in front of them, watching their expressions with satisfaction. He slipped off his tie and rapidly unbuttoned his shirt, throwing it in the direction of the door to the staircase.

The girls took this as an indication of his willingness to service them and drew his trousers down, letting Corin kick off his socks and shoes, and step out of his pants. Laughing, they both whistled in admiration at the size of his erection and then dragged him down towards them so that he disappeared under a mass of floaty chiffon and tousled blonde hair.

Louisa swallowed as she recalled the feel of Corin's hands upon her, but she already found it impossible to drag her eyes away. She could feel Chris's excitement from the intensity with which he was observing the scene that was playing out in front of them, and from the growing erection in his pants that she could feel pressed up against her butt.

In the eerie glow provided by the garden lamps, Corin now sat naked on the end of a wooden bench in front of the girls, who were engrossed in helping each other remove their dresses, but whose attention kept returning to focus on the man in front of them. 'Come on, girls,' encouraged Corin, his lazy smile consuming his face, 'there's plenty to go around.'

In response Davina leaned over and whispered in her friend's ear, and then they clearly came to an agreement as she knelt in front of him to take his huge, exposed cock into her mouth, whilst Alicia stood at his side and began to kiss him and caress his chest, letting him release her breasts from her bra and nuzzle them in return. However, this state of affairs clearly didn't satisfy either of the girls for very long and soon Davina released Corin from her mouth and stood up, pushing him backwards to lie down along the length of the bench. Then, with a nod of approval from her friend who had retreated to the far end of the bench, Davina stripped off her panties. Standing over Corin's hips at the edge of the bench, she lowered herself onto his cock, growling under her breath with each passing inch as she did so.

'What's he like?' called out Alicia, who was watching closely, sliding her fingers down inside creamy satin French knickers.

'Huge,' groaned Davina, squatting down as her hole slowly devoured the last of Corin's penis. Beneath her, Corin lay flat on the bench, his arms draped down to the ground, his legs hanging off the edge of the bench, with his eyes gazing up into the stars.

'Tell me more,' demanded Alicia, shifting her position slightly to get a better view.

'He's wide as well as long,' Davina gasped as she settled her hips fully over Corin's, and starting to gently rock herself against him. 'He's hot and oh fuck, he feels like he's stretching me apart.' She threw her head back on her shoulders and jutted her hips forward, keeping her balance with difficulty as she slid herself up and down Corin's shaft, whilst Corin's fingers reached out to gently stroke at her clitoris, which was just within his reach.

This was clearly too much for Alicia, who inched forward towards Corin's head. Sliding off her wide-legged French knickers and tossing them to one side, she stood over Corin's head. 'Suck me,' she commanded, and he obediently abandoned Davina's clit to her own attentions, using his hands to guide Alicia's cunt to the correct position over his face, and spreading the lips of her vagina apart to lick her out. Like Davina, Alicia threw her head back with pleasure.

'Yes,' she murmured. 'Yes, that's good. God, your tongue is nearly as long as your cock.' Her fingers raced down her front to rub aggressively at her clitoris, and for a moment there was silence, except for the panting sounds of the two women concentrating on their lust and desire.

The movement of Davina's hips became increasingly violent and the final evidence of her excitement was a series of panting groans that started with a low gasp and culminated in an almost inaudible high pitched cry, as she threw her head back once more before leaning forward for one final thrust. She collected herself with a groan and straightened as her breathing returned to normal. After a moment she reached out to attract Alicia's attention.

'Do you want a go?' she asked casually, as though the two girls were there alone. 'He's still got some mileage in him and you know I don't mind sharing.'

Alicia let her hands fall away from her clit and immediately extracted herself from Corin's tongue, moving forward along the bench as Davina eased herself off his cock and away from the bench. 'Sorry, girls,' came Corin's voice from beneath them, 'but I've got to do this my way.' He pushed Alicia further forward and followed her off the bench and then, with apparently no effort whatsoever, picked her up and turned her about, bending her over the end of the bench with her ass in the air.

'What are you going to do?' asked Davina, sitting cross-legged on the grass as she searched through the pile of clothing for her dress. 'I'd like to fuck her in the ass,' replied Corin politely. 'Would that be OK, Alicia?'

Alicia nodded enthusiastically. 'My favourite,' she said approvingly, and Corin took up a position behind her, running his finger along her cunt and then easing the fluid drenched digit inside her for a brief exploration of her butt-hole. Alicia groaned in anticipation and leaned even further forwards across the bench, her ass sticking further out and up.

'Don't piss about. Do it,' she commanded, and in response Corin gently started to ease himself inside her, reaching around from behind to grasp at Alicia's hard erect nipples where they stood out from small round breasts. Alicia gasped as his hands clutched at her breasts, and then cried out loudly as Corin made a final aggressive thrust against her hips, and his cock went fully inside her. Chris and Louisa, watching from the sidelines drew in their breaths as she whimpered for a moment, then she was groaning with pleasure and noisily shouting out words of encouragement to Corin, who was slowly but surely pumping himself into her ass, his hands held lightly against her hips.

Louisa felt Chris move behind her, and he started to draw her dress upwards, first running both of his hands underneath the light fabric, then letting his fingers run around the band of her panties to the front, then inside them and deep down into her damp pubic hair. They watched the couple in front of them continue fucking, unable to draw their eyes away, much like Davina who had pulled her dress on, but was lying on Corin's jacket in the middle of the lawn with her legs spread apart, energetically masturbating her clitoris.

Corin's face was flushed, with a line of sweat breaking out across his forehead. He drew his lips back in a snarl as he kept up a rapid pace, whilst Alicia groaned and cried out at the size of his cock, begging him for harder and deeper and more aggressive sex, and accusing him of holding out on her and reserving his strength for another session with Davina. Corin's response to this was immediate; he leant further over her and took a handful of her hair in both hands, viciously dragging her head backwards. For a moment Alicia shuddered and then she cried out her approval again, before her words were lost in her first panting orgasm.

Chris slid his fingers down further into Louisa's sex cleft, and as the couple in front of them continued their apparently unstoppable bacchanal, he contented himself with stroking her

155

outer lips, making her lean back against him and encouraging her to relax and enjoy the sensations. Chris removed his fingers and drew Louisa further into the arbour where they were hidden from view, but could still see the distant trio. He let his trousers and pants drop down and sat on the stone bench behind him, reaching under Louisa's dress to delicately remove and draw off her panties. She in turn stepped out of them and sat down on his lap, bracing her hands against the bench on either side of him and letting her skimpy dress sit across them, so that any passer-by might possibly think that she was sitting on his lap in an intimate embrace, rather than having intimate relations.

With no further foreplay, Chris lowered her down onto his member. Suddenly his excited cock was filling Louisa's wet hole and she ground herself down on him still further, in order to take as much of him into her as possible, until she could feel the coarse sensation of his pubic hair against her skin. Then, wrapping his hands around her hips for balance and guidance Chris began to work Louisa up and down on his cock, taking control of her as though she was a rag doll in his hands. At first his movements were slow and studied, each time drawing her fully off his cock and then slowly easing her back on, pressing her down so that its full length was consumed by her cunt. However, the pace soon quickened and Louisa found herself penetrated with increasing rapidity as his movements became shorter and quicker, whilst in front of them the couple finally came to their noisy climax.

Corin grunted with satisfaction as he launched his come inside Alicia, his back first arching one way and then another. Like a whiplash his muscles threw his torso forward across Alicia's back, holding onto her shoulders for increased penetration as his hips pumped his cock further into her in his final spasms of climax. In her submissive position bent over the bench Alicia could only accept his actions, whimpering as he made his last thrusts into her until the only sound was Davina's high pitched gasps from the lawn in front of them.

In the silence that followed Chris managed to halt his

156

actions, although Louisa was sure he was desperate to reach a conclusion, and the two sat motionless as the threesome in front of them gathered their things together, giggling and cuddling as they did so. Corin picked up the champagne bottle and tipped it upside down.

'All gone,' he commented unnecessarily. 'Shall we go down and get some more?'

The two girls approved noisily and the three of them went to leave via the metal door. 'Anyway,' Louisa could hear Davina saying to Alicia, 'we can always come back later.'

'Even if it is with someone else,' her friend hissed back, and collapsing into drunken giggles, they disappeared from sight.

'Insatiable,' murmured Chris admiringly as he lifted Louisa from the end of his cock.

'I hope you haven't gone off the idea now that the floor show has gone,' Louisa teased him.

'No chance of that,' Chris replied, swivelling her about to face him. He reached behind and unzipped her dress, letting it drop to the floor, and then guided her to the stone bench where he laid her down flat on top of his jacket. Louisa reached out to pull him down on top of her, her legs spread wide to accommodate him. Instead, Chris took up a standing position at the end of the bench and, taking hold of her ankles and spreading her legs wide once again, he placed his cock at the entrance to her vagina and pushed it inside her.

Both were already highly stimulated by their voyeurism and the combination of the position in which she had been placed and the resulting depth of Chris's penetration meant that soon Louisa was gasping with pleasure beneath his touch as her orgasm rippled up and through her body, until Chris's body spasmed, his cock pulsating inside her and his face screwed up with a desperate sense of release. They slowly came back to reality, and Chris withdrew his cock from Louisa. As they sat on the bench recovering from their exertions Louisa nuzzled Chris's chest. 'So, have you worked out how we're going to sneak back past everyone who's coming out of the party?' he asked.

'Me?' replied Louisa. 'Since when was this my idea?'

'Never mind,' said Chris. 'We may just have to snuggle up together until the morning comes and they've all gone home. Good thing I brought the champagne.'

Chapter 8

Louisa stayed in bed until late the next morning, having cancelled all of her appointments for the day in anticipation of either a great success, for which she would give herself a day off and let the office take care of itself, or a great failure, in which case she had planned to stay at home and lick her wounds. Fortunately the party had clearly been a great success both as a party and as a public relations exercise. All of the right people had been there, the food and wine and entertainment had been excellent and she knew for sure that there would be coverage in the trade mags and probably in some of the newspapers' society pages. And, also to her satisfaction, Scott had been wrong; she hadn't seen any sign of strangers who could possibly have been called 'Mafia types'.

Overall, however, her thoughts weren't occupied by the party, by Corin or even by Chris Dennison. No, now that she was sober and awake the thing she kept coming back to was Tessario and his cousin, Gabriella. Tessario had been very co-operative and relatively subdued. In fact he had been completely unlike himself, and much more like the person who had charmed everyone on the photo shoot in Spain. 'Everyone apart from me, that is,' she thought moodily to herself. And then there was Gabriella. Louisa shivered. She had never been particularly physically attracted to women, but from the moment they had laid eyes on each other in Tessario's office there had been something between Gabriella and herself, although at that time she hadn't realised that she was Tessario's relative, she had simply assumed she was a girlfriend. At the party, however, on those brief occasions when Gabriella had touched her or passed by she had felt a definite frisson of excitement, something that made her feel uncomfortable, particularly when she remembered looking up and seeing Gabriella watching her with an intense, interested expression. Each to his or her own, she thought, attempting unsuccessfully to brush the recollection to one side. She shook her head and wilfully forced herself to change the topic of her thoughts back to work.

For the time being at least, she should have laid the industry gossip and her major worries to rest, and hopefully the business would be reasonably secure, at least in the short term. The next thing was to capitalise on this interest and keep the ball rolling; the agency couldn't afford to lose either pace or its profile at this stage. That meant she must get some more PR organised, and get some bookings confirmed whilst the media interest was at its height. In fact, she thought, she could use the time at home today to plan out some ideas she had been having. She rolled herself out of bed and strolled into the kitchen, picking up her mail from the front door as she went. There were the usual bills, some junk mail, a copy of a magazine and some photos to review. As she was reading the paper and drinking coffee there was a buzz at the door. She sighed in irritation at this unexpected intrusion, but trotted over to the intercom.

'Yes?'

'There's a delivery for you, Ms Dane, requiring a reply. Shall I send the messenger up?'

'Fine,' she replied without enthusiasm and returning to the table she carried on reading her paper. No doubt the delivery would be flowers or something similar relating to the party. However, when she answered the door it turned out to be a single, expensive-looking envelope. She opened it up to find a brief, hand-written note from Gabriella Tessario, inviting her to lunch at 'Sandrine's'. She sat at the kitchen, feeling slightly bemused. Was this a business lunch? And was it with Tessario or a 'girls-only' twosome. 'Well,' she thought, persuading herself successfully, 'it can't do any harm to follow it up, and after all if it gets me closer to finding out more information on him then it can't be bad.' Having made her decision she informed the messenger that she would indeed be accepting the invitation and to advise Ms Tessario that she would join her at 1.30 pm for lunch.

Louisa looked across the table at Gabriella, who was sitting looking as relaxed and cool as ever. Around them the waiters buzzed between tables and there was a noticeable hum from the diners, but, just as she had at the frenetic party, Gabriella managed to bring an enigmatic stillness and tranquillity to the immediate area about their table. The physical similarity between the olive-skinned and voluptuous Gabriella and her cousin was undeniable, but even so Louisa would hardly have placed them in the same league, let alone identified a family relationship. This, she supposed was what mob money could produce when the recipient was nowhere near the streets, or at least she reminded herself, one-step removed from the streets. At the very thought she felt a guilty flush cross her face. There was nothing she knew about Gabriella that could connect her to the low-life of Paolo Tessario or his friends, and she could hardly help her family or heritage. As she pondered these illicit thoughts Louisa became aware of Gabriella's equally close scrutiny from the other side of the table.

'Oops,' she said, attempting to break the silence that had descended. 'Am I thinking with my mouth open?'

Gabriella smiled. 'No, but I think I could follow what you were thinking—'

'Oh?' asked Louisa, feeling the same guilt as before.

'Oh yes. I've come across that expression before. Mostly from East Coast blue bloods. Not from men though, they're usually trying to work out my net worth, rather than where the money has come from.'

Louisa shifted uncomfortably in her seat. 'Gabriella really, I don't know what you . . .' she began.

'No,' said Gabriella. 'Please, don't do that. Let's get this out in the open, with no bullshit between us.' Louisa started at the unexpected swearwords coming from the luscious burgundy lips. 'Paolo has told me that he believes you know at least

161

something about our family connections. Well I can't help my family,' she continued intently, speaking too fast to allow Louisa to get a word in. 'But neither am I going to apologise for them. They are who they are and I deal with that every time I get stopped for a parking ticket, or meet someone who knows a cop and warns them off.' She paused, observing Louisa intently. 'But, unlike some of the more distant members of my extended family I don't get involved with illegal activities. I run my own show and I love my business. And my uncles are simply that, family relatives.' She paused for breath, and fixed Louisa with her large greeny-brown eyes. 'What they do is their business, and I'm not interested.'

'And they don't mind?' queried Louisa. 'That you're not involved?'

Gabriella gave an exasperated sigh. 'There are plenty of family members to go around without worrying about little me. Anyway, some of my uncles are traditional Italian archetypes. Most of my activities would shock them to the core, if you know what I mean.' Confused, Louisa smiled politely in response. After a moment Gabriella continued. 'Anyway, as far as business goes, the very idea of a female being involved in any of their activities would outrage them.'

'But that sort of attitude would never extend to a man,' mused Louisa. There was a silence from the other side of the table and she caught Gabriella giving her a strange, amused expression.

'Like my cousin, you mean,' she asked pointedly. Louisa blushed once again and Gabriella laughed out loud, enhancing her discomfort.

'Tell me about your business,' suggested Louisa, in an effort to change the subject. In response Gabriella leaned back in her seat and waved her arm expansively about her.

'Why don't you tell me what you think?' she countered.

Louisa looked around the restaurant. 'This is yours?' she asked.

'The very same,' Gabriella confirmed. 'I thought you knew.'

'No,' said Louisa, looking around with more interested eyes. 'I had no idea.'

She looked up to see Gabriella casting her eyes to the ceiling, and refilling her wine glass. 'Is something wrong?' she asked cautiously. Gabriella shook her head in irritation. 'Are you sure?' Louisa asked again.

'That asshole,' muttered Gabriella. 'I thought he'd have told you for sure.' She turned her attention back to Louisa. 'Listen, Louisa, I'm sorry to ask you this, but why did you come here today?'

Louisa shifted in her seat, uncertain how to answer. 'I'm not sure,' she said.

After a moment Gabriella continued. 'Well, what I mean is, did Paulo say anything to get you to meet me?'

'Well no,' answered Louisa. 'I haven't spoken to him today.'

'So why are you here?'

'I suppose I just thought we'd get on,' replied Louisa, floundering for a reason, trying to bluff her way through the realisation that she had just wanted to meet with this woman again. 'I guess I thought we could be friends,' she said lamely.

'Even despite your relationship with my cousin?'

'I don't have a "relationship" with your cousin. To be honest we don't get on at all.'

'Hmm,' mused Gabriella. 'And he said nothing else to you about me?'

'I suppose he didn't think it was any of his business,' offered Louisa.

'Hah,' scoffed Gabriella. 'That'd be a first!' They both laughed and Louisa began to relax again, as the moment of tension and uncertainty passed and the subject of Paolo Tessario and his Family was dropped. She looked around the restaurant, the vaulted ceiling and greenery providing a glasshouse effect even in the New York spring day, but giving a feeling of openness, which the packed dining room suggested proved popular with the diners. They were in a slightly secluded area, a few steps above most of the rest of the dining tables, so that their view extended over the main body of the restaurant and out through the glasshouse windows and onto the Manhattan skyline that stretched into the distance ahead of them.

Gabriella informed Louisa that she had taken the liberty of ordering what she thought was the best on the menu for the day. Shortly the waiters brought their hors-d'oevres; plates of bresaola – a cured raw beef – served with a chicory and endive salad in a walnut vinaigrette with walnut bread on the side. The vegetables were crisp and the meat was thinly sliced and mouth-wateringly delicious. For a while they chatted about the party, its success, the people who had been there and what everyone had done and to whom. Louisa was continually amazed that they got on so well and so easily, considering they had only just met.

The entree was a light seafood ravioli, in a cream and champagne sauce, served with a freshly chilled bottle of Chardonnay. The pasta was light as air and the sauce delicate enough to complement the fish, rather than overwhelm it. Louisa closed her eyes as she savoured it and breathed out with pleasure. 'This is heavenly,' she said, 'you must have a great chef.'

Gabriella nodded her agreement. 'I don't know how long I'll be able to keep him,' she admitted. 'He's quite young and this is his first big break. Before I know it he'll be wanting to own his own place, and I can't say I'll blame him, however inconvenient it might be for me.' They chatted a little longer, going over the problems of staffing and running a business as though they were two old friends catching up on time spent apart. Neither wanted dessert and so they moved on to fresh strong coffee, sitting in a comfortable silence waiting for the cafetière to infuse its blend of roasted coffee beans.

'It's lovely here,' Louisa said finally. 'How did you come by this place?'

'It's on a lease from one of my relatives,' replied Gabriella, watching her carefully. 'And I came into some family money when I was twenty-five, so it all fell into place at once. My other places are quite different.'

'You have other restaurants?' asked Louisa. 'Where?'

'Well, I own La Risselle,' said Gabriella, with a knowing smile. Louisa stared at her.

'I took Paolo there when he first came to the office,' she said.

Gabriella smiled. 'I know.'

'He was so—'

'—uncomfortable?'

'Yes,' replied Louisa. 'It was as though it was the first time he'd ever been anywhere like that. I mean, like . . .' Realising the insult she floundered for words once again, but Gabriella unexpectedly came to her rescue.

'Somewhere they had linen napkins and bottled water?'

'Well, yes,' said Louisa lamely. 'I'm sorry. I didn't mean to be rude. But it was very awkward and he was so, well . . .' Gabriella waved her arm in a dismissive gesture.

'Trust me, I know. He told me.'

'But he must have been there before,' said Louisa.

'Of course, many times,' said Gabriella. Louisa shook her head. 'Don't worry about it,' said Gabriella. 'It doesn't matter right now.'

Louisa's face creased up in confusion. 'I just don't understand. You're both so . . . different.'

'Do you think so?' asked Gabriella. 'And some people think we're so similar.'

'In what way?'

'Lots of things,' she replied, dropping her tone so that it could only be audible to Louisa. 'The things we like to do.'

'Like what?' asked Louisa, matching Gabriella's low and confidential tone, feeling that something about their meeting was changing subtly, but still uncertain of the outcome.

'Things like you,' murmured Gabriella, reaching out unexpectedly to take hold of Louisa's hand. Louisa started in surprise and laughed nervously.

'Your cousin despises me. I'm sorry, Gabriella, but you've

165

got this all wrong. We can't stand each other.' She finished speaking, but sat still, uncertain whether to withdraw her hand from Gabriella's touch, which was sending rivulets of pleasure crawling across her skin with each passing moment.

'Are you so sure of that?' asked Gabriella. Louisa nodded, trying vainly to concentrate on the words as Gabriella began to discreetly massage her hand, running her fingers across Louisa's palm with the most erotic and sensitive of movements. 'Well, let's not worry about my cousin right now,' continued Gabriella. 'After all he's not here to defend himself, is he?' She slowly brought Louisa's hand to her lips and ran her tongue over the tips of her fingers, pausing to draw one into her mouth, as Louisa watched her, embarrassed, but unwilling to move or make her stop.

'You know,' said Gabriella, 'I have an apartment at the top of this building. Did I tell you that?' Louisa shook her head, licking her lips nervously. 'Would you like to see it? We could go there if you wanted.' Louisa sucked in her breath. The meaning in Gabriella's words was plain, as was the inference. This was Louisa's decision, she could stop everything right now and walk away, or she could continue and go with Gabriella down a new path. Gabriella placed Louisa's hand back on the table, as if not wanting to influence her decision, but watching her intently for a sign. As she found herself let loose and the warmth of the other woman's flesh faded into memory Louisa came to her decision.

'Let's go,' she said.

Gabriella stood and gestured with her hand. 'This way.' Louisa rose to follow, only now realising that their table's position meant that their exit was masked by a combination of the array of plants and the bustle of waiters. She followed Gabriella down a private passageway at the back of the restaurant and into an office where Gabriella turned around and smiled. 'The rest of the building's flats and offices have other entrances, but for me, having the restaurant and the added complication of my interesting family connections means that I don't always want to have my arrival or departure trumpeted to the world,'

166

she explained. 'So I keep a private way in.' She produced a key and opened an innocuous-looking door to reveal a private elevator, standing aside for Louisa to enter first.

The elevator began to move up the floors. Neither woman spoke or moved, and in the ensuing silence the sound of the commercial music piped through the elevator's loudspeakers was bizzarely loud and cheerful. Louisa stood, slowly tensing up and waiting for Gabriella to make some sort of move, terrified that she would and then mortified when she didn't, but instead stood silently on Louisa's right, allowing the elevator to complete its ride to the top of the building. Finally they were there and strolled down a long corridor to Apartment 2820 where Gabriella fished in her purse for a set of keys, before throwing the door open with a flamboyant gesture.

'"Come into my parlour, said the spider to the fly,"' she quoted as she swept across the threshold, then turning she laughed out loud as she saw Louisa's face. 'I'm sorry, but you looked so horrified in the lift. What did you think I was going to do?' she continued, raising her voice as she walked across the carpet and disappeared into another room, re-emerging a moment later with a bottle of Laurent Perrier. 'I mean, did you really think I was going to go ravish you there in the lift?' She laughed again. 'Well, I suppose I was tempted, but I think I can offer you far more than that.' She paused and looked at Louisa, approaching the sofa. 'You've gone very quiet,' she said. 'Are you having second thoughts?' Louisa swallowed down her growing nervousness and shook her head. 'Good,' said Gabriella popping the cork on the bottle. 'Then let's have a glass of champagne.' Louisa took the proffered glass and sat down on the sofa. 'What do you think about the apartment?' asked Gabriella. She strolled across the floor to the window and looked out to the neighbouring skyscrapers. 'I have to say I'm quite proud of it. I decorated it myself,' she continued, turning back to Louisa. 'It was a mess when I moved in, all jungle prints and caftans. Hideous.' Louisa nodded silently and drank from her glass again as Gabriella walked back to her side and sat down on the edge of the sofa. There was another long pause.

'Louisa,' Gabriella began. 'Look, there's something I need to know. This is your first time, isn't it? With a woman I mean.' Louisa nodded and Gabriella put her glass down, gently took Louisa's glass from her hands and placed that on the table in front of them. 'It'll be fine,' she assured. 'I promise you.' She smiled. 'Just relax and let me take care of you.' As she spoke she let a finger run down the side of Louisa's face and teased a strand of hair back into place, before tipping her chin up and kissing her gently on the lips. At first the kiss was friendly and warming, then her tongue slowly parted Louisa's lips and ran along the edge of her teeth, her moist luscious mouth enveloping Louisa's. As their kiss progressed it changed from a sensuous gentleness and became invigorating and exciting, sending Louisa's senses into overdrive, until she was finally released from Gabriella's grasp, and both girls simultaneously drew in their breath. 'Come on,' said Gabriella, 'let's go to bed.' She took one of Louisa's hands in her own, and picking up the glasses led Louisa towards another door, throwing it open with a flourish. Louisa drew in her breath and stared around her in amazement. This was a bedroom clearly made for sex, not sleeping.

The whole room was a subtle blend of creamy white and antique gold; it had feeling of wanton luxury that emanated from the richness and depth of the furnishings, but it was also curiously light, with the tones of its creamy decor enhanced by a full wall of windows, which were completely draped with a toile that effectively obscured the interior to any curious outside eyes, yet let the light of day filter in. The furnishings were dominated by an antique bed that was covered by a baroque frame and drapes of the same fine toile and around the room were pieces of antique gilded furniture.

'It's upmarket bordello,' announced Gabriella from behind Louisa. 'Just my style.' She leaned across the doorway, effectively preventing any possible retreat, whilst Louisa stood on the threshold looking about her. Then she felt gentle hands on her shoulders, running across the fabric of her linen jacket to slowly ease it from her shoulders, and she knew her seduction was about to move into its final phase. Without turning around she allowed the jacket to slip from her shoulders and heard it fall onto a chair, the silk lining rustling as it slipped from Gabriella's hands. She could imagine the touch of long, manicured nails even before she felt them slide down her bare arms and she leant back into Gabriella's embrace as the taller woman's arms enveloped her and encircled her breasts, gently massaging them beneath the silk of her blouse. Louisa let her eyes close and her head fall back onto Gabriella's shoulder as her gentle hands began to unbutton her blouse. The whole time Gabriella let her lips brush delicately against the lobe of Louisa's ear; tiny butterfly kisses that kept the tension within her body growing to a fever pitch yet which minimised her nervousness and helped to banish her fear of the unknown.

As she finished unbuttoning Louisa's blouse, Gabriella slid one fingernail into the cup of Louisa's satin and lace bra, running its tip around the folded bud of her nipple. Then, tantalisingly, she withdrew her hand, ignoring Louisa's involuntary gasp of disappointment, and continued to undo the remaining buttons, first on the blouse and then on her skirt, letting them both slide from around Louisa's body and onto the floor with a final rustle of silk and linen. Taking Louisa's hand Gabriella led her away from the clothes, discarded like the jacket at the side of the room, and towards the canopied bed. Mute and trusting, Louisa did as she was bidden, although no words had passed between them since they had entered the room.

Gabriella turned her around and sat her down on the end of the bed. 'You're beautiful,' whispered Gabriella. She leant over Louisa, running her long fingers down the cleavage between Louisa's large rounded breasts and on down the central line of her abdomen. 'Magnificent.' Louisa swallowed as nervousness overcame her in a new wave of tension, but Gabriella chose to ignore the wave of panic and indecision that crossed her face. Instead she gently pushed Louisa backwards to lie on the bed, and knelt between her knees. Beginning at her toes Gabriella kissed her way up the inside of Louisa's legs and with gentle nibbles and bites slowly worked her way up to the top of her thighs, where the beige silken stockings finished, exposing the exquisitely soft and lightly tanned flesh at the top of Louisa's legs. With an upward glance at Louisa's supine body Gabriella satisfied herself that the momentary panic had passed, and she let her hands slide between the apricot silk French knickers which hid Louisa's sex flesh from view. She smiled as Louisa gasped and moved spasmodically with surprise before relaxing once again, letting Gabriella's experienced fingers slide up the groove of her flesh and onto her clitoris.

Louisa opened her eyes and looked down into Gabriella's dark hazel eyes, watching her and gauging her reaction. After a moment she lifted her buttocks and still without a word Gabriella eased the panties off to expose her sex, framed only by crisp, blonde curls and the strips of apricot silk suspenders. Gabriella smiled and leaned forward, taking Louisa's sex fully into her mouth and flicking her tongue into the fleshy folds with shallow strokes, whilst she waited to hear and taste Louisa's response. She was not disappointed. Louisa's reaction was clear and she shifted slightly from her position on the bed, her hips bearing down on Gabriella's mouth, clearly desirous of an ever greater degree of penetration from Gabriella's pleasuring tongue. Gabriella eagerly accommodated Louisa's unspoken demands and as her movements became more frenetic Louisa groaned and she stretched her body out, looking for the gradually deepening sensations. When she suddenly came, it was with an unexpectedly loud cry that escaped from her mouth and surprised both of them with its vehemence. Gabriella looked up and smiled as Louisa whispered, 'I'm sorry, I couldn't help it.'

'I wish I could produce the same reaction in everyone I take to bed,' Gabriella said as she stood and moved away from the bed to dispose of her clothing.

Louisa, still clad in her suspenders and bra, looked across

from her position on the bed. Gabriella had a more voluptuous figure than Louisa had previously realised; her hair fell loose as she pulled away its artfully pinned restraints and allowed it to cascade in a chestnut-brown flood down her back and hang loosely around her breasts, which were large and heavy. Her belly was smooth, and slightly rounded, the overall result being to create a lush and erotic femininity that combined a promise of sexual gratification with one of fertility.

Supremely confident, Gabriella strolled back to the near naked figure of Louisa, who rose from the bed to greet her. Deftly she took Louisa's chin in her hand and tilted it up to meet her mouth as she knelt on the bed, first unclipping her bra, then guiding Louisa up to the head of the bed, so that she could rest on the silken pillows. 'I hope you don't mind leaving those on,' she said, indicating Louisa's suspenders and high-heeled shoes. 'But there's something about those sexy shoes that just turns me on beyond belief.'

'I'd noticed,' murmured Louisa, as Gabriella knelt over her once again, covering Louisa's body with her own and working a series of kisses and caresses from one end of her body to the other, her tongue an exquisitely gentle organ of sensuality. Louisa lay back on the bed, lost in a world of delicious feelings as Gabriella continued to rain delicate kisses about her body. She sighed gently as Gabriella moved from spot to spot, and little involuntary gasps and moans crept from her mouth as the sensations of erotic stimulation ebbed and flowed and Gabriella discovered new and more intense erogenous zones around her body. Slowly Gabriella worked her way back up towards Louisa mouth and lay beside her for a moment caressing her gently, running her hands up and down Louisa's arms, gently stroking her naked breasts and letting her manicured fingernails define the rosette of her nipples.

As the caresses continued Louisa's confidence grew and she began to return the kisses more vehemently, letting her hands mingle in Gabriella's hair, and explore the soft flesh that was next to her. Overcoming her nervousness, she began

171

to move her focus downwards, and swivelled herself around to lie alongside Gabriella's body and bury her head in the soft, brown pubic hair. The long, unusually downy strands were chestnut, with soft golden streaks and although she was fascinated by them, stroking the flesh beneath them she was more captivated by the rest of Gabriella's most intimate area. As she continued to go lower she found the folds of the labia and beyond them her search led to Gabriella's sex cleft, familiar yet still so alien.

Tentatively, and still amazed at herself and the instinctive reactions of her body, she licked at Gabriella's hole almost out of curiosity, already knowing the flavour of the musky tang. But she was still surprised and pleased when Gabriella gave a low, sexy moan, an exhalation of breath mixed with a gasp of pleasure. With this measure of approval Louisa found her barriers of reserve dropping, and let her tongue roam inside whilst Gabriella did the same. The two of them used their intimate knowledge of their own bodies to bring pleasure to the other, focusing their efforts on each other's clitoris, working at them viciously in a drive to simultaneously reach a shuddering orgasm, their muffled groans of pleasure filling the room. For a while they lay in each other's arms, a sense of well being suffusing them both. Then Gabriella got up and went over to the cabinet. 'I don't know how you'll feel about this,' she said, returning to Louisa's side, bearing a large black rubber vibrator and a padded black belt. At Louisa's dubious look, she smiled. 'Trust me,' she said. 'I won't do anything you don't enjoy.'

Louisa bit her lip. 'Have you ever had to deal with anyone so nervy before?'

Gabriella laughed. 'I don't do this every day,' she said, 'but yes, I've been to bed with people who've been just as nervous as you and I haven't got them all chained up in the basement; well, no-one who didn't want to be anyway.'

'What are you going to do with that?' asked Louisa, gesturing to the belt.

Gabriella smiled, looking like a tousled-haired goddess of

love. 'I'm going to fuck you senseless,' she said bluntly. Louisa swallowed nervously. 'You're not going to turn chicken on me are you, Louisa?' Gabriella asked with an amused look on her face. Declining to wait for an answer she lay Louisa face down and flat on the bed. Then, kneeling astride her hips, she began to massage Louisa's shoulders, pouring scented oil onto her back as she did so. The fragrance wafted towards Louisa's nostrils and the gentle pull of Gabriella's fingers eased her nerves.

As she continued the massage Gabriella moved further down the bed and as it came within her grasp she eased her fingers through the gap between Louisa's buttocks and reached out to play with Louisa's clitoris, gently massaging the bud of flesh with her oiled fingers, warming it and stimulating it as the slickness of the oil combined with Louisa's sex juices. Once again the sexual tension in the room began to increase, with Gabriella again in control. As she lay there, absorbing the sensations, Louisa realised it was not often she had been so completely submissive to a lover. Normally she would be far more participative, even aggressive in her demands, but right now she bowed to Gabriella's superior experience. Gabriella continued to massage her body, slowly turning Louisa over to face her so that she sat across Louisa's hips, clad only in suspenders and sheer black tights, her chestnut hair tousled and out of place, curling around her face and tumbling down her shoulders. Her deft fingers, soaked in the oil, stroked their way beneath the silk of the suspender belt to Louisa's pubic hair.

'So blonde,' she murmured in wonder, reaching down through Louisa's bush to massage her clit, one thumb rubbing it back into activation, whilst the other hand stroked its way into her cunt. Suddenly Louisa gasped and her head shot up in shock as the heat of her cunt drained away into the oil. Gabriella smiled. 'A little minty surprise,' she said, pushing Louisa back down onto the bed and leaning down to intensify the sensation by blowing gently across the fragile tissues. After the unexpected shock Louisa felt her cunt swell with waves of pleasure, every nerve-ending burning with a cold flame, and she groaned with pleasure.

'Now,' Gabriella said, raising her head from Louisa's sex, 'trust me.' She reached out to pull a pair of stockings from the bedside table and wrapping them around Louisa's eyes she tied them tight enough to block out all but the faintest glimmer of light. Blinded, Louisa heard her move about the bed and then both felt and heard the distinctive buzz of the vibrator that had lain unused at one side of the bed. Slowly Gabriella worked the phallus around Louisa's clit, expertly vibrating the sensitised flesh until she was within an inch of orgasm. Then, although Louisa whimpered in a mute supplication for satisfaction, Gabriella withdrew the cock, and she heard the vibrator turned off and the belt being fastened. She shivered, knowing that Gabriella was fastening the vibrator to herself.

With strong arms Gabriella guided Louisa onto her front and pulled her onto her knees. 'Put your ass in the air, baby,' she murmured. At a heightened pitch of sexual excitement Louisa did as she was told and once again the penis-shaped dildo started to penetrate her, this time easing its way into her cunt from behind, lubricated by her own juices.

Gabriella eased in the penis up to its full length, and then turned on the vibrator. She began to thrust against Louisa, reaching forward to grasp her breasts, hanging pendulously from her body. Louisa gasped and shuddered and thrust her ass further upwards and backwards, spreading herself apart eagerly as Gabriella continued to fuck her. At first the pace was slow, and her inability to see enhanced the stimulation from Gabriella's caressing fingers, running up and down her skin, teasing her nipples, until she finally reached Louisa's clit once again and joined Louisa's begging groans with her own as she thrust harder and faster, the internal vibrations working on her own clit as she worked on Louisa's.

Louisa could take no more. Easing herself away from the cock she pulled off the loosely tied blindfold and rolled Gabriella onto her back. Straddling Gabriella she took the full length of the dildo into her cunt and took over the pace of

174

their lovemaking. She thrust her pelvis against Gabriella's and reached out for her brown nipples with eager fingers, followed by her equally eager lips, biting at the swollen buds with a fascinated delight before moving on to attack and bite at her equally swollen clitoris. They ground their hips together in simultaneous motions and the orgasmic sensations shuddered through their bodies to hit a new level of intensity. Stimulated beyond restraint now, Gabriella screamed out, begging for more in a stream of consciousness and she arched her back in ecstasy, thrusting the dildo upwards into Louisa in a parody of masculine ejaculation.

Their lovemaking at a temporary conclusion, they uncoupled and lay back across the bed, exhausted and gasping for breath. Louisa ran a hand through her hair as she crawled over Gabriella's glorious body and caught sight of the two of them reflected in the mirrors that ran along one side of the room. They were a tangle of pale and dark beige skins, blonde and chestnut hair, apricot and black silk lingerie, and the sight of her lying draped across Gabriella was irresistibly sexy, however exhausted she had thought she felt.

'Wow,' said Gabriella catching sight of the image. 'We're gorgeous.' Louisa laughed and turned her attention back to the woman beneath her. Gabriella smiled. 'And give me a few more minutes and I'll make you even more gorgeous,' she said, reaching up to crush Louisa's lips with a heartfelt kiss. 'How are you feeling?' she asked.

Louisa flopped off her and on to the bed. 'Exhausted.' Gabriella rolled onto her side and looked thoughtfully across at Louisa. 'What is it?'

'Let's rest a while,' Gabriella said. Then getting up from the bed and going to a cabinet at the side of the room she asked, 'Would you like something to look at while we rest?'

'What sort of thing?' asked Louisa, mystified.

Gabriella smiled enigmatically and opened the cabinet for Louisa to see. Inside was a selection of sex aids, ranging from an innocuous-looking small-sized dildo to an aggressive sado-masochist's helmet, complete with zips for the mouth and eyes and a covering of long supple rubber spikes. Louisa stared, caught between surprise and horrified fascination, as Gabriella reached into a drawer at the bottom of the cabinet and pulled out a video, saying, 'I don't think we need to worry about any of that lot today,' and closing the door firmly on the sex aids.

She reached out and pressed a wall switch, and a panel at the foot of the bed slid up and out of a chest, revealing a TV and VCR. Slipping the video inside the machine she returned to the bed and slipped under the alabaster silk sheets, lifting them to allow Louisa to join her as she slipped off her high-heeled shoes.

'Are you sure I'm ready for this?' quizzed Louisa. 'After all, the contents of that cabinet are pretty scary.'

Gabriella smiled back at her. 'I'm sure,' she said. The video flickered into life, showing two women draped around one another, caressing each other and laughing, apparently oblivious to the camera behind them. The voices were clear, but distant, as though they were watching from the far end of a room, and in the background lilting music created an ambience of relaxed sensuality. Both women were clothed in chiffon sarongs, the material hiding the specifics of their bodies but giving a tantalising idea of the contours beneath. One was a redhead, with wild pre-Raphaelite hair falling across her alabaster skin, and with an incongruously youthful sprinkling of pale freckles along the edge of her long slim arms. The other woman was older and more sophisticated; her hair was an expensive golden blonde, cut into a smart business-like bob with a sharp centre parting, so that it framed a heart-shaped face, unusually dark brown eyes and a wide mouth with moist half-open lips.

As she watched the screen Louisa became aware of her freshly growing arousal; a sensation of increasing desire that was slowly enveloping her. She also became aware of Gabriella's hands sliding around her shoulders to draw them closer together. She contentedly slid closer and then further down the bed in order to rest her head on Gabriella's belly, and relaxed as gentle fingers ran through her hair and across her shoulders. The caresses mirrored those on the screen in front of them where the women were slowly undressing one another, kissing, and clearly delighting in the pleasure they were creating for each other.

The blonde watched as the redhead sank onto a chaise longue, lying on her back with her limbs draped delicately across her, then slowly and tantalisingly she let her sarong drift open and fall to the floor. In the background a log fire blazed, casting a flickering light across her skin as she displayed herself for her lover, confident of her nakedness and of the other woman's appreciation. The blonde now knelt at the side of the chaise and leant forward to focus her attentions on the redhead's breasts, her tongue darting out to stimulate the mushroom coloured nipples into erotically shaped rosettes. The redhead closed her eyes and Louisa could hear a low murmur of pleasure as the blonde began to suck at one nipple whilst her fingers continued to stimulate the other. Moments passed, then she deserted the succulent breasts to direct herself towards the mound beneath the copper coloured pubic hair. As her lips descended onto the tiny pink bud of the redhead's clitoris the woman gave a very audible cry of surprise and pleasure, and at that moment Louisa became very aware that Gabriella's hands were playing with her breasts, stroking and gyrating her palm across the surface of the nipples so that they were hard and standing proud of the firm bosomy flesh. Apparently pleased with this result, Gabriella slipped out from beneath her and slid down the bed towards Louisa's groin. In moments Louisa realised that she could now not only watch the couple in front of her but she could feel and participate in their cunnilingus, as Gabriella matched the actions of the blonde, licking, probing and nuzzling at Louisa's sex lips in a practised copy of the movements on the screen. Like the redhead Louisa moaned involuntarily, thrusting her hips towards Gabriella's mouth for more. But on the screen, the redhead grasped the side of the chaise, and arched her back as her lover focused all her attention on bringing her to orgasm.

In contrast Louisa felt Gabriella ease back a little, and she returned to the surface of the bed as the redhead called out in a rising crescendo of gasping cries. Louisa could hardly take her eyes away from the screen as the woman came and then her cries began to slowly fall away into a series of satisfied groans.

She looked up at Gabriella who had been watching her reaction. 'I couldn't let you come yet,' Gabriella explained. 'I wanted to watch you as you watched them, and see what you thought.' She leant further down towards Louisa. 'But I know you enjoyed it,' she breathed with a confidential tone in her voice. 'Your clit is so hard, and your cunt is so wet.' Her voice tailed away as her hands slid back down Louisa's body, and in reply Louisa reached out to pull Gabriella's head closer towards her.

'You're right,' she said. 'I thought it was really sexy. Sexy and erotic and exciting . . . and I am so turned on . . .'

Gabriella smiled. 'Well, that was the desired effect. So what would you like to do now?'

'First of all,' said Louisa, 'I'm going down on you to give you some of your own medicine, and then I'm going to take all night to fuck you senseless.'

'Well,' said Gabriella, with a laugh, 'if you thought that was good you should see the rest of my video collection.'

They finally parted the next morning, and Louisa left via the private elevator, emerging into the crisp morning light to find a car waiting for her as arranged in advance by Gabriella. She returned to her apartment, having promised to meet up with Gabriella for supper in the following week.

The apartment seemed quiet but lacking in atmosphere when compared to Gabriella's extravagantly decorated home, and she wandered about realising that she had spent so much time at the business or at Andrew's flat that she had allowed herself to leave this place bland and uninspiring. There was no real stamp of her personality on it at all. When Scott had admired the decor she had been pleased, but now, she thought regretfully, perhaps that just reflected his own bland personality.

She made coffee and sat down to have a serious think. Over breakfast Gabriella had raised the topic of Paolo once again. The two of them were clearly 'close', although what that meant in practice was not something Louisa had chosen to discuss. The subject of Mafia involvements had also been ignored by the two women, although that subject had also hung in the air.

Gabriella seemed very keen for Paolo and Louisa to talk about their differences, and tried to convince her that Paolo did not dislike or despise her, despite all the evidence to the contrary. Although she thought Gabriella was wrong, now that she had time to think, and now too that Gabriella had slightly quelled her fear of the Tessario family, Louisa also had to consider the fact that she hadn't felt completely turned off by the idea of being more friendly with Tessario. Anyway, she thought, getting closer to Paolo Tessario was what the FBI wanted her to do, and given that Scott was still sitting on his hands waiting for Tessario to make his move then maybe she should take matters into her own hands. Such action could open up new avenues of possibilities for obtaining information and bringing this limbo of uncertainty to a conclusion.

'Be honest,' she told herself. 'If Gabriella is right and Tessario isn't as hostile as you thought, then how would you use that knowledge to your own advantage?' She took a deep breath and looked at herself in the mirror. 'The question is, how far would you be prepared to go to get what you want?' she asked herself. 'Are you prepared to sleep with him if that's what it takes? Will that get you what you need?' Her reflection gazed back at her. 'Right now I would do anything to get this business over with,' she thought. But the other question, of whether she could deliberately provide information for the FBI and then still hold her head up in front of Gabriella was something she didn't want to ask herself right now. She sighed, her good mood dissipating. 'No-one else is going to help you,' she told herself. 'Andrew is completely out of the picture and Scott is following his superiors' instructions to the letter and biding his time, which means doing nothing. Meanwhile you're getting physically and emotionally involved with Gabriella Tessario and you certainly can't discuss any of this with her.'

She turned away from the mirror in disgust. 'And you don't know what Gabriella would do if you told her the FBI were lurking about in the business. She might even turn you in to her family – the less pleasant relatives.' She walked through the apartment and stared out at the city. 'Bugger this,' she thought, coming to a sudden decision. 'It's time for some action. I'll do whatever it takes to get myself out of this mess, so if that means sex . . . Then sex it is.'

Chapter 9

The following Monday morning Louisa dressed with more care and deliberation than normal. Her underwear was pristine white silk, deeply lined with lace; her make-up was delicately applied in soft blush colours, and to top off her appearance she wore a push-up bra beneath a blouse with a deep plunging neckline. From what she knew of Tessario to date, the most likely way for her to get access to any information would be to seduce him and the only question was how she could manoeuvre her way into his office to start her seduction technique without being too obvious about it.

She didn't have to wait too long for her chance. By ten-thirty Scott had called her to say that Tessario was wanting to review the week's work with her. As usual she made him wait a little, and then suggested that as an alternative she meet him in his office after she had finished her phone calls. The last thing Louisa wanted was Scott listening in on her conversation with Tessario and therefore her own office was clearly out of bounds for the time being. Clearly surprised, Scott delivered the message and came back with a positive response.

Taking one last look at herself in the mirror Louisa smiled with satisfaction at her reflection. Her blouse was a heavy creamy satin with wide, almost forty's-style lapels that crossed low down on her chest, giving a big hint of a cleavage that was enhanced by her push-up bra. Her skirt was almost knee length and made from a soft, draped jade coloured silk, in a wrap-over style which gave her a split up the full length of one thigh, something that she planned to take full advantage of. As always she had on high-heeled court shoes and gleaming sheer stockings, so in total the outfit was not so very far removed from her normal working uniform, she told herself, just with a little more cleavage and legs on view than usual. Surely, she thought, this was enough to get any red-blooded American male going, and hopefully a hot-blooded Italian-American male like Tessario wouldn't be able to resist her at all.

She knocked at Tessario's door. God knows what he found to do all day, she thought. He had completed the review of the business files very quickly, but since then she had sent him as little work as possible, so presumably most of the work was for his Mafia friends. She swallowed and tried to banish the thought from her mind. What she was doing suddenly seemed incredibly foolish, if not downright dangerous, and exactly what she was going to do and where she was going to look for this elusive 'information' still wasn't clear.

Finally hearing a call to enter she strolled into the office where Tessario was on the phone. He looked up to wave her in, talking all the time. 'Fine, no, tell them no, yeah that's right . . .' She sat down and crossed her legs and his voice tailed off slightly as he gave her a second surreptitious look, clearly noting both the split in her skirt that revealed her thighs and the enhanced curves in her figure. 'Look,' he finished. 'Got to go. We'll talk. Yeah. Later.' He put the phone down and swivelled in his chair to get a clear look at her. 'Good morning, partner. How are you today?'

'Fine,' she replied.

'I hear you and Gabriella met for lunch,' he continued, shooting her a sideways glance.

'That's right,' Louisa continued brightly. 'We got on very well.'

'She's very, ah, nice, my cousin,' he went on. 'Very popular.'

'Mmm.'

There was a pause, then Tessario carried on. 'She thought we might have dinner together. The three of us, one night.'

Louisa's eyes flicked up at him, wondering if he knew what sort of day she had spent with Gabriella, and what Gabriella would have meant by suggesting they had dinner together.

Her thoughts and her imagination were working overtime at this unexpected development. She instinctively knew that any plans of Gabriella's would inevitably include sex, but why, thought Louisa, would she be thinking of including Tessario in the après-dinner party?

'That might be nice,' she said out loud. 'But I was wondering, as you're obviously here to stay, whether you and I shouldn't spend a little more time together. Alone. To try to work out a workable system for the time being I mean.' Tessario looked stunned at the idea. 'What would you think about that?'

'Well, ah, that would be fine,' he said. Then a suspicious look crossed his face. 'So what's brought on this change of heart?'

Louisa sighed, uncrossed and re-crossed her legs, and casually leaned forward to give him a good look down her cleavage. 'Well, I had a long chat with Gabriella as well,' she said huskily. 'She convinced me that it would be much more sensible to make the best of the situation as it stands. And after all, the party did go well. Thanks to you.'

Tessario stared at her for a long minute, and she was uncomfortably aware of how like Gabriella he was. Then he visibly relaxed, and walked over to lean against the desk so that he was facing her. With his suit jacket off she could see his muscular frame and was very aware of an air, not of menace, but of danger and sexual tension between them. She was suddenly, shockingly, reminded of his near-naked body standing over hers on the sand dunes in Spain, and of her subsequent erotic fantasies that included him as a principal player. In many ways, she thought, the sexuality had always been there, but it was overlaid by her anger at the position in which she had unwillingly found herself and her business, and by his boorish behaviour at every turn. Now that she was consciously suppressing those feelings she was seeing him in the same light as many other women did, as a highly sexual and sexy male.

Almost simultaneously they realised that each was appraising the other, and both dropped their gaze. Louisa stood and stepped forward, the movement putting her provocatively close to Tessario. 'So that's agreed then,' she said. 'We'll meet, and try to work something out.' She was so close she could almost feel his breath on her cheek, but unlike every other occasion when they had been this close he made no move to grab her, touch her or taunt her. He simply nodded, once.

'When do you suggest?' Paolo asked.

Louisa considered. 'How about tomorrow night?'

'Fine,' he replied. 'Where?'

'Somewhere neutral perhaps?' suggested Louisa.

Tessario shrugged. 'How about a restaurant. Sandrine's?'

'No,' she replied too quickly, causing him to raise his eyebrows slightly. 'I don't think we should involve anybody else at this stage.' He nodded acquiescence.

'But dinner somewhere would be fine.'

'I know a quiet place near my home,' he volunteered after a moment. 'Very exclusive, but nice.'

This was it, Louisa thought, the last moment when you can back out. She appeared to give the thought some consideration, then nodded. 'Fine. Not completely neutral, but fine.'

'We could meet somewhere else if you prefer,' Tessario said with a sardonically raised eyebrow.

'No,' Louisa replied, deliberately raising her hand as if to ward off the idea, and placing it briefly on his chest. 'That's fine.' For a moment she was surprisingly tempted to follow her actions with a smouldering kiss, but forced the sensation down. Before she could move Tessario had placed his much larger hand over hers. He dropped his eyes to her level and held her hand in his for a moment, whilst she battled against sexual desire and sense. Then he peeled her hand away from his chest and held it out to her. She turned to leave and threw him a mildly flirtatious glance. 'I can handle it if you can,' she said, leaving him to figure out what she meant, and as she closed the door she was delighted to see a confused expression cross Tessario's features.

Feeling very pleased with herself she turned the corner and ran straight into Scott. He had a grim expression on his face, and didn't speak, but taking her by the elbow he virtually marched her back to her office and threw her through the door.

'What do you think you're doing?' he asked.

Louisa rubbed her elbow ruefully. 'How about you? That hurt.'

'I'll ask you again. What was that little "chat" about?'

'Work.'

Scott folded his arms across his chest and leant back against the door. 'I don't think I believe you,' he said after a minute's thought.

'Why not?' Louisa asked in a tone of hurt indignation. Scott shook his head.

'I'm not sure, but you're suddenly being very nice to your partner. It's all a bit quick.'

'You're in good company,' Louisa said. 'Tessario's just said almost exactly the same thing. But at least in his case,' she continued crossly, 'he doesn't know that someone's been standing behind me telling me, no begging me, to make up to him.' She paused. 'I'm just playing the game. It's what you wanted, isn't it?' Scott watched her in silence, his jaw moving as he silently absorbed the facts. 'What do you want of me, Scott?' she exploded. 'Do you want me to get him to trust me or not?' There was another silence and then he slowly unfolded his arms and walked over to her chair.

'I don't know, Louisa. I'm worried about you. I just don't want you to take things too far, too quick.'

'You mean you don't want me to sleep with him.'

'Exactly.'

'Well mind your own business,' she snapped. 'I'll sleep with whoever I want. After all,' she finished, 'even if you don't have the guts or the libido to take any chances, maybe some of the rest of us do.'

Scott flushed and walked stiffly to the door. 'Fine,' he said, 'just take some advice and don't take too many chances. It could be very bad for your health.'

'Worm,' she hissed and slammed the door in his wake.

185

Louisa sat in her apartment waiting for Tessario's car to collect her and examining herself in the mirror for one last time. It was important, she thought, to try and get the right combination of restraint and attractive availability and hopefully she had hit the right note.

She was wearing a classic evening gown: a high necked, full length and sleeveless black satin dress cut on the bias, deceptively demure and plain from the front but with a plunging backline that stretched down to the base of her spine. She had let her hair dry into soft waves that fell to her shoulders and she hoped she looked classy but attainable. Beneath her dress she wore a very plain, smooth, black satin G-string and matching satin suspenders with sheer black stockings. Finally, in an attempt to meet Tessario's height and also to take away from the severity of her outfit, she wore overtly sexy high-heeled stiletto shoes with ankle straps that were studded with tiny rhinestones that caught the light when she turned and her dress flared out around her ankles.

The car took her to a building in Greenwich Village, making its way through streets that were crowded with people enjoying the pleasant evening; milling about the sidewalks, wandering along with friends and sitting drinking at streetside cafés. The car turned off the main street and took her into a quieter walkway and then up to the entrance to a converted warehouse building. Once inside an elevator took her upstairs to the a loft apartment on the top floor. There was no need to knock, since Tessario was standing at the door waiting to greet her, and looking extremely well turned out in a dinner jacket and bowtie.

'Good evening, Louisa,' he greeted her formally. 'I'm glad you dressed for dinner, you look incredible. Please, come in.'

The loft was huge, with a central fireplace around which the different areas of the room were laid out: a lounge area with huge squashy sofas, a kitchen, and on the other side of the fireplace, a dining area comprising a white marble table top, set with candles and a full set of silverware for two.

'This is a surprise,' she said somewhat archly as she looked around. 'I thought we were going out to eat. Somewhere neutral?'

Tessario shrugged and spread his hands apart in explanation. 'I did say we would eat somewhere exclusive. And in the end this seemed a better option. After all, your outfit isn't really appropriate for dinner in the Village, is it? Anyway, as you can see I've arranged for all our needs to be catered for.' He waved a hand and a waiter appeared at her elbow with a large glass on a silver tray. 'How about joining me for a cocktail?' asked Tessario. 'A martini perhaps.'

Louisa nodded, and took the glass, sipping at the delicious, but very strong mixture of gin and vermouth. She looked over to the kitchen area where several other waiters were hovering and where two chefs were hard at work beneath large extractor fans that prevented any aroma from escaping. 'You seem to have everything very much in control and I would say it smelt delicious if I could smell anything at all.'

Tessario smiled. 'I thought that being here would give us a chance to talk without being overheard and our movements watched. After all, you never know who's marking your actions.'

Louisa looked anxiously at him, but he seemed to be just making a casual observation. He reached out to take her hand. 'Perhaps you would like to take a walk in the conservatory while they're preparing dinner?'

'A conservatory?'

He nodded and a waiter reached out to open up drapes along the outer wall of the building where a long tiled promenade had been created, covered in with glass and filled with greenery. They strolled along sipping their drinks. 'The view isn't that good,' he explained, 'and the plants are much nicer to look at.'

'I would never have thought of you as a gardener,' Louisa noted.

'I have to confess I'm not. I like the effect but I only have to look at plants for them to start wilting.' They reached the end of the deck and turned around. 'Shall we have dinner?' he asked, and she nodded.

The waiters lifted the lid on a silver salver revealing a bowl of oysters on ice. Louisa raised her eyebrows once again. 'I love oysters,' she said.

'I know,' Tessario said enigmatically, then by way of an explanation at her confused expression, 'Gabriella told me.' Louisa nodded slowly in understanding. 'I hope that the dinner will be acceptable,' he went on, 'and if it isn't you can blame my cousin. These are her staff.'

Louisa smiled. 'You've obviously gone to a lot of trouble. Thank you.'

Tessario smiled briefly in return and raised his glass. 'No, thank you.'

The oysters were quickly followed by a dish of steamed turbot in a creamy and lightly flavoured tarragon sauce, served with baby boiled potatoes and a salad of oakleaf lettuce, raddiccio and endive, the crispiness of the leaves contrasting against the warmed sauce, and the soft melting flesh of the potatoes. The entrée was then replaced with a plate of summer berries, surmounted by a crisp lattice of spun sugar that provided a contrast to the sharpness of the fruit. Throughout dinner they chatted nonchalantly about unthreatening aspects of the business, such as the party and recent magazine covers, then about her family and friends. However, Louisa was very wary of bringing up any aspect of Tessario's family, with the exception of Gabriella, and she wasn't sure that she wanted to bring Gabriella into this conversation at this stage.

When dinner was finally concluded they moved to the huge pale cream sofa and sat down together with coffee and brandies. She looked at her watch and realised with a start that it was already almost midnight and that they were alone in the loft, the waiters having slipped away unnoticed after serving their coffee. Until then Louisa hadn't appreciated how relaxed she was or how much she had been enjoying the evening, but that thought promptly re-ignited the gnawing kernel of tension within her. Suddenly she was worrying at what she would need to do to put Tessario sufficiently at his ease for her to gain access to whatever secrets he might have. She hadn't realised that she had stopped participating in the conversation until Tessario placed a hand on hers and she rocketed back to reality.

Just as she had been aware of the sexual tension between them in his office, she was suddenly very aware of a new erotic charge that set her nerves alive. 'You were miles away,' Tessario said with a smile. 'Was I boring you?'

'No,' she replied. 'I was just lost in thought for a moment.' She realised as she spoke that his hand was still on hers and taking a deep breath she continued. 'I was thinking that we should get closer. But as business partners, I'm not sure how close that should be.'

Tessario sighed with exasperation. 'Let's forget about the business, for God's sake, Louisa. Let's just be here alone, that's why I brought you here tonight. I wanted you to see that there is much more to me that you initially assumed.'

She bit her lip. 'Truthfully, all I have seen is that you like plants and have good taste in interior design, or else you just have a good interior decorator.'

Tessario sighed again, this time more edgily. 'I don't think you mean that,' he said. 'This is me. Surely you can see that.' He was clearly exasperated and for a moment she thought he was going to blow up in a rage as he had so many times before. Instead, in that moment he leaned forward and kissed her on the lips, tenderly and softly. It was a romantic kiss that had none of the aggression that she had associated with their prior contact, and it took her completely by surprise. Slowly his hands crept around her waist to the expanse of skin exposed at the back of her dress, maintaining his hold on her lips until finally drifting his touch to encompass her throat and shoulders. Louisa's skin tingled; she was shocked at the way her body was betraying her desire and subconsciously amazed at the sensitivity with which Tessario was caressing her, touching her and seducing her. Slowly she allowed herself to be eased back into the mass of oversized cushions, with Tessario at her side, finding her supposed sacrifice rapidly turning into a willing partnership with a man that up until tonight she had feared would not be capable of more than brutish abandon.

Louisa closed her eyes and felt the well of desire grow even more strongly as Tessario's teasing hands ran down the front of her dress, stopping to gently outline the shape of her breasts beneath the tightly stretched fabric. Against the background of gentle music she distinctly heard him groan with poorly suppressed desire, a faint noise that heightened her own excitement even more, as he found and focused on her nipples, standing erect against the cold satin of her dress. All of his actions so far seemed to suggest a level of interest that was far greater than the uncaring conquest and sexual domination she had anticipated and she instinctively found herself responding to his caresses with ever increasing enthusiasm.

Eventually Tessario's rain of kisses eased slightly and Louisa took the opportunity to stand, pushing him slightly so that they could exchange places, he now on the sofa, she standing in front of him. 'Louisa . . .' he began, but she laid a finger on his lips to silence him and with trembling fingers she found the button at the high collar of her dress and released it, letting the expensive and erotic fabric fall from her breasts then slither unchecked from her hips to the floor. Tessario reached out and drew her towards him, placing more kisses precisely and delicately around her bellybutton, whilst his hands moved up her torso towards her breasts, which he tentatively covered with his palms. His restraint was as intoxicating as it was surprising, and for the first time Louisa allowed herself to display the signs of her stimulated senses. Her head rolled back on her shoulders and she let out a long and unrehearsed 'Ahhh,' of pleasure and release.

Tessario's hands deserted Louisa's breasts and moved

downwards, exploring for the first time her thighs and buttocks, deliberately and wilfully avoiding her genitalia whilst he completed his examination of the remainder of her body, identifying every erogenous zone across the surface of her skin. His hands slid down her legs to her ankles, closely followed by his lips, caressing and kissing every inch of covered and uncovered flesh, whilst Louisa stood in front of him, her head hanging back and eyes closed, shuddering with an overwhelming desire for him to find and explore her private parts. Perversely, the shoes she had chosen with such care delayed him longer than she could have imagined, as he ran his hands around the ankle straps, and stroked their curves as though they were a part of her.

The room was very quiet now, and Louisa's breath was coming in short low pants as her sense of expectation continued to rise unabated. Abruptly Tessario stood and putting his hands about her hips he looked Louisa straight in the eyes.

'Do you want this?' he asked.

'Yes,' she whispered, surprising herself with the truth. Draping her arms around his shoulders she repeated herself. 'Yes, I do.'

To her momentary surprise Tessario walked away from her and towards a door at the far end of the room. He pushed it open to reveal a darkened room with a single candle burning in the depths of the shadows and the edge of a bed just visible where she stood. At the entrance he held out his hand. 'Come,' he said. Obediently Louisa stepped out of her dress and walked towards him. Then, just as she reached the bedroom door he swept her into his arms and pressed her up against the wall. It was the first sign of aggression she had seen and it came as a sudden, devastating shock.

'Don't try to mess with my head, Louisa,' he whispered in her ear. 'Don't try anything like that, because I'll know if you do.' Then he swept her up in his arms and half carried her into the bedroom, depositing her gently on the end of the bed. Moments later Tessario was standing at her side; tall and brooding and sexy, tearing his bowtie from around his neck and pulling off his jacket, shirt and trousers as quickly as possible.

He rested his hands on either side of her head as he reached down to kiss her lips once more, and then at last his attention was diverted towards her private parts. He knelt at the end of the bed, and ran his fingers down her flanks and towards her sex, caressing the taut length of suspenders. Tessario ran a finger down the central strip of her satin G-string, and lifted it to expose the blonde hair surrounding and hiding Louisa's sex. She sighed with pleasure and let her arms stretch out across the width of the bed, whilst Tessario gave himself fully to the task he had chosen.

Slowly his hands eased the delicate sliver of satin out of the way and he cautiously ran a single finger along her sex flesh for the first time, until it eventually disappeared inside her, engulfed by her flowing juices. Louisa groaned. Her senses were alive with need and she felt that she could wait no longer. 'Please,' she begged, 'please, do it now.'

'Shhh,' whispered Tessario, 'I want to see all of you first,' and he slipped the G-string from her hips, drawing it away and over the sexy rhinestone shoes. Towering over Louisa's prone and vulnerable form he took another moment to run his fingers through her exposed bush of golden hair, contrasting vividly with the black satin suspenders and stockings that framed her sex. Once again Louisa was overwhelmed and surprised by the care and attention of his movements and then, finally, he knelt fully above her and without further ado eased his cock inside her as she shuddered and gripped at his shoulders.

Louisa suddenly came awake with a start, sitting upright in the bed and looking around for a clock. It was four o'clock in the morning and she was still wearing her stockings and suspenders, the candle was still burning in the corner of the room and Tessario was asleep on the other half of the bed, lying face down with his hands stretched out across the pillow.

She lay back down, her mind full of a million thoughts. The dinner in the loft, Tessario's sensitivity and his eagerness to pleasure her; all this had been a complete and very enjoyable surprise. Louisa stopped herself abruptly, recalling the one moment of his aggression, which reminded her exactly why she was here and what she had planned to do. She needed to focus on the job at hand, get up and look for information.

She slid her legs over the side of the bed and stood up, searching on the floor around the bed for something to put on and finding that Tessario's discarded shirt was nearest to hand.

'What is it?' came a sleepy voice from the other side of the bed.

She froze midway between pulling the shirt across her shoulders. 'I need a glass of water.'

'Hmph . . .' was the reply and she stood, waiting. There was no other sound for a moment, and then she heard a light gentle snore and realised that he had fallen asleep once again. Suddenly she was horribly aware of her heart beating loudly, as though it was trying to fight its way out of her chest, and she swallowed as a wave of nausea flooded over her. Then she forced herself to move again, and slowly made her way towards the door.

Once inside the main loft area she walked straight to the kitchen and poured herself the glass of water in question. Then, alibi in hand, she began to look around the lounge, searching for a computer, a desk or anything that looked as though it might hold files, documents or important papers. In the far corner of the room she spied a small filing cabinet and crept across the hardwood floor towards it, hearing the noise of every creak in the floorboards as though they were alarm bells. Carefully, she eased her way around the cabinet and drew it open. As the early dawn light filtered in through the shuttered windows behind her she tried to work out what the files inside were about. Disappointingly, a cursory glance suggested that they were personal letters, official documents, and scrap pieces of paper; notes and comments on brochures, menus and guide books. She shuffled through one set of files and then the next, hampered by the fact that she wasn't sure what she was looking for, and all the time she was on edge, trying to keep alert for any noise from the bedroom, and expecting to be discovered at any moment.

There was nothing that she could see that could be of any possible use in the filing cabinet and she regretfully slid it shut and turned to look for a computer. At that moment Tessario appeared at the door to the bedroom.

'The kitchen's over there,' he said, rubbing the sleep from his eyes and pointing to the other side of the room.

'I know,' Louisa answered, her voice somewhere between a squeak and a gasp. 'I've got some here. I was just going to check out the weather.' Tessario strolled over to the window, and opened the shutters to their full extent.

'There,' he said, 'now you can see clearly.'

'I didn't want to open them up and disturb you,' she blustered in explanation. 'I thought I'd left the door to the bedroom open.'

'Well you didn't,' said Tessario. Dismissing the subject he reached out a hand and took hold of hers. 'Let's not waste time here. Come back to bed.'

'I should probably be thinking of going home,' she murmured. 'I've got to change and do some work.'

'Don't be ridiculous, it's four o'clock. Come back to bed,' he repeated, more awake now. 'Do I have to work out how to persuade you? I understood that you didn't tire so easily.'

Louisa flushed. 'I don't know what you're talking about.'

'Oh yes you do,' Tessario said, yawning.

'Look, now I'm up I probably should go home and get some rest,' she went on. 'Perhaps we could meet up later today.'

'What? At the office, for a bit of evening work?'

She shrugged. 'Maybe.'

'What a good idea,' he said sarcastically. 'But I've got a better one.' He grabbed Louisa's wrist and, pulling her across the floor, he pushed her face forwards over the back of the sofa. 'I've clearly been far too gentle with you,' he murmured in her ear. 'Far too nice for you to want to stay,' and he slid his hands underneath his shirt and inside the stocking tops, before returning to reach into her sex. 'Still nice and wet I see,' he murmured. 'That's useful.' Without warning he pushed his cock into Louisa's vagina, simultaneously forcing her further over the sofa and clamping his hands around her hips to keep her in place. Louisa gasped in indignation and surprise, and made to wriggle free, beating the air with her hands, but Tessario simply laughed. Pausing for a moment, he grabbed hold of her hands and pulled them forward, restraining them easily with one of his own. Wrapping his free hand around her waist to hoist her forward once again, he forced his cock further into her and then reached for her clit.

Realising that she had no chance against his superior strength, Louisa finally gave up any attempt to break free. 'That's better,' Tessario grunted as her struggles subsided and he thrust himself inside her. 'This is what you want, isn't it? You expected me to fuck you and finally you're getting what you wanted.'

'Yes,' she snarled back. 'Yes I did, so fuck me, you bastard.'

Tessario leant over her back. 'No problem,' he hissed in her ear, and standing upright once again he reached down to grab her hair and drag her head backwards.

Louisa groaned. 'That's it,' she gasped. 'Fuck me. It's what you know, isn't it? Doing it hard and fast.' She hurled out insults, no longer caring what they were, every word driving her own senses half crazy with desire and knowing that Tessario was experiencing equal degrees of stimulation. Suddenly he withdrew and rolled her over against the back of the sofa. Refusing to relinquish his hold on her hair he dragged her backwards, forcing her hips upwards onto the back of the sofa. 'I want to hear you say that again,' he hissed. 'To my face if you dare.' Then his cock was inside her cunt once again, forcing its way upwards inside her in a series of harsh aggressive thrusts, his face above hers in a position of absolute power.

'You've wanted to fuck me all along,' she snarled. 'You couldn't wait to get your paws all over me. Well now you have, so fuck me as hard as you can. It won't be enough.'

'It'll be better than that preppy boyfriend of yours,' he hissed back. 'I'll bet he hasn't even got a dick.'

'At least he knows what to do to satisfy a woman.'

'And you've been whimpering for me all night,' he finished, cutting her off. 'You wanted my cock inside you so bad you were begging for it.' He paused. 'And you're still begging. Maybe I should let you beg a bit longer.'

For a moment she had the bizarre thought that he would exercise total control and withdraw from her, leaving her unsatisfied and hovering at the point of orgasm. 'You're right, you bastard,' she screamed, losing any remaining vestige of restraint or self-control. 'You're right. I'm begging. Don't stop. Fuck me and don't stop until I'm done. Make me come.' For a moment she was mortified to see a slow smile spread across Tessario's face and then it was replaced with an expression of concentration. He resumed his thrusting and, completely in his power, Louisa groaned and whimpered, all thoughts of insults gone as she wrapped her legs around his hips and urged him on until they both came in a simultaneous burst of orgasmic climax.

Louisa finally left Tessario's apartment at six-thirty in the morning. Despite her initial protestations that she could get a cab, she eventually let him drive her home, rather aware that her appearance and clothes signified a night spent away from home to any casual passer-by. At her apartment he drew the car into the underground garage and paused for her to get out, letting the engine idle. For a moment neither spoke, then Louisa said awkwardly, 'Thank you for dinner.'

Tessario snorted with laughter and after a moment she joined in.

'You have a great way with words,' he said. 'But I think we've gone a bit beyond that.' There was another pause. 'So when shall we do this again?' he asked bluntly.

'I'm not sure,' she said. 'I have appointments all afternoon and I think I would like to stay home tonight.'

He laughed again, derisively this time. 'Sure you would. No problem. I'll see you in the office later.'

'Oh, right,' Louisa replied, slightly taken aback at his laissez-faire attitude. She opened the door. 'I'll see you at the office then.'

'Fine,' he called after her as she emerged from the car. 'Ciao,' and then he was revving up the car and was gone.

She stared after him for a moment, and then hurriedly went into the elevator before any prudish eyes could see her and pass judgement. She emerged on her landing and let herself into the apartment. Catching sight of her reflection she was a little horrified. 'No doubt about what you've been doing,' she thought, looking at the evening dress and sexy shoes, her bare legs, from which she had removed the shredded stockings, and the slightly tousled hair, which despite her best attempts had refused to settle back into place. She stripped away her clothes and stepped into the shower, uncomfortably aware that she had failed in her intentions, succeeding only in enjoying sex with Tessario, where she had simply planned to endure it, and failing to find information of any sort. She scowled at her reflection, shivering with embarrassment as she recalled how she had begged him for more sex, lost in the throes of passionate abandon.

'Great,' she said to herself. 'He'll certainly trust you to wander about his office from now on. But I should think he'll tell the whole of the Village what a dirty slut you are.'

When Louisa got into the office things were just the same as always. She ran the gamut of Scott's suspicious gaze, settled at her desk and began to work her way through the messages and queries in her in-tray. However, there was no sign of Tessario until around midday, when Scott passed on a message.

'Your business partner would like you to join him for a late working lunch. In his office.' Louisa opened her mouth to decline, but Scott continued. 'He says he knows you don't have a lunch appointment and he has provided an agenda for your meeting.' He flourished a sheet of paper in front of

Louisa's face before letting it settle on the desk. She stuck her chin in the air in defiance. 'Fine. Tell him I'll be there at two.'

At two o'clock she dutifully went to Tessario's office and knocked on the door.

'Come in,' he called. As she entered he was straightening up from behind his desk, 'Hey, Louisa,' he said. 'I thought it'd be you. How's it going?'

'Fine,' she replied, guardedly. 'I gather you wanted to have a working lunch, and it's pretty late so let's get to it.'

'OK by me,' he said. 'But let's have a break first. Take a seat.'

Louisa sighed. 'OK,' she said.

'Here you go,' continued Tessario. 'Have a glass of wine. You like Chardonnay, don't you?'

'I shouldn't,' she said. 'I've got a lot to do this afternoon.'

Ignoring her reply Tessario filled a glass and passed it to her. 'Believe me. You should take this and relax.' She reached out and took the proffered glass and Tessario turned away. 'I've got a surprise for you.'

'What sort of surprise?'

Tessario moved behind the chair. 'You seem very tense today, Louisa,' he said, reaching down to massage her shoulders. She shifted in her seat, enjoying the sensations, but feeling surprisingly awkward in the office environment.

'What sort of surprise?' she repeated.

'Well, now, we had such a nice time last night,' he began. 'Didn't we?'

'Well yes,' she admitted. 'But that was outside office hours, and I think it should stay that way.'

He laughed. 'Well I have a fifty per cent vote here, and I think it shouldn't.'

Louisa stood up. 'Sorry, Paolo,' she said. 'I can see where this is going and I can't get involved in this right now. I have too much to do and so do you.'

He laid a hand on her arm. 'Relax,' he said softly, 'I'm

winding you up. This is for later.' She sighed heavily and sat down again. 'That's better. No I just wanted to suggest that we set a post-work agenda for this evening.' Standing behind her he ran his hand down her arm, and she shivered. 'I just thought perhaps we could meet at your place.' She opened her mouth to object, but he continued. 'I know you said you wanted to spend tonight on your own but we both know that's not true. Anyway,' he went on, ignoring her expression, 'obviously I want you to enjoy yourself this evening, but I was thinking you'd do something for me this time.'

'You're not trying to tell me you didn't enjoy yourself,' she demanded with a note of scorn.

He laughed. 'No, Louisa. But you know, you could do more.'

She flushed and stood. 'I am not used to having my, my—'

'Technique?' he interjected helpfully.

Louisa glared at him, '. . . my behaviour in bed criticised by anyone.'

'I'm sure you're not,' he scoffed gently. 'But I just thought, as you're so eager to keep me happy, you might follow a guideline or two. Just to be sure.'

Louisa bit her lip. 'I am not doing anything to keep you happy,' she objected.

'Of course you are,' he said equally smoothly. 'Hey, I don't care. If it keeps us ticking along that's fine. But like I said, here's a tip.' He dropped his voice a tone. 'Don't you remember? I like leather. There's something about it that just turns me on.'

Louisa looked away. 'Really?' she said in a deliberately bored fashion.

'Oh yeah,' he said. 'So I got you some.' He reached behind the chair and brandished a package. 'Don't open it now though,' he said. 'You'll get me all excited and who knows what could happen?' He turned away and went back to his desk. 'I'll see you tonight. About eight? Your place?'

'How dare you?' she demanded. 'You are so totally insensitive. You can keep this and don't even think about coming round to my apartment.'

'Your choice,' he said blandly, from behind his desk. 'It's just a suggestion. But it's still a gift I thought you might like, and if you insist on leaving it here I'll just have to call for Scott to come and collect it. It's up to you.' She glared at him, then snatched up the box. 'Great,' he finished. 'Now shall we get back to my agenda?'

'Get stuffed,' she snapped and stormed out of the room and back to her own office.

Louisa finished work at a reasonable hour that day, and made her way home, carrying the unopened, but surprisingly heavy package with her. She had no idea whether Tessario would turn up or not, but she was confused that the caring sensitivity had disappeared and the base animal behaviour had emerged once again. She was also beginning to wonder at the quicksilver way these personalities varied. 'He's either got multiple personalities,' she thought as she poured herself a gin and tonic and sat down with a thump, 'or I'm missing a trick somewhere.' The package sat on the sofa next to her. She stared at it and finally gave in and pulled open the wrapping. She hadn't been sure exactly what to expect, but inside, perhaps unsurprisingly, was an overtly sexy piece of leather attire.

'Bastard,' she thought instinctively. 'He was right, it is sexy.' She got up and went to her bedroom to try it on. It was a dark cherry red, two-piece outfit; the top half a scoop-necked croptop that finished above her midriff, sealing up the front with a long silver zipper. The bottom half was a pair of tight-fitting red leather hipster shorts complete with a zip-up split in the crotch. Finally, the box also contained a pair of cherry red lace-up, knee-length boots with four-inch spiked silver heels. When she had finished changing Louisa stared at herself in the full-length mirror. With her blonde hair tousled from the day and the exertions of both lacing up the boots and sealing herself into the leather, she looked like a cross between a barbie-doll and a red leather cat-woman.

Cautiously she let her fingers slide over the leather, which sat on her body like a second skin. Her fingers crept downwards and, still watching herself, she undid the zipper in her panties and let one finger reach inside the panties and run around her outer labia. Whatever she might have said in Tessario's office, this was already making her feel very horny. She stopped and removed her fingers with a passing feeling of guilt but that was immediately replaced with an overwhelming urge to caress herself. Well, she reasoned, there was no guarantee that Tessario would turn up and in any case, she thought, there was no point in taking all of this leather off again.

Louisa slid to the floor and lay down on her side, facing the mirror which was wide enough for her to see the full length of her body and examine its curves. She ran her hands down her side, exploring the curves and bumps beneath and then, inevitably, she let her fingers roam further downwards towards the slit in her panties, except that this time she let her fingers slide inside the slit and into her hole.

Being unable to see her pussy or her tits, yet feeling them grate against the soft leather and sensing the moistness inside her was almost unbearably titillating. Forcefully, she roamed further inside herself, stroking herself as she attempted to keep her eyes open and fully experience the display she was giving for herself. On an impulse she swivelled around and crawled to her bedside cabinet, retrieving the vibrator that Andrew had given her, then she crawled back to the mirror and looked at herself, swivelling around to a sitting position to face her reflection full on.

The slit in her panties showed her cunt as a swollen mass of dark pink flesh, the tiny tongue of her clitoris just visible through the honey blonde of her pubic hair. Turning on the vibrator she paused for a second, then ran it carefully across her breasts, watching her nipples rise within the tight leather sheath as it passed across them. Then, moving slowly and carefully, she positioned the vibrating phallus at the entrance to her sex, allowing the moulded head to gradually penetrate her, splitting the crease of flesh in two.

Louisa lay back and watched, fascinated, as her sex absorbed the fullness of the vibrator, then eased it out, setting up a rhythm in and out of her, manipulating the machine and working her hips against the weight of it within her. She groaned with pleasure, uncertain whether the rapid upsurge in desire was created by the motion of the vibrator within her, or the sight of her sex exposed in the mirror ahead of her. Then she leaned back against the bed behind her and gave herself up to the thrusting rhythm, grasping at the vibrator. She closed her eyes and focused on maximising the rippling sensations that were growing within her belly and cunt, rotating her clitoris with sensitive fingers to create new sensations as she moved and writhed on the floor.

In the distance Louisa was suddenly aware of the doorbell ringing. 'No,' she hissed to herself. 'No, not now. Go away.' Brought down from a heightened sense of sexuality, frustrated and groaning, she contemplated leaving the caller to their own devices, until she realised that she could hear Tessario's voice calling loudly through the door. In a panic she removed the vibrator and, scrambling to her knees, she threw it in the direction of the bedside cabinet.

'Louisa,' she could hear him shouting. 'Louisa, are you in there? Answer the door. Louisa!'

'All right,' she shouted back. 'I'm coming.' With no time to spare she grabbed at a voluminous cotton kimono and threw it around her, then rushed to throw open the front door before Tessario could make enough noise to have her evicted.

Chapter 10

Louisa threw open the front door with her wrap pulled tightly around her. Without a word Tessario walked straight inside and she slammed the door shut behind him.

'How the hell did you get in here and past the doorman?' she demanded. 'And how dare you make all that noise outside. This is a nice apartment block, not the docks, in case you hadn't noticed.'

'Well, you're in a good mood,' Tessario snapped back. 'What's the matter? Did you forget about our date?'

'What date?' she snapped back automatically. 'I don't remember agreeing to any date.'

Tessario opened his mouth to reply and just as quickly shut it again. A broad, knowing smile spread across his features. 'Well,' he replied, 'I don't think you're telling the whole truth there, Louisa.' He reached out and switched at the bottom of her robe. 'Nice boots. Were you warming yourself up for me?'

She flushed. 'I was trying them on and you rang the bell.'

Tessario smiled. 'I don't think so. You should look at yourself.' He walked past Louisa and into the kitchen, opening the fridge door and retrieving a bottle of wine whilst she cast a surreptitious glance at her reflection in the mirror on the lounge wall. He was right, damn him; she looked tousled and a little bit flushed.

Tessario returned from the kitchen with two full glasses of wine and held one glass out to her. 'Come on, Louisa,' he said. 'There's no shame in trying it on. And let me at least try to get you drunk; I'm desperate to see you in that outfit.'

She grimaced and took the glass of wine. 'What is it with you?' she asked. 'You always turn up at the wrong moment.'

'I thought we had an arrangement for tonight,' he reminded her and despite herself she shivered in expectation. Her interrupted masturbation had left her aroused and unfulfilled, and although there were some conflicting images and recollections from their previous sexual encounter, the most compelling memory was one of satisfying and orgasmic sex. All these thoughts ran though her mind in an instant, as Tessario quietly moved to stand behind her, stroking her hair and gently running his hand along the back of her neck and just inside the cotton kimono so that she gave up any thoughts of rejecting him.

Louisa stood up and turned to face Tessario, finishing her wine as he smiled at her obvious acceptance of the situation. She reached out to take his hand and led him to her bedroom where he looked around with interest, taking in the simplicity of the room; the broad bed with four posters but no canopy, the plain mahogany furniture comprising bedside bureaux and a chest of drawers and the wall of mirrored wardrobes facing the base of the bed. Before Tessario could speak or pass comment Louisa turned and reached out for him. He let her draw him closely towards her, kissing her as his hands roamed across her body and then moved down to cup her rounded buttocks in his hands, the leather still hidden from view beneath her long robe.

Eagerly Tessario reached out to open up the cotton kimono, but Louisa pushed him away. 'Not yet,' she said. 'You wanted to see, well here I am.' She moved away from him and towards the other side of the room whilst Tessario threw himself across the bed in expectation. 'You seem to like to watch me strip,' she went on. 'Well OK, but let's see you manage this. The tables are turned and this time I want to see you beg.'

'What do you want me to do?' he asked.

'Get your clothes off and get into the bed,' she commanded, turning to the bureau where she had thrown the vibrator. With a quizzical smile he did as he was told, climbing between crisp white cotton sheets and throwing off all the covers so that his form was almost visible through the fine woven linen.

'Well?' he asked.

Louisa strode towards him, revealing in her hands two pairs of handcuffs that had been lying in her drawer, a legacy of Andrew's tenure. She dangled them in front of Tessario and as he made no movement she promptly snapped one around his wrist and the other around the bedpost, then moved to repeat the process with the other wrist as he sat complacently in the bed.

'You don't seem particularly worried that you're chained up,' she commented as she completed the job.

He shrugged. 'It depends what you're planning to do.'

'I want to hear you beg for it.'

He shrugged again with a smile. 'I want you, Louisa, you know that. I'm already begging.'

'Don't be so naive,' she retorted. 'You're going to beg for release. And I can wait a long time.' She strode out of the bedroom, and refilled her glass with wine, waiting and looking out across the buildings outside as she sipped her drink and cooled off. Eventually she made her way back to the bedroom.

Tessario lifted his head up at her entrance. 'OK,' he said. 'You've made your point. You can make me wait. But while you're leaving me in here I might go off the whole idea, so what will you do then?'

Louisa laughed. 'Don't be ridiculous,' she said, crawling onto the bed. 'You'll just end up suffering for longer.' She crawled up to his crotch and ran her hands across the sheet that covered his erection. 'Oh yes,' she said mockingly. 'I can see just how uninterested you are.' Leaning down she caught his solid cock in her teeth, holding it, protected only by the cotton sheets, as his breath hissed out of his mouth in a gasp of shock. 'I think you're very interested,' she murmured, releasing him and straddling his groin, with her hands gently rubbing up and down his shaft. 'Very interested indeed.'

Tessario's lips reached out to hers, but with a spring Louisa stood up on the bed, towering over him in the spiked heels of her cherry red boots. 'I think you ought to learn you can't have everything your own way, Paolo Tessario,' she announced. 'You wanted me trussed up in red leather, well here I am. And if you do what you're told I might let you touch me, with one part of your body or another. However, in the meantime I think I should be able to keep one eye on just how excited you really are.' She got off the bed and pulled the sheet back, exposing Tessario's groin to her gaze, then threw off the kimono and struck a pose in front of him, with both hands on her hips and her legs slightly apart. 'So,' she said. 'Do you like it?'

Tessario nodded. 'Very much,' he murmured, running his eyes over the tight shiny leather.

'I do too,' she said. 'Particularly this bit.' Slowly Louisa reached down the front and unzipped the panties, running her finger inside the entrance of the split and down into the cleft of her sex. Tessario watched her with narrowing eyes as the soft blonde pussy hair slowly crept out, the swollen pink lips of her vagina just visible beneath them. 'You know,' she said conversationally, 'I am incredibly wet. I guess it comes from fucking myself with my vibrator before you came. It's very long and thick, and even bigger than your cock, Paolo. And it's very, very satisfying.' As she spoke Louisa stood with one hand over her groin, rubbing her thumb against her clit as other fingers slid inside the split panties and explored her sex.

Unable to drag his eyes away, Tessario swallowed and she could see his erection grow. She smiled. 'In fact,' she went on, 'I think I may have to pleasure myself with my vibrator right now. Should I do that, Paolo?' He nodded. 'Would you like me to do that?' He nodded again. 'What was that?'

'Yes,' he said hoarsely. 'I would like to see you fuck yourself with your vibrator.'

'Did I say I was going to let you see?' she asked, and walking to the bureau she picked out the vibrator and set it buzzing for a moment.

'Louisa,' Tessario pleaded, but she cast him a dismissive glance and retreated to the end of the bed. 'You're going to have to beg a lot harder than that.' From her vantage point close to the base of the bed, she knew that Tessario could only catch the occasional glimpse of her, although she could clearly see his anguished face as he strained against his restraints. Louisa smiled to herself and lay down along the edge of the bed, watching his reflection in the glass as she set the vibrator buzzing again and slid it towards her sex.

Although she was watching for Tessario's expression Louisa couldn't stop a grunt of satisfaction as she finally slipped the vibrator inside her, feeling it shiver its way in and out of herself. For the first time Tessario really tried to remove the handcuffs, shaking at the bedstead as he tried to drag himself further down in order to be able to see her. His face contorted with fury as he realised her sighs and moans were all that he would be able to experience, and his struggles finally subsided as he settled to listen to her.

At the base of the bed Louisa experienced a perverse thrill at making him suffer, emotionally if not physically. Watching him slump back in the bed she continued sliding the vibrator around and inside her sex, and began taunting Tessario as she did so. 'I'm sliding it into my panties, and my sex slit is so wet I can send it all the way in with one stroke,' she groaned. 'I'm so swollen up with sex juice. Now I'm running it over my clit, to make it hard and hot. Do you want to see me, Paolo?'

'You know I do,' his voice hissed from behind her. 'Please, Louisa. I'm begging now. I want to see you putting it inside you.'

Louisa rose to her feet and stood against the end of the bed. Tessario's cock was red and swollen and standing obscenely out from the mass of his dark curly pubic hair. Slowly, Louisa half unzipped the brassiere top and her tightly restrained breasts sprang forward, swollen mounds of flesh that were visible almost as far as the edge of her nipples, but no further. Tessario drew in his breath and writhed impotently on the bed as she leaned slightly backwards and eased the silent vibrator towards the darkness of her sex. She made no sound as she turned it on and ran it down the front of her panties, across her

207

clitoris and finally, slowly, inside her cunt. Tessario groaned with frustration as she closed her eyes and began to masturbate herself.

'Louisa,' he hissed. 'Let me do it. I can fuck you better than that thing. You know it's true.'

Finally Louisa paused in her actions and opened her eyes again. 'Maybe you can,' she agreed and removing the vibrator she scrambled onto the bed once again. Pinioning him below her she ran her hands over his chest, and sat across his groin.

'Let me out of these,' he begged, but she only laughed as she sat above his cock that was almost straining for her and then slowly lowered herself on top of him. His swollen penis disappeared inside her in one swift movement and they both shuddered in unison at the sense of impending release.

Louisa leaned backwards and began to manoeuvre herself up and down on Tessario's member as his hips butted from the bed against her. 'Stop,' she hissed. 'I'll do this.' Reluctantly he ceased his movements and changing her position Louisa now squatted vertically above Tessario's shaft so that it sank directly in and out of her cunt. In her position of control she was able to set a faster pace for their union and as she moved the moisture seeped out of her, covering Tessario's member with her slick juices. Unable to restrain herself any more Louisa sank forward onto her knees and covered his body with her own, sliding herself up and down his cock and working herself against him until she felt the muscular contractions of her orgasm rippling through her, the sensations driving Tessario towards a climax which came as a shuddering finale to their coupling. They sank back into the bed, Tessario still chained to the bed posts, both groaning with their exertions. After a few minutes he nudged Louisa. 'Hey,' he said. 'Get these things off me, will you?'

She propped herself up on one elbow and looked across at him. 'I don't know,' she said teasingly. 'At last I've got you where you belong. Maybe I'll just leave you there for a while.'

* * *

Early in the morning Louisa woke to find Tessario emerging from the shower room with a bath sheet tied tucked around his hips. She groped for the clock, squinting in the light that was creeping through the folds of the bedroom curtains. 'What's going on?' she croaked.

Tessario bent over the bed, fresh and clean from his shower. 'I meant to tell you last night. I have to go away for a few days. I'll probably be back Friday. Can you keep the office ticking over till then?'

'Bloody nerve,' she muttered. 'I've only managed it every day until now.'

He laughed. 'I've been doing my share,' he admonished her as he collected his clothes from the far end of the room and started dressing. Louisa temporarily gave up any thought of sleep and dragged herself into a half sitting position, looking blearily at him from below the sheets she had drawn up to her neck.

'Where are you going?' she inquired.

'Out of town,' he answered vaguely. 'Not on Dane Agency business though.' He finished dressing and slid on his shoes. 'It's a private visit.'

Louisa curled her lip. 'Please yourself,' she said in a prim tone.

'I'll be back later this week,' he assured her, 'and we can talk then.'

'About what?' she grumbled absently at his departing form, sinking slowly back into sleep once again.

The alarm woke her once more at seven-thirty and she struggled awake, dragging herself into the shower and turning the taps full on to stand underneath the shower in a stupor until her brain kicked back into life. She groaned as she thought about her behaviour. 'You have no backbone,' she thought. The thought struck her that the fact she so enjoyed Tessario in bed was obscuring the issues and blinding her to the main problem and the reason he was there: mob money. Their continuing liaison had been infinitely more pleasurable than she had expected, but her aim had always been to investigate Tessario and his activities, and come up with some information that she could use to get him out of her hair. Now, she thought, with Tessario out of the office for a couple of days perhaps this was the time to get her act together and look for information in his office. In any case, if she did find some information then even if she didn't go to the FBI maybe she could use it herself to force Tessario out of the business.

She paused. The trouble with all of this was that the more time she spent with Tessario, 'this version of Tessario,' she reminded herself, not the thuggish one she had seen so often in the past, the more she found it hard to believe that he would actually do her harm. In addition, confusing the issue still further, there was Gabriella; she couldn't believe that Gabriella would have anything to do with Tessario if he really was the thug he had originally appeared to be. She sighed with confusion. Nothing seemed to be becoming any clearer.

She finally left for the office and a full day of meetings. First of all she had back to back meetings with the editors of two different magazines, one about a potential story on the Dane Agency and its plans for the future and the second a meeting with Venetia Hall on the final layout for the Spanish photo shoot. In the afternoon she was meeting the director of an advertising agency which was considering using Nadine in a major nationwide campaign selling toothpaste and finally, at the end of the day, she had scheduled a review meeting with her Chief Booker, Claudia. They were long overdue an opportunity to review the state of the 'model boards' and today's meeting would give them a chance to go over the status of the models on their books and discuss who should be taken off from the 'new faces' and promoted to the 'main board'. This was a big step for a young model since it would mean that the agency would be more selective about the type of jobs the model was sent on, and therefore it would also probably mean less work for a while. However, on the plus side it was intended to improve and redirect his or her career over the longer term. In addition to this task, the recent media interest in the business had meant that the number of new applicants to the agency had risen dramatically and she and Claudia needed to formulate some plans on the recruitment of new staff and discuss how the business should develop and expand on the booking and sales side.

By six-thirty Louisa and Claudia had sorted through the model boards and had beaten out a basic plan for filtering the increased number of potential models who were appearing at the door or sending in photographs, and agreed to recruit four bookers-cum-administrators at different levels, one highly experienced and the others to be trained; all to be brought into the business as soon as the building work was finished and they could be accommodated in the offices.

Once work was completed the two of them sat in Louisa's office having a chat over a glass of wine, the first time they had been able to relax together for weeks. 'So where's Paolo?' asked Claudia casually.

'Away for a few days,' Louisa replied as Claudia nodded sagely. 'Why?'

'Oh I just wondered,' Claudia said, giving Louisa a sly glance. 'He's rather cute.' Louisa shrugged. 'Oh come on, Louisa,' she went on, dropping the casual facade. 'It's obvious you two are hot for each other.'

Louisa blushed. 'We are not.'

Claudia snorted with laughter. 'Rubbish. I noticed that poor boy you took to the party didn't have a chance once you started seeing Paolo.'

'I don't know what you're talking about,' Louisa repeated. 'Chris Dennison and I just saw each other a few times and then let things drop. It has nothing to do with Paolo Tessario.'

Claudia stood to leave. 'OK,' she said, 'have it your way. But you should probably know that the whole office has been waiting for you two to get it together. They don't talk to me about it of course, but even I can tell that the place is buzzing.'

'I would prefer not to be the centre of gossip by my own staff,' replied Louisa stiffly as Claudia walked to the door.

'Sorry, Louisa,' she said with a smile. 'You haven't got a hope of that. That's what people do with bosses, they talk about them. Thanks for the wine, I'll get on with the recruitment straightaway.' With a smile and a wave she slid out of the door, passing Scott who put his head into the office.

'Are you done?'

Louisa nodded. 'Come on in and shut the door.'

Scott walked in and sat down. 'So,' he said, 'you decided to take things into your own hands and get a lot more friendly with Tessario.'

'Mind your own business,' snapped Louisa. 'That's what your boss wanted, anyway. Its not my fault that Tessario turned out to be good in bed.' Scott stayed silent. 'And no,' she went on, 'I haven't found out anything useful, even though I've been trying. Anyway, if you're so worried about me what have you been able to do about it?'

'Nothing so far,' he replied. 'I've told you before that we thought this was going to be a long-term operation. That's what I wanted to talk to you about. We propose to tone down our surveillance and investigation.'

'What does that mean?' asked Louisa suspiciously.

Scott shifted in his seat. 'Mr Krysakow thinks that the lack of evidence to date is an indication of a duplicate operation, an attempt to divert our attention, and on the basis of this suspicion we are planning to minimise our surveillance activities for the foreseeable future.'

Louisa sat back and digested this information. 'Behind all the waffle and double talk what does that mean exactly?'

'Mr Krysakow thinks the mob are playing us for fools. That they became overtly interested in your business to divert our attention from something else, something more significant. They may even know that you are under FBI surveillance and protection.'

'What protection?' she scoffed, and then more seriously she asked, 'And what do you mean by "surveillance"?'

'I haven't been the only one assigned to this case,' he admitted. 'I probably shouldn't mention this but we know everything you've been doing since this started.'

'I'm going to pretend I didn't hear that,' Louisa said. 'I don't think I can handle that right now.' She paused, digesting the information. 'So what you mean is that you think you were fed information and Tessario was placed here in order to get you focused on me.' Scott nodded.

'In essence, yes.'

'Do you have any reason to think that?'

'Yes, but obviously I can't go into that. I'm only telling you this so that you can extricate yourself from any relationship with Tessario, if you should wish to.'

'But my business is still being funded by mob money?' Scott shrugged.

'Possibly true, but there's nothing we can do to make certain of that now. Anyway they don't appear to be laundering dirty money through the business. That's it. The fact that we are withdrawing from the business may give them some indication that their plan has failed and that we are stepping up our investigation into other areas. But you can still contact us if there is any information or change in the situation. You know how to get hold of us.'

Louisa gaped at him. 'So that's it?' she said incredulously. 'After doing absolutely nothing for me you're dumping me and moving on? Leaving me to handle the mob and Paolo Tessario by myself.'

'There won't be any trouble to "handle", Louisa,' he said soothingly, 'they're not interested in you. It was us they wanted to keep running around.'

'Oh,' she sneered back, 'and how would you know? You've been so very well informed all the way through this, so why should I believe you now?' She swivelled her chair, fighting the irritation. 'Anyway,' she went on, 'have you actually looked for any information?'

Scott nodded. 'Of course. We've been monitoring Tessario's computer files, but there hasn't been anything of interest.

213

We've also followed his movements all the way through, and apart from that mob-owned bar he took you to . .

'. . . ZanZi,' Louisa murmured. 'That's why they let us in, they must have known him . . .'

'Yes of course,' replied Scott. 'Apart from that and the use of his mother's apartment in the Middleton he's been remarkably low key on Family associations.'

'Do you know where he is right now?'

Scott shrugged. 'He's gone to see his mother I believe.'

'Is that it?'

Scott rose from his chair. 'I will be working out the week and then moving on. Obviously you will need a new PA. I hope everything works out for you, Louisa. I am sure it will and that soon you will find that business returns to normal.'

'So that is it,' Louisa finished blankly. Scott shrugged slightly, and walked to the door.

'Goodbye, Louisa,' he said and left.

'My heroes the FBI,' Louisa muttered to herself as she threw the last of her wine down her throat. She sat at her desk letting the dusk fade, stunned by this development and contemplating what to do next. Finally, as the evening closed in she made a decision. She would go and have a look at the PC in Tessario's office and see whether he had any information there, or anything that she could retrieve. If she could find something useful she could go ahead and try to negotiate with him to get him out of the business. If not, she would have no choice but to carry on regardless into uncharted territory and hope that Scott was right, that the mob really had no interest in her business.

She went down the deserted corridor, let herself into Tessario's office with the master key, turned on the computer and went into the File-Master section. Tessario's notes were filed under a range of directories from 'Office' to 'Home', 'Social' and 'Notes'. None were protected by password and as far as she could tell so far they had all been about the business or trivial matters, and had no reference to anything that was in any way incriminating.

214

'Damn,' she muttered to herself, 'come on, Paolo, where would you have put something important . . .'

She rummaged around his filing cabinet looking for something useful but again to no avail. Finally she gave up and went into his fridge in search of a drink. There was a split of Laurent Perrier champagne inside and behind it, quite unexpectedly, she saw something wrapped in tin foil and stored in the corner, and she knew she had found the disc she had been looking for.

'At last,' she said to herself, emerging with the champagne and the disc. 'There must be something in here.'

'That depends on what you're looking for,' said a languid voice from the door. She sat bolt upright and stared at Paolo Tessario, framed against the light of the corridor.

'Paolo,' she gabbled nervously. 'I didn't think you were back until Friday.'

'Obviously,' he replied. There was silence as he entered the room and then stood, watching her. 'I might ask what you're doing delving around my computer files in the middle of the night,' he said, walking over to the desk. 'But I think I can probably guess.'

'I was looking for the newest version of those files I gave you,' she babbled.

'Crap,' he shot back. 'You can do better than that, Louisa.' There was another pause and Tessario settled himself into the chair opposite the desk. 'So?' he asked. 'What's the deal?'

Louisa looked across at him and was more angry with herself than scared at her situation. 'Dammit,' she said, 'you know what I'm doing.'

'Just enlighten me.'

Suddenly all of Louisa's irritation at being forced into this situation in her own business bubbled to the surface. She looked across at Tessario and was angry with him and all the other men that had messed her about and messed with her business. 'You bloody well know what it is,' she snapped. 'I want my business back. You can't blame me for that. I want you out; you, your Mafia friends and the FBI. You can all go

215

to hell as far as I'm concerned so long as you leave me alone and piss off.'

Tessario's expression hardly changed, but he raised one quizzical eyebrow. 'Ah,' he said, 'so you want the Mafia out.' He nodded. 'And as far as the FBI are concerned would you be talking about the redoubtable Agent Scott?'

Louisa stared at him. 'You know about him?'

'Louisa,' Tessario went on reasonably, 'Agent Scott has FBI stamped all over him. Anyway,' he continued, 'I was expecting someone to move into the business fairly quickly and he arrived right on schedule. It had to be him.'

Louisa stared at him. Finally she found her voice again. 'So you know?' she asked weakly and to Tessario's obvious amazement she started to laugh.

'What's the matter?' he asked.

'Why don't you just fill me in with your version of events?' she suggested.

'This isn't easy to explain, Louisa,' he began.

'Try,' she suggested.

'Look,' he said. 'You obviously know about my family. Well, you should also know that my contact with the 'Family' is a loose one and I'm not involved in any of their operations.' He shrugged. 'I'm quite boring really. I'm what they call a legitimate businessman. But I do have a certain obligation to my family, and this 'opportunity' to be in your business presented itself by way of a request from my uncle. It was something legal, it would be useful and I was assured that it would be sufficient demonstration of my, well let's say my commitment to fulfil my Family obligations and enough to keep me out of any other aspect of mob business in the future.'

'Do you believe them?' she asked.

He smiled. 'Of course. They're my family.'

'Including your second cousin Anthony?'

He grimaced. 'Even including him. I have to admit I brought him along to convince Agent Scott and yourself about my mob credentials, but he played his part far beyond my expectations.'

216

She shook her head. 'You've been one enigma after another. Nice then nasty.' Tessario shrugged.

'Well, you were being a queen bitch, and it got a little out of control sometimes.'

'So how come you're telling me this now?'

'I was here to play a part. If the FBI wanted to trail me around then that was their problem. When they finally realise that your business is not a priority for the Family then my usefulness here will be over. After all, there are a lot of other things they would be better spending their time investigating.'

'What happens then?' she asked.

'I leave the business after a suitable period and you continue on as normal.'

'What about the money in the business?' she asked.

'That's not going to be a problem,' he said. 'The money originally came through the venture capital firm and funds will be re-diverted and set up as prior to our involvement. The venture capitalists will take back control and put someone else into the business. Someone with business experience and no Family connections.'

'And in the meantime?' asked Louisa.

'As soon as we know that the FBI have moved on then I can think about moving out.' He looked closely at Louisa. 'You don't seem awfully surprised by this.'

'What's on the disc?' she asked coming round from behind the desk and ignoring his comment, forcing herself to suppress a smile as he confirmed everything Scott had told her.

Tessario laughed. 'Nothing of any interest.'

'No?'

He shrugged. 'Just a little something Anthony downloaded from the internet and I never got round to deleting.' Louisa raised her eyes in a query. 'Some rather risqué pictures that I didn't want Agent Scott to access in one of his tedious searches of my computer and then use to get me downtown on some sort of pornography or indecency charge.'

'So why are you telling me all this?' she asked.

Tessario stood and walked towards her where she was leaning against the side of the desk. 'I'm telling you so that you know the business will be safe. And because I want you to trust me. Gabriella and I talked it out with my uncle. I don't want you to go on loathing me because of what you think I am.'

'So,' Louisa said, musing. 'You've got pornography in your office, and I've got a confession. So I suppose if Agent Scott had this information, then you could be in trouble.'

'I might be,' Tessario replied cautiously.

She nodded. 'I see. So this information could be quite valuable, if used correctly.' He sat down beside her.

'But you're not going to tell Agent Scott anything,' Tessario said confidently.

'No?' Louisa queried. 'And you're sure about that, are you?'

'Are you threatening me, Louisa Dane?' he asked curiously, a smile playing across his features.

'I could be,' she said flirtatiously. 'I might need to be persuaded not to go straight to Agent Scott. In the morning that is.'

Tessario leaned across and ran his fingers along the line of Louisa's shoulders and down towards the front of her blouse. 'Would this be enough persuasion?' he asked.

'Oh no,' she replied, reaching out for him hungrily. 'I'm sorry, Paolo, but you're going to have to work much, much harder than that . . .'